THE MIDNIGHT SEA

Fourth Element Book #1

KAT ROSS

The Midnight Sea

First Edition

Copyright © 2016 Kat Ross

This story is a work of fiction. References to real people, events, establishments, organizations, or locales are intended only to provide a sense of authenticity and are used fictitiously. All other characters, and all incidents and dialogue are drawn from the author's imagination and are not to be construed as real.

Cover design by Damonza

Map design by Robert Altbauer at fantasy-map.net

ISBN: 978-09972362-1-7

For my Dad, who always carried around at least one book—and usually several.

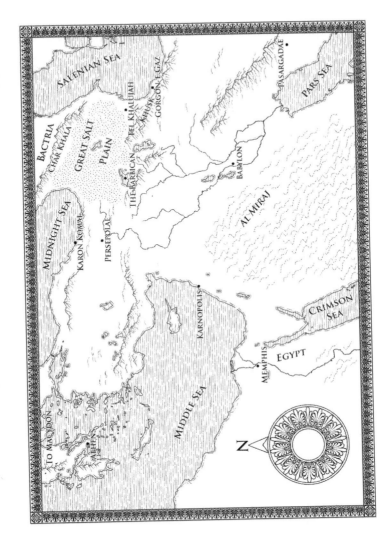

Out beyond ideas of wrongdoing and rightdoing there is a field.
I'll meet you there.

—Jalaluddin Rumi

※ I ※

The wind whistled through the high passes as we picked our way up the trail. Slow-moving shadows signified the long train of people and animals stretching ahead, but the snow was blowing too hard to make out much more than that.

The Khusk range was an unforgiving place, I knew. It was my twelfth year crossing these mountains and so far, the hardest. The snow had begun weeks earlier than usual. It piled in drifts against the rocks and concealed crevasses that could swallow a man and his horse whole. But we couldn't turn back. That would mean certain death by starvation, while the crossing was only possible death—generally without warning. A foot placed wrong. A quiet weakening of the snow shelf until the slightest movement set off an avalanche. Most of us would make it to the other side, I knew. Most, but not all.

Higher and higher we climbed, into the teeth of the storm. I squeezed my sister Ashraf's hand. We leaned into the wind, hoods cinched down tight. The sheep bleated plaintively as they scrambled up the steep, winding trail. They

I

weren't happy, but they too had made this crossing before and knew better than to try stopping. Our animals were as hard and stubborn as we were.

On a clear day, you could stand atop these icy cols and see to the edges of the earth. But now the visibility was perhaps a dozen feet in any direction. I knew we would stop for the night soon. The journey to the spring pastures in the foothills took eight days, the reverse more than twice that. Our route passed a series of fixed campsites that hadn't changed in generations. One of those lay perhaps ten minutes ahead, a dent in the spine of the mountains that offered some shelter.

"Here, let me take him," I shouted to Ashraf.

My sister looked up at me. A puppy squirmed inside her sheepskin coat. It had been a gift from our father for her seventh birthday. He had wanted to tie the dog to his saddle, but she insisted on carrying it. I could feel her steps lagging. It was the end of a long day and she was exhausted.

I unbuttoned my own quilted *arqalok* and held out a hand.

"Come on," I said. "I'll give him back when we camp."

Her dark brows set in a line. "I'm as strong as you, Nazafareen."

"I know that," I snapped. I was exhausted too. "Just give me the dog."

Ashraf scowled but she eased the puppy from her coat. He wriggled and squirmed. I cradled his warm body in one hand while I made space for him among my layers. And then he gave a loud bark and kicked his hind legs. Sharp nails gouged my wrist. I loosened my grip for a moment, but that's all it took. The puppy was off and scampering into the storm.

Without a word, Ashraf ran after him. In a heartbeat, she'd vanished behind an outcropping. I muttered a curse and followed her.

We had been warned never to leave the path. To always

keep our place in the long train of the Four-Legs Clan. But I thought I knew these mountains well enough to find my way back, even in such severe conditions. And Ashraf had left me no choice.

I followed her footprints, calling her name. The wind whisked my voice away the moment it left my lungs. How far could a little girl and her puppy get?

Not far, it seemed. I rounded a pile of fallen boulders and the footprints stopped abruptly. "Ashraf!" I yelled. "Where are you? It's too cold for games."

I turned in a slow circle, panic rising in my chest when I saw how close I was to a ledge that dropped away into the swirling snow. I couldn't tell how far down the fall was. A hundred feet? A thousand? Five thousand? The footprints didn't lead to the edge though. They stopped dead about six feet away. Past that, the snow looked undisturbed.

"Ashraf!" I yelled again.

And then I heard a low whine. It was the dog, shivering in a crevice. I approached with my palms out. He eyed me warily.

"Come on, stupid dog," I said.

I had just knelt down to reach for him when a low growl rose in his throat. The dog tried to squeeze deeper into the crack. His eyes were fixed on something behind me.

I had a small knife in a sheath at my waist. I fumbled for it now. There were wolves in these mountains, although they'd never been known to attack a human in broad daylight, so near the entire clan. Maybe the harsh early winter had made them desperate.

I spun around and let out a relieved breath. It was my sister. She stood in front of the ledge, the wind blowing at her back and streaming her long hair in front of her face. I could scarcely make out her features in the darkness of her hood.

"Thank the Holy Father," I said. "Come on, we have to be getting back before they leave us behind."

Ashraf didn't move. The dog's growling turned into a pitiful, high-pitched whine that set my teeth on edge.

"What's wrong with you?" I asked. The wind dropped for a moment, leaving a pocket of silence. My breath plumed white in the dying light. It would be dark soon. "Ashraf?" I stepped toward her. "You're too close to the ledge. Come away."

"Shut up," my sister told the dog, and her voice was not her own.

My heart started to thud, slow and painful.

"Stop it," I said. "Just stop it."

She didn't reply. I wanted to pick up the dog, stuff him in my coat and get going, but suddenly, I didn't want to turn my back on her. Where had she come from? Why did the footprints stop?

She was just a little girl. My irritating sister, who followed me everywhere and never gave me a moment's peace. Who begged me to braid her hair exactly like mine, and always put her share of barberries on my plate because she knew they were my favorite.

"If you don't come now, I'll tell Father," I warned.

"*I'll tell Father,*" she said. My own voice now, thrown back at me. The hair on my neck rose.

I don't know how long we stood like that in the snow. Long enough that it started to accumulate on her hood and shoulders. Long enough that the last bit of daylight bled from the sky. I felt frozen, unable to think. I didn't understand what was happening, only that there was a tangible *wrongness* to my sister and I had no idea what to do about it. I felt trapped in a nightmare, the kind where every movement is heavy and ponderous, like an ant floundering in honey.

Ashraf's breath, I noticed distantly, made no fog. It was the same temperature as the air.

I don't know what would have happened if the dog hadn't started to bark. A frenzied yapping and snarling. It broke my trance and I took a step toward her. Pulled her hood back. Saw the eyes, no longer a soft blue but something else, something dark and sentient. It had devoured the whites so they looked like hard black almonds in her face.

I dropped my knife. Urine trickled down the insides of my thighs.

Her teeth snapped together and she leapt at me, knocking us both to the ground. We tumbled through the snow. I could feel the ledge yawning at my back. My fingers scrabbled over the icy rocks, searching for anything to grab onto. Then I was kicking over empty air. Terror made me wild. I thrashed, trying to throw her off, but she was too strong. Freezing breath panted in my ear.

I screamed, sliding inexorably over the edge. And then hands grabbed me and hauled me up. I saw the face of my uncle. He looked angry and confused.

"What in the name of the Father are you two doing?" he demanded, releasing me.

I scooted away on my bottom. He still held Ashraf by the arm. I couldn't speak, but I could point. He looked at her for the first time and finally understood, stepping back as confusion turned to fear. Her mouth curved in a smile. And I knew what she meant to do. My uncle was tall and strong. Whatever was inside her would take him, and then it would take me, and then it would walk back to our camp and take us all, one by one.

I whispered a wordless prayer and scrambled for my knife, half-buried in the snow.

"Druj!" he hissed.

Druj.

I had never seen one, but I'd heard them spoken of when the embers of the campfires burned low. How they'd come from the north in an endless tide, Undead things with iron swords, and shadows whose touch meant death. How some of them, the ones called wights, wore human bodies, except that their eyes were as black as the deepest crevasses...

In a blur of movement too fast to track, Ashraf knocked my uncle down and straddled his chest, mouth stretching wide to reveal black gums. A dark mist oozed out of that mouth. Creeping toward my uncle. The knife trembled in my fist.

"Ashraf," I begged, tears freezing on my cheeks, but I didn't move. I was too afraid.

It would have had my uncle if the ledge hadn't given way. There was a thunderous crack as the ice shifted. And then Ashraf was sliding into the void. I bit down on my tongue and tasted blood as a small hand caught on the rim. Over the wind, I heard a thin voice call my name.

"Nazafareen."

I crawled over, sobbing and shaking. Ashraf dangled over a league of swirling snow.

"Please, Nazafareen, help me. I'm slipping..."

I looked at her face and for a second, I saw my sister as she used to be. Just a little girl of seven summers. She seemed so small and frail against the ocean of darkness beneath.

"Please, Nazafareen," she cried again, and this time her voice was her own, high and sweet. And terrified. Somewhere behind me, the dog howled and howled.

How could I let her die?

I seized her hand and started to pull her up. That's when her other arm shot up and grabbed my hair. I still had my knife but I couldn't use it on her. Not even to save my own life. So I didn't understand when the blade sunk into her throat.

I looked numbly at my hand. My knife was still there. It was my uncle's that lay buried in Ashraf's flesh. She jerked once, twice. Her claw-like fingers released me.

I watched as the thing that had taken my sister tumbled into blackness.

❧ 2 ❧

"**W**ater Dogs!"

I set aside the cookpot I'd just finished scrubbing and took another from the pile, not bothering to look up.

"Very funny," I said. "This would go a lot faster if you'd do your share instead of teasing me."

My brother Kian dropped to his haunches. "Not teasing. Have a look."

I sighed and pushed the hair out of my face. A moment later, I was on my feet, shading my eyes with one hand. Two mounted figures picked their way up the grassy hillside. They wore scarlet tunics and matching *qarhas* that wound around their heads, leaving only the eyes visible.

Everywhere, people were emerging from their goatskin tents to see what was going on. Tension and excitement buzzed through the Four-Legs clan as the figures reined up.

"Are they really Water Dogs?" I whispered.

"No one else wears the red," Kian replied.

I had never seen Water Dogs before. All I knew about them was that they belonged to the King, and they hunted

Druj—wights, liches, revenants. Like the one that had killed my sister a year ago. I felt a surge of bitterness. *You're too late*, I wanted to scream at them. You've come too late to do any good.

"Come on." Kian grabbed my hand. "Let's go see why they're here."

I ran down the slope with him, the familiar anger burning in my stomach. No one blamed my uncle for what he'd done, not even me. Once a wight takes possession of someone, it can't be driven out. It will use its victim up until that person drops dead from starvation or cold or sheer exhaustion. And then it will find another. Ashraf was beyond saving. Everyone knew it.

And yet I still saw her face in my dreams. Still saw her falling into the abyss, night after night, for months after her death.

At least I prayed my sister was dead. Her body had never been recovered.

"People of the Four-Legs Clan!" The first rider unwound his *qarha*. He was young, just a few years older than me.

"He looks like a barbarian," my brother said under his breath.

I'd never seen a barbarian, but this Water Dog had copper hair and grey eyes. It was a striking combination. He had an air of calm authority, an impression heightened by the royal seal—a roaring griffin in a circle—emblazoned on his scarlet tunic.

"We come in the name of King Artaxeros the second and Jaagos, Satrap of Tel Khalujah," the young man said in a ringing voice that carried to the far reaches of the assembled crowd. "We come to ask who here wishes to serve the Holy Father as a Water Dog. Only those between the ages of twelve and sixteen are eligible to test."

No one spoke. We rarely saw outsiders and had an innate

suspicion of anyone whose bloodline wasn't Four-Legs Clan for at least a dozen generations—no matter how many distant authorities they claimed to speak for.

"Your families will be well compensated." He held up a bag of coins and shook it. A small murmur went through the onlookers. Most of us were very poor, if you measured wealth by silver or gold. My family's only source of income was our animals. We traded milk and cheese, and my mother used the wool to weave shawls that she sold at the market in Tel Khalujah twice a year. A bag of coins that size was more money than we would earn in a decade.

"What does it mean to be a Water Dog?" His eyes roamed across the sea of faces, pausing on those who were close to my age. "It means you will champion the innocent, protect the powerless, punish the wicked. You will be the hand of the Holy Father, protecting our borders from the Druj to the north. And yes, you will use daēvas to do it."

"Demons to hunt demons," someone muttered.

I was very fuzzy on what exactly a daēva was. The older kids claimed they were Druj too, and that they had magic powers. I didn't understand how the Water Dogs could control such creatures, but apparently they managed it somehow.

"Who here has the courage to step forward?" the Water Dog asked. His companion lounged in the saddle, *qarha* still wound tightly. Something in the shape of the body told me it was a woman. "We will test any who are willing. Let me be clear: We are not here to forcibly recruit anyone. This is not a burden, but an honor. There's no place for cowards in our ranks."

This comment provoked some grumbling in the crowd. The Water Dog held up a hand.

"I mean no offense. The Four-Legs people are known to be among the strongest and toughest in the empire. How else could you eke out a living in these hard lands? You are descendants of the great hero, Fereydun. I only hope that his blood has not run thin."

I caught my father's eye. He stood with his arms crossed, felt hat pushed back on his head. His expression was unreadable.

Then a boy came forward. "I wish to be tested," he said.

The crowd buzzed. Two more boys approached the riders. They stood in a tight knot, grinning nervously.

"Anyone else?" The Water Dog's eyes swept the crowd. They passed over me without stopping, although they lingered for moment on Kian. My brother looked down at his feet. "No? Then we'll begin the testing."

He started to wheel his mount up the slope.

Demons to hunt demons.

My heart beat faster. I wasn't sure what it meant, but I suddenly saw a way to make Ashraf's angry, restless spirit stop haunting me.

Kill Druj.

It would mean walking away from my family. My clan. If I was chosen, I might never see any of them again. And in our world, those ties were everything. If the community cast a person out, they were as good as dead. It only happened for serious crimes like rape or murder, which were almost unheard of among my people. But when it did, that person became a ghost. Their name was never spoken again.

Leaving wasn't quite the same, although that was unheard of too. There was the Four-Legs Clan, and the soft, fat people beyond the mountains. Only the first mattered.

Please, Nazafareen, help me...

Yet I knew in my heart that Ashraf would never give me peace. Not until I avenged her.

"Wait!" I stepped forward. "I wish to be tested."

The Water Dog hardly looked at me. "Come along, then," he said.

I felt the stares of the crowd as we followed the two riders to a tent they had commandeered. Kian was pale with shock, but he didn't try to stop me. Nor did my mother, who stood wringing her shawl with weathered hands. They couldn't. I had volunteered, and I would be tested whether my parents liked it or not.

· One by one, we were summoned into the tent. I squatted on the ground outside, trying not to fidget, the other volunteers' eyes on me, hot and disdainful. I was the last to be called. When my turn came, I walked with my head high, although I expected to fail whatever test they had planned. I knew how to use a bow and knife, but I'd never handled any other weapon before.

The Water Dog who waited inside was the one who looked like a barbarian. He wore a sword at his hip, and I wondered if I was going to have to fight him. If so, I was doomed.

"My name is Ilyas," he said. "What's yours?"

I told him.

"Nazafareen," he said. "I want you to wear this and tell me what you feel."

He placed a gold circlet around my wrist. I noticed that he wore one too.

The gold was warm against my skin, but that was all.

"Close your eyes," Ilyas commanded gently. "Let your mind drift free."

Easy for you to say, I thought, wiping sweat from my palms.

I closed my eyes. A minute passed. I began to grow impatient. My leg ached. A muscle cramp, I thought, flexing my bare toes with a wince.

"What is it?" Ilyas asked.

"Nothing."

"Tell me."

It wasn't a question.

"Just growing pains. That's what my mother calls them."

"Where?"

"Here." I touched my calf.

Ilyas smiled. He pulled up his pant leg. There was a vicious scar, half-healed.

"I fell from my horse two weeks ago. My leg struck a rock."

I stared at him, uncomprehending.

"That's my injury you feel, Nazafareen," he said.

"Oh." I frowned, rubbing my calf. It was a strange sensation. My pain, and yet not mine, at the same time.

"You have the gift. Only one in a thousand does. These—" he pointed to the circlets—"are cuffs. When two humans wear them, there is a degree of empathy if the wearers are gifted. When a human and daēva wear them...well, it's more intense." He looked very pleased with himself. "You're the first we've found in a long time."

"What happens now?" I asked.

"We take you to Tel Khalujah. To the satrap's palace. That will be your new home." His grey eyes grew serious. "Are you certain you want this? It's not an easy life. I won't lie to you."

"That's all right," I said. "My life now isn't easy either."

He laughed. "I imagine it's not. Come, let me speak to your father."

"Ilyas?" The name spilled awkwardly from my tongue. "What are daēvas? Are they really Druj?"

"Yes, they are Druj. But they are tame Druj. The magus will explain it to you." He smiled. "We almost didn't come this way. Zohra thought we should skirt the mountains. But then we saw a herd of goats and followed it. Perhaps the Holy Father wanted us to find you."

I made the sign of the flame, the first two fingers of my left hand brushing forehead, lips and heart.

Good thoughts, good words, good deeds.

Ilyas nodded in approval. "We are the light against the darkness," he said. "Never forget that, Nazafareen."

We left the next day. The scouts gave my parents a bag of silver. At first, my father refused it. He was too proud. So I gave the money to Kian and made him promise to hide it until we were gone.

My mother wrapped me in her favorite shawl, a beautiful thing sewn with tinkling copper coins, and hugged me close. Her hands were stained with dye from the weaving, her cheeks rough and wrinkled from the harsh wind. She'd never been a sentimental woman, and I could see she wasn't about to start now.

"Keep it," she said. "Never forget where you come from. That you are Four-Legs Clan. And try not to get yourself killed."

"I won't," I said. "And the Druj will be the ones to die."

She stared at me. "I hope so. Now go before your father does something to bring the satrap's wrath down on all of us."

No one ever left our clan. I was the first in memory. It was a strange feeling to ride behind Ilyas, to leave the tents and familiar faces behind. I had always hated the smell of goats. Now I missed it already.

Five days later, I had my first glimpse of Tel Khalujah. We came out of one of the high passes and the city nestled in the foothills below, the domes and spires of the satrap's palace at its center. My mother and brother had been to the market there but I was always left behind, no matter how much I begged and sulked.

It was the grandest thing I'd ever seen, although that wasn't saying much since my whole world up to that point had been either the mountains or the Salt Plain. I had never set foot inside a house, let alone lived in one.

"You'll go to the magus first," Ilyas informed me. "He'll answer your questions. Then you can choose a bed in the novice barracks."

I nodded, feeling suddenly afraid. What if Ilyas had been mistaken? What would they do to me when they discovered I didn't have the gift? They'd send me back to my clan in shame. I imagined the smug faces of the volunteers I'd beat out.

And what if I *did* have the gift? I didn't even know what it was, not really. Neither Ilyas nor the other Water Dog, Zohra, had told me anything more during the journey. I'd listened to them talking but I couldn't understand half of what they said. They lived in a different world entirely. One I was about to be thrust into.

My stomach roiled as we rode up to the gates.

The guards made the sign of the flame and waved us through. The satrap's palace was made of timber and marble. Even the servants hauling water in the courtyard were far better dressed than I was. Four-Legs women wore layers of brightly colored skirts and pretty scarves, but I preferred the loose pants and tunic of the boys. Since Ashraf's death, I'd been a wild, dirty creature, and even my mother had given up hope of taming me. Now I wished that I'd at least combed my hair before we left. I took her shawl out and wrapped it around my shoulders. The smell of her—wood smoke and the sheep fat she oiled into her braid—made me feel slightly less alone.

They took me straight to the fire temple. This at least was something familiar. The Four-Legs Clan followed the teachings of the Prophet Zarathustra, although we set our fires beneath the open sky.

It was a simple stone room with a brazier burning at the center. The magus kneeled before it. His head didn't turn when Ilyas brought me inside and left me there without another word. I stood for a moment, unsure what to do. Finally, I walked forward and joined him, lowering my head in prayer.

Grant me strength and wisdom, Father. Show me the right path.

"What is your name, child?"

I didn't dare look at him so I kept my face down.

"Nazafareen."

"How old are you?"

"Thirteen," I said. "Almost fourteen."

"Why did you volunteer for the Water Dogs?"

"I..."

My mind went blank. I knew the answer, but I didn't want to tell the magus about Ashraf. Didn't want to tell him about the hatred in my heart. How for the five nights we travelled through the mountains, I had dreamed of killing faceless creatures. Of stabbing them with a sword while another faceless creature—my daēva?—laughed at my side.

Perhaps it was because underneath that thirst for vengeance, I was afraid. Terribly afraid. Monsters were real, and the grown-ups had failed to save us from them. Only the Water Dogs could do that. It was my secret—the only thing I had left that was truly mine—and I didn't wish to share it with a stranger.

The silence lengthened. It was too hot in the temple and I

could feel beads of sweat trickling down my ribs. The magus waited.

"To serve?" I finally managed.

"You say it like it's a question. Why do you wish to be a Water Dog?"

"To serve," I repeated, more firmly this time.

"To serve whom?"

"The King...the King and the Holy Father."

"Ah."

I could feel his eyes on me.

"Do you know what the bond is?"

"It's..." My shoulders slumped. "No. Not really."

"It's a responsibility," he said, turning my chin up. "A great responsibility."

I have to admit, I was disappointed when I saw him. He didn't look at all like a proper magus, or at least what my childish mind expected a proper magus to look like. He didn't have a long white beard. He seemed far too young, about the same age as my uncle. But his brown eyes were kind.

"What do you know of daēvas?" he asked me.

"They're wicked," I responded immediately. This was safe ground. "Demons. They used to be loose but now they're chained."

"Do you understand that the bond is the chain? That you will be holding one end of it?"

"I...yes."

I had a vague notion of this from what Ilyas said, and stories I'd heard, so it wasn't a complete surprise.

"Where did they find you?"

"I am of the Four-Legs Clan."

He took in my amber eyes and light brown hair. "You have the look. A nomad then. Can you adjust to life under a roof?"

"Yes, magus."

He sighed. "Let's go to my study. I'd prefer not to conduct this entire interview on my knees."

I couldn't tell if he was joking, so I said nothing. The magus led me outside the temple and through a side door into the palace. I goggled at the rich furnishings, the floors inlaid with ebony and lapis lazuli and carnelian gathered from across the breadth of the empire.

We reached a small room and the magus took a seat behind a plain wooden table.

"Sit down, Nazafareen," he said, gesturing to a chair opposite the desk.

We looked at each for a moment.

"You're wondering why I'm so young," the magus said.

I shook my head and he laughed.

"Yes, you are. I can see it in your eyes. In truth, I am more than a hundred years old."

My jaw gaped open. I couldn't help it.

"The reason I look young is that I was bonded. A warrior magus, although there are not many of us left. Daēvas, you see, live a very long time. No one knows how long. They grow to early adulthood and stay that way. When you are bonded, the same will happen to you. If you were already older, you would stay the same."

I tried to understand. "So I'll be...immortal?" The thought shook me to my core. I couldn't decide if it would be a blessing or a curse.

"Not immortal, but something very close to it. You will inherit some of your daēva's strength and ability to heal." The magus sat back. "But you can still die from violence, and very likely will. Eventually. The life of a Water Dog is not quiet." He smiled gently. "That's why we need new ones."

"Yes, magus."

"The daēvas here were raised with the bond from birth. Like us, they follow the Way of the Flame." He pressed his palms flat on the desk and leaned toward me. "We need their power, Nazafareen. The Druj are stirring in the north, and Eskander's wolves are at our door to the west. If the war comes—when it comes—we'll need daēvas to keep them both from our throats." The magus sighed. "But that's not for a novice to worry about. I don't suppose you can read?"

I shook my head. I had no idea who Eskander and his wolves were, but it wasn't news to me that the Druj were stirring.

"We'll do it by rote then," the magus said. "I hope you at least learned some of our history?"

His tone was friendly, but I still felt like a savage. "Yes, some."

"Tell me what you know, and I'll tell you how much is true," he said, smiling.

Again, my mind went blank. "A long time ago there was a war," I said in a rush. "Everyone was going to die but then the Prophet Zarathustra came and fixed things. The daēvas are wicked but they serve us now."

The magus laughed. "That's the short version, yes. Two centuries ago, the Druj swept down from the north in numbers never seen before. They served Queen Neblis and her necromancers. Daēvas fought in their ranks as well and the city states were quickly overrun. Thousands died. And then, in our darkest hour, the Prophet was sent a vision from the Holy Father. It showed him the secret to making the cuffs. Once we leashed the daēvas, forced them to fight with us instead of against us, the tide turned. The Druj were driven back. And the empire was unified under King Xeros the First."

"What happened to Neblis?" I asked.

"She reigns in Bactria still, but over a broken, barren land. Since we leashed her cousins, she hasn't dared to attempt another invasion."

"Her cousins?"

The magus blinked his owlish eyes. "Nebh
thought you knew."

I shook my head. I hadn't known that, but I s
made sense. If she was still alive, she certainly ʋuldn't
be human.

"We may not be at war, but Druj still occasionally harry
our northern border, and it is the job of the Water Dogs to
hunt them down and keep their countrymen safe." The
magus clasped his hands. He had long, elegant fingers. Unlike
mine, the nails were very clean.

"They should have killed her," I said, scowling. "It was
foolish to let her live."

"You think so, child?" The magus raised an eyebrow.
"These lands were already bleeding from a thousand wounds.
The King did what any intelligent leader would do. He
regrouped. Xeros expanded the army and installed the satraps
to ensure the loyalty of the provinces. Then he set about
building an empire. Roads, cities, irrigation. I suppose you
would have gone haring up to Bactria with a few daēvas,
leaving every other border unprotected? Why not just send
the barbarians a formal invitation?"

I squirmed a bit in my seat, although his tone was mild.

"Now, listen. You were correct in one thing. The daēvas
are wicked, but their magic is different from the magic of the
other Druj," he said. "It is what we call natural magic, while
the revenants, wights and so forth use necromancy. It's a
complex subject, but in essence, daēvas draw their power
from the elements—air, water and earth, but not fire. Their
Druj nature rejects the holy flames. If they try to work fire, it
will kill them. But they also heal from injuries that would be
fatal to a human and they do it quickly. That's why they make
such good soldiers."

I nodded, trying to memorize everything, but it was a bit

...rwhelming. I had no idea what *necromancy* meant, or how any of this actually worked. Not for the first time, I wondered what I'd gotten myself into. Unlike my brother Kian, who spoke slowly and had a cautious nature, I tended to leap into the first course of action that occurred to me—a habit that had gotten me into fights and worse. *Reckless* was the word my father used most often, although he said it with a hint of pride. My mother preferred the term goat-brained.

"It goes without saying that you and your daēva will become close," the magus continued. "The bond is a very special gift. But you must never forget what they are."

"Druj," I whispered. That single syllable sent a thrill of fear through my belly.

"Yes, Druj. You will serve the Holy Father, then the King, then the satrap. Those are your loyalties. Nothing else matters. Do you understand?"

"Yes, I think so."

"Good. Ilyas will take charge of your training. We usually have a dozen novices, but you're the first with the ability the scouts have managed to find in over a year. You will have chores in the morning, followed by weapons training. In the afternoons, you will report to me. Then chores again. Do you have any questions?"

I thought. "Yes. How long will I be a novice for?"

"The usual period is four years."

"And when will...when do I..."

"Bond your daēva? Not until I decide you're ready."

"Where do I go now?" I asked.

"The novice quarters are in the barracks next to the stables. There are plenty of empty beds, you can choose the one you like. Just stay away from the river. That's where the daēva quarters are."

"What will my chores be?"

"Kitchen duty to start, most likely. Go, child." He waved a

hand in dismissal. "Ilyas will sort you out. You can find him in the training yard."

I could see his patience was wearing thin, but I didn't want to wander around lost. "Where's the training yard?"

"Between the barracks and the stables. Just take the road you came in on."

I followed his directions to a dusty courtyard. Ilyas wasn't there, so I wandered into the stables. I loved to ride and wondered if they would give me a mount of my own when I became a Water Dog. The warm animal smell inside reminded me of home. I walked down the stalls, admiring the satrap's horses. I didn't think anyone else was there, so I jumped when a young man suddenly appeared, leading a glossy chestnut mare.

He looked me over, his expression more curious than hostile, but I still felt like a trespasser. He had short golden hair that curled up at the ends and a slender but powerful build. I guessed he was about twenty. I had never seen anyone —male or female—so beautiful. It was almost ridiculous. Then he took a step toward me and I realized that his leg was twisted at an odd angle. A club foot.

"Hello," he said. "Are you the new recruit?"

I nodded. "I'm looking for Ilyas. Do you know him?"

He seemed amused. "I know him."

I felt my cheeks grow warm. Of course he knew Ilyas. He lived here. I looked at his sky-blue tunic, identical to Ilyas's in every way except for the color.

"Are you a recruit as well?" I asked.

"Novices wear the grey," he said. "My name is Tommas."

"You're a Water Dog then?" I asked, confused.

His eyes, the green of a spring meadow, darkened a fraction. "Yes."

I was opening my mouth to ask why he didn't wear the red when Ilyas strode into the stables.

"I see you've met my daēva," he said to me, ignoring Tommas entirely.

I took a step back. I couldn't help it. His *daēva*? I'm not sure what I expected. Horns and a forked tail, perhaps. A creature as ugly on the outside as it was on the inside. But they looked just like us.

Tommas nodded to Ilyas and led the horse past us out to the courtyard. He moved with a startling grace despite his infirmity. Like an animal. A predator. Ice touched my spine.

"Let's see what you're made of," Ilyas said. "Take a practice sword from one of those barrels."

I'd never held a sword before, not even a wooden one. It was heavier than I expected.

"Get your feet apart," Ilyas said. "Right leg forward."

I did as he ordered. Several of the serving girls had paused in their chores. Half of them were watching Tommas saddle the horse. The other half were laughing at me behind their hands.

"Blade up," Ilyas said.

I lifted my sword and he slapped it aside with his hand.

"Up and steady!"

I raised it again, and this time held it firm when he tried to knock it from my hands.

Ilyas took his own practice sword from the barrel.

"Today, all I want you to do is keep that in your hand," he said.

I nodded, muscles tense. A moment later, my sword was flying through the air. Ilyas had flicked his wrist as casually as swatting a fly, and suddenly, my sword just wasn't there anymore.

"Pick it up," he said calmly.

I picked it up.

Again and again, he disarmed me. Again and again, I picked up the sword. The girls were laughing openly until

Ilyas walked over and said something too low to hear. They scattered like a flock of chickens.

By the time the sun was setting, I could hardly lift my arms. But I refused to quit. Ilyas wouldn't break me so easily. I was Four-Legs Clan.

When he saw I was on the verge of toppling over, Ilyas clapped me on the back and smiled.

"You did well, Nazafareen," he said. "I'll see you in the fire temple for morning prayers. They'll feed you in the kitchens. I left some novice tunics for you in the barracks."

I nodded, suddenly too tired to speak. As I trudged toward the palace, I wondered what my family was doing now. Probably sitting around the fire, laughing and talking while the dogs begged for scraps.

I'd given Ashraf's puppy to some distant cousins. I couldn't stand to look at it. If I'd just let her keep the cursed thing, my sister would still be alive.

4

It soon became clear that almost everyone at the satrap's compound considered me a savage. I wasn't accustomed to eating at a table, and my clumsy manners were a great source of entertainment for the serving girls. They pretended to sniff the air when I entered the kitchens, then turned their noses up in disgust. I had never realized the contempt most people had for nomads.

The only ones who treated me like a human being were Ilyas and Tommas, and the magus. The other Water Dogs spent most of their time on patrol and I saw little of them at first. Eventually, I managed to keep the sword in my hands while Ilyas battered me, but the first few weeks were sheer misery. Every night, I dreamed of Ashraf. Sometimes it was my knife in her neck. Those dreams were the worst, and I would wake shaking in the darkness of the empty novice barracks.

Clearly, my sister had an axe to grind.

So I would light a stub of candle while I waited for the dawn (trying to sleep again was useless) and I would vow to her that I'd do whatever it took to earn my place in the Water

Dogs. To start killing Druj. But Ashraf had never been patient—she was only seven, after all—and I knew she would hound me until I made good on my promise.

It didn't take long to learn my way around the satrap's sprawling complex. There were two sets of Water Dog barracks, one for daēvas and one for humans. The servants had their own quarters, as did the harem. The fire temple, where I prayed with Ilyas in the mornings, was a simple stone structure on the east side of the gardens. Our faith held that fire was the holiest element, followed by water, and then earth. The flames symbolized the light of wisdom banishing the darkness of ignorance.

Ilyas would kneel next to me, eyes shut tight, lips moving silently. There was a strange intensity to his prayer, as though he sought forgiveness for some perceived sin, although his behavior seemed in all respects proper, if a touch rigid.

"The world is in an eternal struggle against good and evil," he would say to me. "But the most important war is fought here." Ilyas would tap his chest. "It is not the barbarians, nor even the Druj, that we must fear the most, Nazafareen. It is the enemy within."

I would nod and pretend I knew what he was talking about. Did he mean the daēvas? Being bonded? Or just the temptations of sin in general? All of those things? Several times, I nearly asked, but something in his grey eyes held me back. As though Ilyas would be terribly disappointed in me if I failed to understand.

I hoped that the afternoons I spent with the magus might clear up my confusion. I knew almost nothing. My people lived an isolated existence and the larger workings of the empire mattered little to us. So I would sit in my hard chair while he lectured me on politics and history and other subjects too boring to name. The only time I perked up was when he discussed the daēvas. They fascinated me in a shivery way, like panthers viewed through the bars of a flimsy cage.

"Only the Immortals—the King's personal division of the army—use daēvas as a large fighting force," the magus said. "The satraps have a small number for their Water Dogs, but not too many. The most powerful and wealthiest merchants are permitted one or two. Daēvas equal power, Nazafareen. If the satrapies had their own armies, they might consider rebelling. The King can't risk that."

"What about the magi? You said you were bonded too."

"I was." He looked out the window. "Some of us choose the bond, but not all. Fewer now. Most magi fear the taint too much."

I wanted to ask why he wasn't bonded anymore, but it seemed an impertinent question and for once, I managed to keep my mouth shut.

"Why don't they try to break free?" I asked instead.

"It's impossible. If a daēva so much as touches the cuff of their human bonded, they will suffer severe pain. Punishment can also be inflicted directly through the bond if the wearer wills it. But all our daēva soldiers have been raised in the light. We've trained them to overcome their wicked natures."

"But you still don't trust them," I said. "That's why they're cuffed."

The magus smiled but it didn't reach his eyes. "Yes. They are still Druj. The bond doesn't change that."

"Are they Undead? Like the wights?"

"Not Undead. Not human either. Something else."

I thought of Tommas. He seemed so *nice*. "How do you know they're Druj then?"

"They fought on the side of the Druj," the magus said stonily. "They fear fire. They have unholy powers. What more do you want?"

I considered what I knew of the Undead. Some said liches

were the souls of murderers, or of human-daēva offspring that had been abandoned to die of exposure. Whatever they were, a single touch would kill. Revenants were some kind of soldier. They had been the most feared in the war, after the necromancers, because of their strength and size. They were the main force of Neblis's army.

And wights...Well, I knew about wights. Their substance looked something like liches, but they knew how to creep inside a person. They didn't kill with a touch. What they did was worse. Before people knew the signs—those black almond eyes, for one—a single wight could turn an entire family in minutes, each killing and infecting the next. Whole villages fell in this way.

But the daēvas were *alive*. They talked and ate and laughed like the rest of us.

"I don't know. Where do they come from? What did they do before the war? Did daēvas always exist?"

He tapped a finger impatiently. "We seem to be straying from the point of this lesson. No doubt they came from the same place as the rest of the Druj."

"Where's that?"

"Bactria, of course." The magus leaned forward. "If you are to become a Water Dog, you need to be very, very clear about what you are dealing with. I understand that the daēvas you see now are the ones we've raised in the Way of the Flame. But their fundamental natures are deceitful, impure. That is all the word *Druj* means, Nazafareen. It is not some kind of..." He fluttered his hands. "...scientific classification. We are speaking of the soul. The main thing you must remember, above all else, is that you must always hold the leash tightly, unless you are in danger. Always."

I thought about this for a moment. "But they *can* kill Druj? I mean, the Undead kind."

"Oh, yes." He smiled at me, pleased to be back on familiar

ground. "Greater Druj, like Revenants, must be beheaded. In theory, a human can do it, but it's very difficult. The same for Lesser Druj like wights. But liches? Their substance is shadow. They must be unknit with air. Only a daēva can accomplish that."

"When I'm bonded, will I have that power too?"

"No. But you will hold your daēva's power in the palm of your hand. He cannot touch it without your consent." The magus made a fist. "When you need him to use it, you just... open your hand." He let his fingers relax.

"I think I see. When will I get my daēva?"

The magus sighed. "Not yet, Nazafareen. You still have a lot to learn. I might consider it in another year or two." He waved a hand. "You can go to your chores now."

I started for the kitchens, my feet dragging. Another year of scrubbing pots and dodging blows from the cook while the household maids shot me poisonous looks. One of them had spit in my breakfast that morning but I saw her do it and knocked the bowl to the floor before she could hand it to me. The cook had wanted to beat me. Then some of the harem girls came in asking for sweets and distracted him long enough for me to slip away. But I knew he hadn't forgotten.

I decided that I would risk being late and getting a worse beating to stop at the barracks and ask Ilyas if he would let me serve in the stables instead.

His door was open. Ilyas stood by the window, watching Tommas spar with another daēva in the courtyard. They were both soaked in sweat, their movements a blur almost too fast for the eye to follow. I made a small noise so Ilyas would know I was there. He spun around, an almost guilty look on his face. It softened when he saw me.

"Nazafareen. Do you need something?"

"Yes. I don't want to work in the kitchens anymore."

"Why not?"

"They treat me like I'm a barbarian."

Ilyas stiffened.

"I don't mean any offense," I said hastily. "You're not..."

"A barbarian? No, but my mother was." He fingered his red-gold hair. "I have her look, although my father is Satrap Jaagos."

He said this lightly, as though it didn't matter. I never would have guessed. The noble women of the palace wore veils, but I'd seen the satrap's wife in the gardens. She had long, dark hair. No one in all of Tel Khalujah had Ilyas's coloring.

"Your father is the satrap?" I said carefully.

"He brought me back with him after one of the campaigns in the Middle Sea. Against Eskander's father. I was just an infant."

That name again. "Who's Eskander?"

Ilyas laughed. "Hasn't the magus been teaching you anything?"

I tried not to sulk like a child at his dismissive tone. "Things about the daēvas. Some history and geography. I'm learning the names of all the satrapies, and their capitals. What goods they produce." I scuffed my toe on the floor. "I don't really see the point. I'll probably never leave Tel Khalujah."

Ilyas studied me. "You think it doesn't matter?"

I shrugged, sensing one of my captain's lectures coming on.

"How about Macydon? Ever heard of it?"

"Um...One of the Free Cities?"

"Their enemy, actually. And ours now, as well. Eskander of Macydon is the new thorn in the King's side. Rumor has it he's offered sanctuary to any daēva who manages to escape the empire." Ilyas pulled his boots on. "He's a heretic. If Eskander has his way, we'll all be food for the carrion birds."

The thought was disturbing. "Will he try to invade?"

"At the moment, he's busy snapping up Athens and the other Free Cities. But it's only a matter of time before his eyes turn east."

"What about the Immortals?" I said. "We have ten thousand human-daēva pairs in the capital. Nothing can stand against them."

"Likely not," Ilyas agreed. "And he's a pup. Just eighteen years old, I hear. No doubt luck and the advice of his father's generals have been behind his victories."

Ilyas strode out the door. I had to jog to keep up. "So will you let me switch to the stables?"

He looked at me sharply. "You wish to work under Tommas?"

"I don't care who I work under," I said truthfully. "It's just that I'd prefer to be with animals. The serving girls and the cooks hate me and nothing I do can change that."

Ilyas paused and I saw sympathy in his expression. It occurred to me that he knew what it felt like to be an outsider. To be despised for the way you look.

"I'll see that it's done," he said, stalking into the practice yard and grabbing a spear from the rack. "Tommas!" he shouted.

Ilyas's daēva wiped the sweat from his forehead and walked over. Summer had come to Tel Khalujah, and it was much hotter than I was used to in the mountains. There was a place we used to swim in the river, a deep pool with rocks you could jump off. I imagined my brother and the other kids laughing and screaming, the sublime moment of weightlessness before the water rushed up and grabbed you, and felt a stab of homesickness.

"Nazafareen is switching to the stables," Ilyas said. "I expect you to make her useful."

Tommas nodded. "You can start today, if you like."

"I've cared for horses before," I said quickly. "I won't get in your way."

"It doesn't matter if you can't tell the front end from the back," Ilyas snapped, irritated. "He'll do it because I told him to do it."

I felt awkward, but Tommas didn't seem offended by his tone. It wasn't the only time I'd seen Ilyas go out of his way to chastise his daēva. At best, he was coldly polite. At first, I thought that all Water Dogs were expected to act that way. The daēvas were Druj, after all. But then I saw the others in the yard, joking easily with their bonded. Clearly, Ilyas had some grudge against Tommas. Or perhaps he just felt the need to hold himself aloof.

"Come by in an hour," Tommas said to me with a smile.

As he limped away, Ilyas's eyes followed him, and for some reason, his words came back to me in that moment.

It is the enemy within we must fear the most, Nazafareen.

☙❧

AND SO TOMMAS BECAME THE FIRST DAĒVA I EVER GREW acquainted with. He turned out to be as easygoing as Ilyas was stern. I already knew how to saddle and groom a horse, so he put me to work straightaway. At first I felt shy being alone with him, but he kept up a gentle patter of questions about my family and life with the clan, and soon we were speaking like old friends. That may sound strange, considering that he was Druj. But I knew that he couldn't touch his powers without Ilyas's consent, and although Tommas was inhumanly strong, I could see from the way he treated the horses that there was kindness in him, whatever the magus said about his soul.

Tommas told me that he had grown up in the islands of the Middle Sea, keeping the wind steady for merchant traders. When his ship, the *Antikythera*, was attacked by wights, Tommas showed an affinity for combat, killing half a dozen Undead at the tender age of nine. His owner thought he might be suitable for the Water Dogs, and Tommas had fetched a high price from the satrap. He had been bonded with Ilyas since he was ten, Ilyas twelve.

It was Tommas who told me that Ilyas's mother was not only a barbarian, but a Macydonian, like Eskander.

"That must be hard," I said, as I brushed down a long-legged piebald mare.

"He was singled out for ill treatment by the other children when he was younger," Tommas agreed. "But once he became a Water Dog, they knew better than to cross him."

"Does the satrap acknowledge him as a son?"

Tommas glanced up at me from the water trough he was filling with a bucket. "He told you about that?"

"Just today."

"Yes, Jaagos has treated him decently."

"Why is he so mean to you?" I blurted out. "Ilyas, I mean."

"You're very plain-spoken," Tommas said with a wry smile.

"Rude, you mean," I said. "I'm sorry. My mother says my tongue is like a dog. It makes lots of noise, but very little sense."

"No, you can ask," Tommas said. "Although I'm not sure I know the answer. He's a complicated man, and his life has not been easy. More than anything, I think he wishes to prove himself."

I sensed that Tommas knew more than he was letting on, but decided I'd pressed my luck enough. "How old is Ilyas?"

"Nineteen."

"He prays a lot," I said, stroking the horse's neck. "I always see him at the fire temple."

"Yes, he's very devout." Tommas reached into his pocket

and took something out. "A welcome gift," he said, handing it to me.

I studied the wood carving in my hand, feeling pleased and slightly embarrassed. It was a fish, the scales and fins so detailed and lifelike I half-expected it to begin flopping around.

"Thank you," I said. "You made this?"

He nodded. "Do you like it?"

"Very much." I wished I could return the gesture, but my possessions were few. Then I remembered something I'd hastily packed the morning we left the Khusk range. "Wait here." I ran next door to my room in the barracks and searched through the small goatskin bag I'd brought from home. When I returned, Tommas was sitting quietly on a bale of hay.

"It's all right," he said. "You don't have to—"

"No, I want you to have it." I offered my prize, and his eyes lit up.

"It's the tail feather from a mountain eagle," I said. "I found it on a ledge."

Tommas's slender fingers riffled the snowy white barbs, which faded to a darker brown at the tip.

"Air is my favorite element," he said. "This is a treasure. Thank you."

We shared a smile, and I thought that if my own daēva was like Tommas, it might not be so bad to be bonded after all.

❦

NOW THAT I WAS FREE OF THE KITCHENS, MY LIFE AT TEL Khalujah became a much happier one. Daily sword practice and generous food rations put some muscle on my bones. We ate apart from the daēvas, but I got to know the other Water

Dogs. There were only three bonded pairs besides Ilyas and Tommas. They were all much older and a tight-knit bunch, so when I heard that a new recruit had arrived, I was both excited and wary.

We met when she walked into the barracks and sat down on my bed. She was very pretty, with dark skin and a multitude of braids held back with a gold band. Like me, she wore the grey tunic, but this girl made it look like a gown fit for the satrap's wife.

"Are you the nomad girl?" she demanded.

"My name is Nazafareen," I said, giving her a look that dared her to say something rude. I was no longer the skinny thing I'd been when I arrived. I knew how to fight with my hands and feet as well as with a weapon. And I was past tolerating other people's ignorance.

"Nazafareeeeen...I like it." She smiled. "North star."

"How do you know that?" I was shocked. Not many knew our dialect.

"I know a lot of things, nomad girl." She had a lilting, musical accent. "I come from Al Miraj. Do you know of it?"

I tried to picture the map the magus kept in his study. "The burning sands to the south," I said.

"The very same. My daēva's name is Myrri."

"You have a daēva?" I felt a stab of jealousy.

"Bonded since we were small children. We do things differently in Al Miraj." She flopped back on my bed and sighed. "And we don't call them daēvas there. We call them djinn."

"They haven't given me one yet," I said glumly.

She eyed me closely. "They'll have to soon. Have you had your blood yet?"

I blushed a little at her bluntness, although my people weren't shy about such things. "Yes. A while ago."

"Hmmmm. I suppose you follow the Way of the Flame?"

"Doesn't everyone? I mean, all civilized people?"

She laughed. "Oh, nomad girl. No, we have our own gods in Al Miraj. We've been loyal to the King since the war and he's too smart to take our customs away from us. That's the best recipe for rebellion."

"So why are you here?"

"My father is very rich," she said languidly. "He's good friends with the satrap of Al Miraj. I told him I wanted to go kill Druj and he refuses me nothing. So here we are."

"You haven't told me your name," I said.

She grinned, flashing a set of even white teeth. "I'm Tijah," she said. "It means sword."

And then she proceeded to pull out a wicked-looking curved blade that she said was called a *scimitar*. I decided right then that I liked this girl very much.

"What does it feel like to be bonded?" I asked.

"I've been told it depends on how strong your gift is. It's different for everyone."

"What about you?"

She thought for a moment. "I sense Myrri there, almost as if I have a second body, but it's...ghostly. Faint. Sometimes I know what she's feeling, but not always."

"Can you read each other's thoughts?" I asked, greatly fearing the answer.

"No, nothing like that. Much more subtle."

"Thank the Father."

She laughed. "Are your thoughts so terrible?"

I saw Ashraf for an instant, bloody and accusing. "Sometimes. The point is that they're mine, and I don't want anybody rifling through them. What's she like, Myrri?"

"Brave. Loyal. She's a sister to me," Tijah said. A shadow crossed her face, but she covered it by standing and tossing her bag on the bed next to mine. "So you've had the place all to yourself. I hope you don't mind company."

"I'm glad for it," I said honestly.

"How long have you been here?"

"Since last winter. Have you met Ilyas yet?"

"Yes, he said we are to train together. What do you think of him?"

"Hard but fair," I replied, helping her shake out a blanket and tuck it in. "He'll push you to your limits, but not beyond. He's been good to me." I lowered my voice to juicy gossip level. "He's the satrap's bastard. His mother was Macydonian."

"A barbarian!" Tijah exclaimed in delight.

"Not really. He looks like one, but he was raised here." And then my tongue was off and running, filling in my new friend about the other Water Dogs and their daēvas.

Zohra, who was even shorter than me but could leave four men weeping in the dirt at practice. Sanova, who always wore a sneer on her face and should be avoided at all costs. Behrouz, who could throw a boulder twenty paces but had a singing voice as sweet as a nightingale.

"Then there's Tommas, that's Ilyas's daēva. He's handsome and nice, but Ilyas is very cold with him. I think he doesn't like being bonded."

"Can't he just take another daēva?"

"No, the magus says the Water Dog cuffs are for life. It didn't used to be so, but the last satrap was caught trying to sell his daēvas on the black market. Now they lock the cuffs on. Only the magus has the keys."

"Well, I hope you get a good one then," Tijah said. "Since you'll be stuck with them forever."

I fell back on my bed and stared at the timbered ceiling, suddenly feeling a little ill.

"So do I," I said.

On my seventeenth birthday, the magus summoned me to his study.

I sat down and waited while he shuffled through a stack of papers. Finally, he looked up.

"I've found you a daēva," he said.

I sat very still, hardly breathing.

"His name is Darius. He was raised by the magi in Karnopolis. By all accounts, obedient and devout. And powerful." The magus held my eyes. "Very powerful. The strongest in generations, if his keepers are to be believed. You were chosen because I can't leave you unbonded much longer. You're nearing the time when your mind will become too rigid to accept him, Nazafareen. And so that is my present to you. Are you happy?"

"Yes, magus. Very happy." I was happy. I was also extremely nervous.

"Do you wish to meet him?"

My heart lurched. "He's here?"

"In the yard, waiting for us. Oh yes, and his curse is a

withered left arm. I thought the fact that you are left-handed would be a nice complement."

I let out a long breath as we walked outside. Bonding my daēva meant I could hunt Druj. Go on patrol with Ilyas and Tommas. Tijah had already been promoted several months before. Now the six of us would be a unit. I'd been waiting for this moment for more than three years, and yet part of me still wanted to run in the other direction as fast as I could.

We came around the corner of the barracks and there he was. A boy still, although not for much longer. I took in the close-cropped brown hair and pale, serious face. His sky-blue tunic matched his eyes, which were not particularly warm. More along the lines of one of the glacial lakes I'd bathed in as a child.

I walked right up to him, refusing to be cowed. It seemed prudent to let him know who was in charge immediately.

"I'm Nazafareen," I said.

Darius nodded. His face was perfectly impassive, but did I see a spark in those eyes? Of fear? Contempt? It came and went too fast to tell.

I had no idea what to say next, so we just stood there in awkward silence for what felt like an eternity. Finally, the magus spoke.

"Come. Satrap Jaagos and the other Water Dogs are waiting."

The bonding ceremony took place in the audience chamber of the satrap. It was a cavernous room, with vaulted ceilings of gilded tile and three marble pillars. The walls were carved with bas-reliefs of horses, their arched necks and braided manes rendered in exquisite detail.

Jaagos sat on his throne, his Water Dogs arrayed to either side. Half of them wore tunics of sky blue, the other half of a deep, bloody red.

I'd seen Jaagos from afar a few times, but this was the

closest I'd ever been to him. In the moment before I prostrated myself, I saw a chubby man dressed in a rich gown of
silver thread. He was bald as an egg, with thick lips and
sloping shoulders. A housecat among lions.

I pressed my forehead to the stone. To my right, Darius
did the same.

I was keenly aware of the eyes of the Water Dogs on me.
They were the ones I wanted to impress, especially Ilyas. I
didn't give a fig about the satrap, except that I knew I didn't
want to make him angry. His authority was absolute, the hand
of the King in Tel Khalujah, and if he wanted me dead, he
had only to make the slightest gesture and it would be done.

"Get on with it," Jaagos said after an appropriate amount
of time had passed for the obeisance.

The magus stepped forward. "You are Water Dogs, the
holiest of all dogs," he said. "Without water there is no life,
yet water has the power to destroy as well as to create. May
your impurities be washed away." The magus slowly poured
the contents of a silver bowl over our heads.

"May the Holy Father keep you and guide your actions,"
he intoned. "May the bond bestowed this day be true and
pure. May you always serve the cause of light and shun the
darkness."

He set the bowl aside and pulled on a pair of leather
gloves. Then he took out a gold cuff, thick and worked with
snarling lions. Had he touched it with his bare hands, he
would have bonded Darius himself instantly.

The magus's face swam in my vision as he knelt before us.
Darius had gone a deathly pale, but he looked at the cuff—
the twin of one already encircling his right arm—without
wavering. I resolved not to show him how afraid I was. Not
to give him that victory.

"You will fight as one, live as one," the magus said. "You
will carry out the will of the Holy Father, as directed by your

King and satrap. Good words, good thoughts, good deeds. By the Prophet and the Holy Father are you bonded."

Then he snapped the cuff around my wrist and locked it with a tiny golden key. I may have cried out. I probably did. Because I wasn't alone anymore. Floodgates opened in my mind, releasing a torrent of alien emotions. Next to me, Darius drew a sharp breath as the same thing happened to him, although I barely heard it. Panic surged through me, followed by an aching loss so deep it tore a hole in my heart. I didn't know if it was mine or his, or both feeding off the other. And I felt his power, a deep, churning pool of it, held tight in my fist.

"It is done," the magus said.

My knees trembled as I stood. Darius offered me his hand but I was afraid to touch him so Ilyas took charge of me, leading me from the audience chamber to the fire temple. We knelt there together. I tried to pray, but my teeth were chattering.

"It gets easier with time," Ilyas said in a soothing tone, as if he was talking to a small child. "You'll learn to tell the difference between your own feelings and his. To separate them. To hold onto yourself."

I nodded but I didn't believe him. I just wanted to tear the cuff from my wrist. To get Darius and his bottomless despair out of my head. But that was impossible. It was locked in place.

"Look into the flames," Ilyas said. "Imagine them burning your fear away. Scouring your mind clean of thought. Feed it all to the holy fire. You have the gift, Nazafareen. Now you must learn to control it, or it will destroy you."

I tried to do as he instructed. For a moment, I felt as though I'd broken the surface, that the torrent was easing a little, but then it came back stronger than ever.

I jumped to my feet and just made it to the courtyard before I threw up.

They let me go to my bed after that for the rest of the day. Everyone left me alone. They understood that I couldn't bear to be near even a single other person. I had enough of them in my head already.

❧

MY EYES FLEW OPEN AT THE CRACK OF DAWN. I GROANED and rubbed my forehead. My scalp tingled, an icy, unpleasant sensation. I knew right away where Darius was and what he was doing. It was another side effect of the bond, I'd discovered. I could feel his heart beating. I knew that one of his boots was too tight. I could shut my eyes and tell you exactly where he was, even if he was hundreds of leagues away.

Why had no one told me what it would be like? I supposed Tijah did, but this was much worse than I'd expected. Much, much worse.

I threw on my new scarlet tunic and marched down to the river. Tendrils of mist swirled through the dead reeds at the edge. It was late autumn and the air had a dank chill that promised snow.

My daēva stood there, stripped to the waist, pouring water over his head with his right hand. He wore a gold faravahar on a chain around his neck, its eagle wings spread wide. His left arm lay at his side, grey and dead. I stared at his shoulder, at the juncture where smooth skin met rough. His Druj curse.

It slowed me for a moment, seeing that pathetic arm, but I wasn't yet ready to forgive him for waking me. That was my excuse, anyway. Of course, what really angered me was the terrible realization that I was burdened with a sorrow not my

43

own, but that bled me nonetheless. What really angered me was *him*—everything about him.

He was calmer this morning, but I wasn't. I stopped about twenty feet away. He didn't turn around although he knew I was there.

"It's nice that you're so pious," I said. "But don't you think it's a little early to be down here performing the morning rites?"

He paused, then dumped the last of the water from the bowl. I felt the cold trickle down my spine and my lips tightened.

"I was taught by the magi to come at first light," Darius said. "Did you expect to sleep in? I'm afraid that's not the way it works for Water Dogs." He smiled, and we both knew it was fake. "I'm sorry if I've offended you in some way."

I stared at him, at the dark hair plastered across his forehead, his stubborn mouth. He looked so human. And yet there was something in the way Darius held himself, perfectly at ease in his own skin. Still but *coiled*, like the wolves I'd seen in the mountains.

"You haven't offended me in the least," I said. "I suppose you need the blessing more than I do."

I spun on my heel and walked away, knowing I had wounded him. A small stab to my own heart. And I felt slightly ashamed. But that wasn't the end of it. Then I felt his satisfaction at my shame. And my own anger that he knew and was glad.

And then his amusement at my anger!

I stalked off, determined to think nothing, to feel nothing, ever again.

If only it were that easy.

I DIDN'T SEE DARIUS AGAIN UNTIL ILYAS BROUGHT ME TO the training yard that afternoon. He wanted me to watch our daēvas fight each other.

Tommas was already waiting. He grinned when he saw me and tilted his head in greeting.

"Mine," Ilyas said, with a possessive edge to his voice. "And here's yours."

Darius walked up. Tommas got a nod. I didn't. If Darius was nervous, I couldn't feel it. If anything, his emotions were flat, blunted, like he'd found a way to hide them from me. Well, good for him. I hoped I could learn to do the same.

They each selected wooden practice swords. The daēvas began to spar, slowly at first, testing each other's infirmities. Tommas's leg versus Darius's arm. Tommas was taller, but Darius moved like a striking serpent. Soon, they were slashing the air so fast I could only follow their sparring by the sharp crack of the wooden blades coming together with bruising force. When they shattered their fourth staves, Ilyas called an end to it. I found myself as flushed and sweaty as the combatants, which made him laugh.

"I've almost forgotten what it's like in the beginning," he said. Then his face hardened. "But you must learn to separate yourself, Nazafareen. To keep focused. In a real fight, it can kill you to let the bond take control. To think that what he's experiencing is real. It is real, but it's over here." He made a pushing motion with his hand. "You must use your will to keep him in one part of your mind. Like a box. You're aware of what's happening in the box, but it's not yours. Do you understand?"

"I think so."

I closed my eyes, tried to find the place where I ended and Darius began. I could almost feel it, like the edges of a bubble. Something tangible, at least. I imagined the bubble shrinking, growing smaller until it fit into the palm of my hand. He receded, and for the first time since the bonding ceremony, I felt some measure of control over the contents of my own mind.

Then the bubble burst and he came hurtling back. But it was a start.

"Now we fight in pairs," Ilyas said to me. "Get a sword."

I pulled one out and went over to Darius.

"On his left," Ilyas snapped.

I reddened and moved over. Of course, I was supposed to compensate for my daēva's infirmity. That was my purpose. To keep Ilyas out of the way, while Darius engaged Tommas.

We squared off, Ilyas on the side of Tommas's bad leg. An instant later, Ilyas lunged, and it was like my first day in the yard. Before I could blink, my sword was sailing through the air.

I stood there for a moment, dumbfounded. I had fought Ilyas countless times, but I had never seen him move like that. Had he been toying with me the entire time? Embarrassment and fury flooded me as Darius lowered the tip of his own sword to the dirt while he waited for me to retrieve my stave. How could my captain leave me so unprepared? Was part of my training to make me look a fool in front of my daēva?

I gritted my teeth and pulled the sword out of the horse trough.

"Blade up!" Ilyas commanded. "Come, Nazafareen. You can do better than that."

I adjusted my grip on the hilt and managed to keep it for about ten seconds before Ilyas disarmed me again. This process repeated itself several more times, until he mercifully called for a break. I had staggered over to the well for a drink of water when Darius came up behind me. I expected pity or scorn, but that wasn't what I sensed from him. It was something closer to frustration.

"Listen," he said. "You have some of my strength and speed, if you'll just use it."

I opened my mouth and he held up his good hand.

"I'm not asking you to let me in. I understand that you don't want to do that, and frankly, I don't either. But if you loosen your grip on the power, just the tiniest bit, you'll get what's called backflow. It will help you. Ilyas is using it." He tilted his head, and I didn't need the bond to see his amusement. "Unless you enjoy playing fetch."

I stared at him. One advantage of the bond was that I didn't need to come up with a cutting response. I could just let my opinion of his patronizing attitude leak straight into his brain.

"Thank you," I said stiffly, turning my back.

I could feel it, lapping at the edges of my mind. Not the dark power of the Druj I was so terrified of. Something full of life, bursting with it. I took a deep breath and let go of his leash. I was clumsy that first time, feeling the power surge and then clamping down in fear again, until I felt just a trickle come through the bond. But that trickle was enough. My reflexes quickened, as did my awareness of Darius's position just behind and to the right of me. The yard snapped into sharper focus. Even from ten paces away, I could see the tiny patch of red-gold stubble on Ilyas's jaw that he'd missed while shaving that morning, the sweat beading between his fingers.

I felt Darius's satisfaction as I kept Ilyas at bay for a full five minutes before he disarmed me. The next time, it was ten. To his credit, Ilyas realized what I was doing right away and didn't reprimand me for it. He could be strange sometimes. I think he'd wanted me to figure it out on my own.

But I knew I wouldn't have if Darius hadn't helped me.

IT TOOK ME A LONG TIME TO LEARN TO CONTROL MYSELF. To control *him*. He wasn't as nearly obedient as they claimed. I woke every morning to the sensation of cold water trickling down my spine. My complaints to the magus were ignored. Apparently, Darius's need to purify his Druj nature at the river, regardless of the season, took precedence.

But one thing came out of it that surprised me. From the day we were bonded, my nightmares stopped. I still dreamed of Ashraf, but they were good dreams. Of lying in the high grasses and swimming in the river. My sister had returned to me as she was in life rather than death.

And I started to notice that at certain times of day, usually the early evenings, Darius seemed to go away. I knew where he was physically, but his mind was so tranquil, I barely noticed him. Or I noticed him in a different way. It's hard to be completely unaffected by someone else's mood when they're living in your head. If he felt angry or depressed, my own thoughts grew dark. I would worry about Neblis and her Druj, and what I would do the first time I had to face one. I worried about dying in battle, and I worried about *not* dying. About what it meant to live for hundreds of years, never truly alone in my own mind. Yoked to a demon for all eternity.

But then...there would be these moments of serenity. They lasted anywhere from fifteen minutes to an hour, and left me feeling clean and new. Like a little kid again, without a care in the world.

I began to wonder what he was doing. So one day, when the birch leaves were just starting to turn gold, I went looking for him. Well, not looking, really. I knew where he was. A grove of trees near the river.

It was a beautiful early autumn afternoon, the sky bluer than blue and the air with that crisp edge to it that lets you know winter is coming but not for some weeks yet. If I had been home, the clan would just be starting the long trek across the mountains.

I followed the path, which wound in and out of the woods, through blackberry brambles and dark pines. As I reached the river, a cormorant winged by overhead, its serpentine neck extended in flight, and I paused to watch it for a moment.

Just past the bend was an overgrown orchard enclosed by a low stone wall. Darius sat beneath a pear tree, the very same that Tijah and I had poached fruit from in summer. His eyes were open. He wore his blue tunic and baggy trousers tucked into short boots. The left one was still too tight. I thought I would ask Ilyas to give him new ones.

Darius must have known I was there, but he didn't stir.

I had planned to...not confront him. Just ask what he was up to. But seeing him there like that, his face and hands relaxed, I changed my mind. If he could find a moment of peace, who was I to take that away? I watched him for another few seconds, and then I turned and walked slowly back to the barracks.

☙❧

WITH PRACTICE, IT GREW EASIER TO MAKE A BOX IN MY mind and stuff Darius inside it. He wasn't gone—my daēva was never gone—but it was the difference between someone whispering into your ear and the murmur of voices in a distant room. It was something I could live with. I had no choice.

I came to recognize these second-hand sensations, to sort them from my own direct experiences. As soon as I encountered a feeling that I knew wasn't mine, I shoved it into an out-of-the-way corner of my brain and ignored it. If I hadn't learned to do this, I would probably have gone crazy very quickly.

We trained every day, first with Tijah and Myrri, and when they grew tired, with Ilyas and Tommas. Despite their strained relationship, when my captain and his daēva fought together, they were like one mind in two bodies. I suppose it was because they had been bonded so long. It was beautiful to watch them move, like silk cloth rippling in the wind or water flowing over stones. Like a dance where the partners were perfectly in tune with each other.

By contrast, Darius and I were horribly awkward. I kept stepping on his feet, and he kept getting in the way of my sword arm. But slowly we learned the other's strengths and weaknesses. We learned to anticipate each other. To let go of the walls we had built, if only for those hours in the yard, and allowing the other to be fully present.

Managing his power was different. I still fumbled with it, although I had become used to its constant presence. A faint, pulsing thing, like starlight seen out of the corner of your eye. I hadn't seen him use it yet. The power was to be released only to kill Druj, nothing else, and the border had been quiet.

When I asked the magus what it was, he gave me a long-winded answer that left me more confused that I was before. Tommas said that power was the wrong word. It wasn't something you seized, like a force, but something you *became*, which made even less sense. All I knew was that it didn't belong to me, although I could feel it, hovering just out of reach. And if I trusted Darius enough, I could let him touch it when the need arose.

That turned out to be the hardest part.

❧ 6 ❧

"Hold!" Ilyas held up a fist.

I reined up. The village we sought lay just ahead, a collection of mud-brick houses the exact color of the dusty landscape. We were close enough that we should have heard the shouts of children playing, the barking of dogs. But a heavy stillness lay over the streets. The buildings crouched together, dark windows like broken teeth, and I knew the reports weren't mistaken. Something bad had happened here.

We were four hours' ride from Tel Khalujah in the foothills of the Char Khala mountains that marked the empire's northern border with Bactria. For two centuries, the jagged range had acted as a barrier against Queen Neblis and her necromancers. It was even higher and more treacherous than the Khusk range I'd grown up in and stretched all the way from the Salenian Sea to the Midnight Sea, which hemmed Bactria to the east and west.

There was no trade with Bactria, of course, and little news. Anyone foolish enough to travel that way didn't return.

But our side of the mountains had always been reasonably safe.

Until a few months ago. According to Ilyas, people were starting to disappear from the border settlements. Just one or two in the beginning. It was attributed to wolves. This was the first time an entire village had vanished.

That's what the trade caravan passing through Tel Khalujah had claimed, at any rate. That the dwellings were all intact but the people were gone. They hadn't lingered to investigate and I couldn't blame them. Despite the bright noonday sun, the place had an ominous air.

"We search house by house," Ilyas said. "Bonded pairs. Are you ready, Dogs?"

I shared a glance with Tijah. She flashed a cocky smile, but I could see she was gripping the amulet she wore to ward off bad luck. Behind her, Myrri stared into space with a dreamy look. We both rode with our daēvas on massive stallions bred for a double saddle. Ilyas and Tommas chose to ride apart, but they didn't stray far from each other.

We all made the sign of the flame—head, lips, heart—and galloped into the village of Ash Shiyda. Our hooves kicked up a cloud of dust. I wound my *qarha* around my face. There were no bodies, no overt signs of trouble, but I felt Darius's unease. It mirrored my own.

"Anything?" Ilyas asked Tommas brusquely as we reached the main street. It was lined with one and two-story dwellings, some with shops on the ground floor. An awning cast a knife-edge shadow across a table displaying wooden figurines of the Prophet. Next to them was a brazier with the charred remains of esphand seeds, burned to ward off evil. I wondered if these people had reason to fear something. If they had fled.

"Nothing living," Tommas said. "Not that I can sense." He looked at Darius and Myrri. They shook their heads.

"We'll take the houses at the end of the street," Ilyas said. "Nazafareen, you have the left side. Tijah, take the right. We meet back here in ten minutes. If either of you find anything, come get the rest of us. Understood?"

"Yes, captain," I said.

I nudged the horse into motion with my knees and rode up to the first house. Laundry flapped on a line in the yard. A pair of boots sat next to the doorstep. I shielded my eyes against the sun, but it was too dark inside to see anything.

"Breathe, Nazafareen," Darius said. "You're giving me a stomach ache."

I scowled and tried to relax. We'd been patrolling together for more than a year now, but we'd yet to encounter any Druj. So far, we had broken up fights in the wine sinks of Tel Khalujah's seedier district, arrested a man trying to sell a pair of daēva cuffs (fake, of course), and hauled in several members of a new sect sympathetic to Eskander.

I was itching to kill a demon. But I was afraid too. I wasn't happy that Darius knew it, but there was nothing I could do about that. Strong emotions were impossible to hide from him.

We dismounted and went inside, swords drawn. There were only two rooms. Both were empty. The stench of rotten food hung in the air. Whatever had happened, these people had been eating dinner when it came. Their bowls of stew were still on the table, crawling with flies.

The next house was the same.

"Are you sure you can't sense Druj?" I demanded.

I knew Darius was a skilled tracker. He'd done it with the barbarian-loving traitors. They'd tried to flee Tel Khalujah and Darius had led us straight to them.

"They're Undead," he replied. "I can only feel life. It comes from—"

"Yes, yes," I said impatiently. "The nexus. The magus already told me."

None of that mattered at the moment. I wanted only to use it to kill as many Druj as possible.

"Come on," I said, striding into the next house. "Let's get this over with. If the demons were here, they've come and gone."

It was larger than the others, with a narrow flight of stairs leading to a second story.

"I'll look up there," I told him. "You check these rooms."

"We're supposed to stay together," Darius said. His eyes glowed like a cat's in the dim light. "Unless I misheard our captain, he said to search in bonded pairs."

"You'll know if I need you," I said, heading for the stairs. I could feel his annoyance and it gave me a grim satisfaction. Let him think I'm a coward now.

Thick carpets covered the floors, masking my footsteps as I entered the first bedroom. It faced away from the street. A child's room, judging from the toys scattered across the carpet. My chest tightened. It had been five years since the wight took my sister, but the flames of my guilt and hatred had not dimmed. If anything, they burned hotter than ever. I had fed them everything I was, everything I had. In many ways, they were all that was left of me.

I left that room and went to the next. It was bigger, with a wooden bed and large chest in the corner. Dust motes danced in the beams of light streaming from the narrow window as I walked over to the chest. It was a pretty thing, with silver trim and a painted border of flowering vines. The owners of this house had been prosperous.

I used the point of my sword to ease the lid open a few inches. I suddenly had a terrible vision of finding a corpse in there, or something worse, but it turned out to be full of folded cotton tunics.

If Darius had discovered anything downstairs, I'd know about it by now. I let out a breath and closed the trunk. We still had a dozen more buildings to clear, but I was starting to think that whatever had happened here, it would remain a mystery. I'd yet to see signs of a violent struggle, not in this house or the others. There was no blood, no overturned furniture. Perhaps the people had simply left in a hurry.

I was turning to leave when I heard a creak. Soft, but definite. It came from underneath the bed.

I jumped back, blade leveled at the gap.

"Come out," I said, adjusting my sweaty grip on the hilt. "If you're human, I won't harm you. I'm a Water Dog, sent by the satrap in Tel Khalujah."

There was no response for a long moment. Then a woman crawled out. She looked about my mother's age but her skin was pale and soft. A merchant's wife.

"Praise the Holy Father," she said in a cracked whisper.

She wore a blue headscarf that emphasized the hollowness of her cheeks, the sagging jowls. A woman who had once been plump, but whose flesh had been slowly winnowed away. I wondered how long it had been since she'd eaten anything.

"What happened here?" I asked. "Where is everyone?"

"I'll tell you," she said. "Help me up. My legs are cramped from hiding for so long."

I hesitated for only an instant. The light was dim, but I could see her features. Not like my sister, who'd been hidden behind a curtain of dark hair. I held out my hand. She was starting to reach for it when her eyes fixed on something over my shoulder. The woman visibly recoiled.

"Darius." I didn't bother turning around. "You're frightening her."

"Step back, Nazafareen," he said, and it was not his tone that made my pulse leap, although that was warning enough. It was the rush of emotion through the bond. Pure hatred.

Druj.

Without thinking, I swept my sword in a lightning arc at her neck. I was only two feet away. Her head should have toppled to the ground. But she slithered away like a snake, and when she looked at me again, her eyes were hard black almonds in her face.

"She knew you would come," the wight hissed. "Water Dog heroes. She left you a gift."

Rage blurred my vision. I leapt at the Undead, not caring if I lived or died. Only that if I did, I took it with me. The woman it had possessed was as good as dead. Worse. There was no saving her body. Only her soul.

I swung again and my blade sunk deep into its flesh, but that hardly slowed it down. I could feel Darius battering at the bond in a panic, shouting my name. I shoved him away. The wight dodged and wove, inhumanly fast. But I was fast too, and my bloodlust lent me its own unnatural strength.

Finally, I drove it into a corner. I stabbed and stabbed. I was raising my sword to do it again when Darius grabbed the front of my tunic and spun me around.

"Release me!" he screamed. "Let go of the bond, Nazafareen! Let go!"

And I realized that I'd been gripping our leash with white knuckles, holding all his power tight in my fist.

"I have to chop its head off," I mumbled, sagging against the wall.

"You already did," Darius said. "And the liches are coming. For the love of the Holy Father, unchain me!"

I looked down. The wight's head lay between my feet, tongue lolling. When I looked up again, I saw them. Twin shadows darker than night. They billowed through the door like smoke, long tendrils reaching along the floor.

"Now!" Darius shook me again.

I closed my eyes and let go of our invisible leash.

A second later, the shutters banged open and a hot wind roared through the room. I staggered back. The *qarha* kept the dust from my mouth, but it felt like a huge hand was clamping down on my lungs and *squeezing*. Breath whooshed from my mouth in an arid croak. Then I was searching madly for something to hold onto as my feet began to lift off the ground.

A keening scream rent the air. The liches fought, shredding apart and reforming. Darius's hair whipped around his face. I knew he was only using a fraction of what he could have. That he was still holding back. I could sense the shining pool of power, how deep it was.

He pushed me to the floor, careful not to touch the cuff, and braced his legs against the bed. The gold alloy felt both searing hot and freezing cold against my skin. Darius's mind stilled.

That's when the roof blew off.

Sunlight poured into the room. I watched as Darius lifted the liches high into the air and ripped them apart, the shreds dissolving in black wisps against the blue of the sky.

When it was done, he collapsed onto the bed. I felt him release the power but my breath still came in hard, sharp gasps, as did his. I lay on my back, stunned at what he'd just done. I could still feel echoes of that tremendous surge through the bond. It thrilled and terrified me at the same time.

"What just happened?" I finally managed. "Did the liches touch you?"

He rolled over and gazed down at me with mild scorn. "Do I look dead?"

"No."

"Then obviously they didn't. It's the price of using the power."

"The price?"

"Do you truly not know? Daēva magic is sympathetic. When I manipulate an element, my own body responds to it too. Water affects blood, earth affects flesh and bone. And air..." He took a shuddering breath. "Didn't the magus explain it?"

"I...yes, of course." I vaguely recalled his droning voice warning me that I *might* experience a *slight sensation* when the power was used. "I just didn't think it would be so intense."

"Well, now that you're enlightened, we should find the others," he said.

Darius rolled to his feet and we ran down the stairs. Five steps outside the door, he stopped abruptly and grabbed my arm. A ragged crevice had opened up in the ground, running the entire length of the street. On the other side of it stood Ilyas and Tommas. The thing they were fighting could only be a Revenant. One of the Greater Druj.

It towered over them and wielded an iron sword nearly five feet long. I saw right away that they couldn't get close enough to put it down. Strings of silver hair swung past empty, colorless eyes as the Revenant parried a thrust by Tommas and nearly severed his arm on the backswing.

The magus said they were ancient warriors returned from the grave. A forgotten race resurrected by Queen Neblis's necromancers. Whatever the truth was, I understood now how the Druj had overrun our cities in the war. Because as bad as the wights and liches were, this thing was worse.

It wore mailed leather streaked with some kind of black mold. I could see old wounds on its body. Terrible wounds. I knew they were old because nests of maggots squirmed inside. But they didn't seem to affect the Revenant's brutal strength. I heard the high whistle of metal cutting through air as it drove the Water Dogs back toward the crevice. Tommas had probably sundered the earth under the

Revenant's feet but it had escaped somehow. Now both he and Ilyas were about to tumble in themselves.

"Can't you use air again?" I turned to Darius, frantic. The gap was too wide to leap across or I would've done it in a heartbeat.

"Not without risking them as well," he said grimly.

The Revenant swung its huge sword again. Tommas leapt to the side, but the tip sliced through his tunic and blood started to run freely from his right shoulder. Tijah and Myrri were nowhere in sight.

Darius closed his eyes. A low stone wall on the other side of the street began to tremble. I felt a sharp pain in my side, like the stab of a needle. Three seconds later, half of the wall smashed into the Revenant's back. It staggered a little. Then it growled and drove its sword against Tommas's in a blow so hard that the blade flew from Tommas's hands.

I watched in horror as his legs buckled and he dropped to his knees at the Revenant's feet. The blow had affected Ilyas as well. He looked stunned.

"No!" I screamed, running for the crevice, knowing I wouldn't make it in time.

The Undead raised its sword high, the point poised down for a killing stroke.

Tommas's head was bowed, but I could see he was smiling. Why was he smiling?

And then Ilyas stepped neatly inside its guard and, with a single two-handed sweep, cleaved its head from its shoulders. There was no hesitation. He'd known exactly what his daēva intended. A second slower and Tommas would have died.

Tommas had to have known that too. But he took the chance. He trusted Ilyas with his life.

Even decapitated, the Revenant was a foot or so taller than the Water Dogs. It swayed for a moment, that terrible sword still clutched in one mailed hand. When it finally toppled over, the sound was like an oak tree falling. Darius started to laugh, then winced in pain. He'd cracked a rib throwing the wall.

"An old trick," Ilyas called to us. He was panting, his hands braced on his knees. "Give them a taste of blood and they forget what they're facing. Not two Water Dogs, but one."

I glanced at Darius and my cheeks flushed. We'd come within seconds of dying today because I'd pushed him away. In my lust for revenge, I'd forgotten he was even there.

He pressed his right hand to his side, the same place I'd felt a stab of pain when he threw the wall. One of his ribs had cracked. The price of sympathetic magic. I hadn't realized it was so high, and that he alone would pay it. It seemed unfair somehow. But I understood now why Tommas hadn't simply dropped a building on the Revenant. It would have broken every bone in his own body.

Tommas got to his feet and limped down the street. That's when I saw that his horse was badly injured. It lay in the dust, sides heaving. Tommas crouched down and stroked its muzzle. I thought he was weeping. I knew how much Tommas cared for that horse. He had named it Abraxas.

Ilyas sighed and pulled a knife from his belt. He walked over and whispered something to Tommas. The daēva shook his head. Ilyas laid a hand on his shoulder. Abraxas's hind legs kicked weakly. It emitted a low groan. Finally, Tommas nodded. I turned away as Ilyas put the horse out of its misery.

For once, Darius and I both felt the same things. Pity and sorrow, mingled with a deep, simmering anger.

Then Tijah and Myrri came around the corner. Tijah was carrying a head by the hair. Another Revenant. She was grinning until she saw Abraxos.

"They laid a trap," Ilyas said, walking over to us. "Neblis

took the people and left the Druj, knowing we'd turn up sooner or later."

"What does she want them for?" I asked, fearing the answer.

"Slaves. And when they break, she gives them to the necromancers."

I thought of the toys on the floor of that room and felt sick.

"Any chance we can catch up to them?" Tijah asked.

Ilyas shook his head. "The raid came at least a week ago. They'll be over the mountains by now."

Tijah swore in her native language, something filthy by the sound of it.

We stood silent as Tommas approached. His tunic was soaked in blood. I couldn't tell how much was his and how much was the horse's.

"Let me see your wound," Ilyas said gently. It was the first time I had ever heard him speak to Tommas in a tone that wasn't cool or distant.

"It's nothing," Tommas said.

"You'll take my mount," Ilyas said. "I'll run back to Tel Khalujah."

Tommas looked at him. He seemed in a daze. "No, I can walk."

"That's an order," Ilyas said, grey eyes hardening. He lifted the edge of Tommas's tunic up and I stifled a gasp. His entire back was an angry red that would soon turn into a spectacular bruise. That wasn't from the Revenant. That was from working with earth.

"I'll ride with you, Tommas," I said quickly. "I'm the smallest. The captain's horse can take us both."

They stared at me.

"No one needs to walk," I said. "Ilyas can ride in the double saddle with Darius."

"Fine," Ilyas muttered, stalking away.

Tijah tossed the head into the crevice and shared a look with Myrri. Her daēva was mute, cursed with a missing tongue, but the two of them were so close, they didn't seem to need words. When they did, they used a complex system of hand gestures. I'd learned some of them, but most remained a mystery.

Myrri made a fist and waggled her pinky. Tijah nodded in agreement.

"We ride hard," Ilyas said, swinging into the saddle behind Darius as the rest of us followed suit. "But we stop at the villages along the way and warn them to get out. Move south." A muscle feathered in his jaw. "This border is no longer secure."

7

Dark had fallen by the time we arrived in Tel Khalujah. Ilyas went straight to the satrap to report what had happened to the village of Ash Shiyda. Tijah and I headed to the bathhouse together. I couldn't wait to get the stink of the wight's blood off me.

Water was one of the holiest elements, so even Tijah was required to kneel and give thanks to the Holy Father before entering. The hour was late and we had the place to ourselves. In the four years we'd known each other, I'd noticed that she always made sure to come here alone. I assumed Tijah was modest, although it didn't really fit with the rest of her personality. But women were treated harshly in Al Miraj, the magus said. Not like the rest of the empire, where they could own land, enter into contracts and hold fairly high positions. Rich women, like the satrap's wife, veiled themselves, but it was by choice, and more a sign of their status than anything else.

Tijah quickly peeled her tunic off and slid into th but not before I caught a glimpse of her back. brown skin was covered with a welter of old

She knew from my expression that I'd seen it. She had *let* me see it. We were quiet for a moment.

"What is your father like, Nazafareen?" she asked in a soft voice.

I thought about it. "He taught me to ride and shoot a bow. Not a soft man, but no one in the Four-Legs clan is soft. In truth, I think he was closer to his horse than he was to his children. But he kept us alive." I smiled and sank deeper into the water. "He has a very fierce mustache. It always tickled my face when I kissed him."

Tijah smiled, but there was something sad in it. "I grew up in my father's palace, the youngest of five girls. We had every luxury, but it was an empty life. As children, my sisters and I were treated like pretty little ornaments for my father to show off when he had guests. I realized later that he viewed us in the same way as his carpets and spices. Objects to be bartered for more wealth and power. One by one, he married my sisters off. When I turned thirteen, he betrothed me to a business partner." She scowled.

"Fat and ugly?" I guessed.

"No. He was handsome enough. Tall and broad in the shoulder, with the eyelashes of a girl. But my sister Saalima had also married him, several years before. I rarely saw her afterwards, but when I did, I could tell she was a broken thing. The light had died from her eyes." Tijah splashed water under her armpits, gold bracelets jangling. "This man had two faces, you see. The one he showed to the world, and the one he showed to his wives. My mother saw it too. She begged my father to wait two more years before the wedding took place. He reluctantly agreed."

I dragged a comb through my hair. "He sounds like a monster. What happened?"

"The two years flew by. My dread grew so intense I opped eating. But my father would not be budged. He was terrified of offending this man, for he was the son of the satrap."

I shook my head in disgust. "Many marriages are arranged in the Four-Legs Clan as well, but care is taken to choose someone suitable. And the girl has the right to refuse."

"Then you nomads are far more civilized than my people," Tijah said wryly. "If I hadn't had Myrri, I might have taken my own life. I saw no other way out."

"How did you come to be bonded, if girls are valued so little?"

"My father had no choice. The satrap rewarded him with a daēva for a service he performed, and I was the only one he trusted that had the gift. I imagine he expected to take her from me once a male heir capable of wearing the cuff was born. But my daēva made me even more valuable to my future husband."

"He did that to you?" I asked, looking at her back.

"My father did that to me," Tijah said flatly. "Or rather, he ordered the servants to do it, the coward. He didn't want me looking emaciated on my wedding day. When I refused to eat, he had me beaten. And when I still resisted, he made them whip Myrri. He knew I felt her pain as my own. Greater, in some ways, since she had done nothing to deserve it."

I thought of Tijah's daēva, mute, unable even to scream. "What a bastard. He didn't fear her power?"

"She was afraid I would be harmed if she fought back. But after that, we'd both had enough. She told me we would both end up dead if we stayed, and I knew she was right."

"So you ran away."

"Yes. The night before the wedding, I stole a horse from his stable. Myrri laid a false trail leading south. Then I chose the most remote satrapy I could find. One where they would never think to look."

"Why the Water Dogs?"

She shrugged. "I spoke the truth when I said I wanted to kill Druj, although I had never seen one before coming here. A Water Dog is...it is the opposite of everything about my old life."

"And your scimitar?"

She gave that wicked grin. "My father's. It was purely ceremonial. I thought it should be put to good use."

"You know they won't give up, don't you?" I said. "They will hunt you to the ends of the earth. Men like that...to be humiliated by a girl. It is the worst shame imaginable."

Her lovely face hardened. "I know. Which is another reason I joined the Water Dogs. By the time they come, they will find not a frightened girl, but a warrior with blood on her sword. Let them try to take me back."

I leaned over and kissed her lightly on the cheek. "You won't fight them alone, if it comes to that," I said.

"Thank you. I wanted to tell you before, but..."

"I know. My mother used to say that secrets begin as pebbles and grow into boulders. Yet still we would rather carry them around than give them to another for safekeeping."

Tijah yawned. "Your mother was a clever woman."

We dried ourselves off and put on fresh tunics.

"I suppose your name isn't really Tijah," I said as we walked to the barracks.

She turned to me, brown eyes blazing with a kind of crazy determination, and I thought if those men valued their manhoods, they would stay far away from this girl.

"It is now," Tijah said.

***

I WAS BONE-TIRED, BUT I COULDN'T SHAKE THE SHAME OF my failure at the village. It touched a raw nerve in me, something that had festered for years. After Tijah's confession, I felt a powerful need to apologize to Darius, to explain myself. We'd been bonded for more than two years now but I hardly knew him. Yes, I could tell what he was feeling, but not *why* he was feeling it. Not always. I couldn't read his mind and he couldn't read mine. Thank the Holy Father for that.

We saw each other only at practice. In every other way, the daēvas lived separately from us. They slept apart, ate apart. I prayed at the fire temple, but Darius couldn't enter it so he prayed by the river—as I knew all too well.

Rain pounded the roof as I lay there, unable to sleep. I knew I'd have no chance to speak to him privately tomorrow. We were never alone. Finally, I threw off my bedclothes and slipped outside.

I'd never been to the daēva barracks but I knew where they were. I ran down the hill and through the gardens. It was late summer and the rain had brought out the sweet, heady scent of jasmine. When I neared the river, I saw a sagging three-story wooden building on the bank. I touched the bond lightly, felt for him. A moment later I frowned.

I'd expected him to be sleeping, but he was on the roof.

And his mood was not happy.

I stood for a moment, dripping. I almost went back. I should have. But instead, I found my feet leading me to a rickety ladder that leaned against the eastern wall of the barracks.

"Go away, Nazafareen," Darius said the instant I reached the top.

He lay on his back, staring up at the storm. For a crazy second, I wondered if he had made it. But even Darius couldn't be that strong.

"I'm sorry," I said, climbing out onto the roof. The tiles were slick with rain and I chose each step with care.

"For what?"

His careless tone irritated me.

"For holding you back. I didn't mean to."

"Oh, that."

"Really," I said. "It won't happen again."

"You could have killed us both," Darius said mildly.

"I know. I'm sorry."

"You still don't trust me, do you?"

"It's not that."

I wanted to tell him about Ashraf but I couldn't. I'd kept it in too long, and the words stuck in my throat like sharp stones. Or boulders.

Darius turned to look at me for the first time. "It's because I'm Druj." He clutched the gold eagle-winged faravahar he wore around his neck with his good hand. An unconscious gesture I had seen many times. It was the symbol of the Prophet. The symbol of the empire.

"No! I mean, I suppose you are. But you walk in the light like the rest of us."

He laughed then, a bitter sound. Since that first flood of emotion at the bonding ceremony, Darius had kept a tight rein on himself. He rarely smiled and seemed indifferent to pain. Sometimes, I suspected, he sought it out.

"Yes, the magi taught me well," he said, and something dark and feral in him seemed to stir.

I squinted through the sheets of rain. "Why are you up here anyway? Was it another nightmare?"

Darius didn't respond. I should have let it go, but I suddenly wanted to crack that emotionless shell. It was a stupid impulse, like dangling a dead rabbit in front of a hungry wolf.

"They wake me up sometimes," I said. "What do you dream about, Darius?"

"I don't remember."

"That's a lie," I said.

His walls went up, hard and fast.

"Do you dream of fire?"

It was just a guess, but on those times when I woke up with dread oozing through the bond, there was also a sensation of heat, of a wild, untamable power that would consume me if I let it.

"What do you want, Nazafareen?" Darius demanded hoarsely.

"Just the truth."

He stared at me, dark hair dripping, and the look in his eyes made me want to run.

"All right. Sometimes I hate this." He held up the cuff around his wrist. "If you really want to know, sometimes I hate *you*."

I wasn't ready for the anger that burst through the bond then. It staggered me. I put a hand to my head, dizzy, and tried to keep my balance. But my feet slipped on the rain-slick tiles and a moment later I was sliding toward the edge.

Darius cursed and lunged forward, grabbing my arm. My legs kicked over empty air. And just like that I was back to the icy ledge, a terrified child of twelve, except that this time, it was me who was about to plunge into the abyss.

He grunted with effort, hauling me up. The spell broke and I realized I'd just done it again. He could have lifted me with air as easily as a kitten, but I was gripping his power tight.

Darius shook his head. He laughed again, although this time it was more darkly amused than angry. I put my head in my hands.

"A fine pair we——" he started to say.

And the edge of the roof just gave way. The wood must have been old and rotten. I suppose the satrap had decided that they were only daēvas and didn't need decent housing.

I didn't fall, but Darius did. Three stories to the stone courtyard. The pain of the impact took my breath away.

I scrambled down the ladder as fast as I could and ran to him. I knew without even looking that he was terribly hurt.

"I'm sorry, I'm sorry," I whispered. Blood ran in a thin trickle from the corner of his mouth. His blue eyes were clouded. I took his hand. It was the first time I had ever touched his bare skin. It was warm. But such a strange sensation. I could feel the contact through him as well, like looking at my own reflection in a hall of mirrors.

"Nazafareen," he whispered. "You don't..."

He never finished what he was going to say because shock set in. Darius's head rolled to the side and his eyes slipped shut.

Holy Father, please don't let him die...

I screamed for help and Tommas came limping out the door of the barracks, golden hair tousled from sleep, wearing only a pair of pants. Normally, I would have enjoyed the sight of him half-naked, Druj or not. But the only thing filling my mind at that moment was Darius.

"Run and get the magus as fast as you can," I said. "I think his back is broken."

8

"**I**'d like to see him," I said, folding my hands primly in my lap.

"Why?" The magus gave me a hard stare. He'd aged in the four years I'd known him. His brown hair was now streaked with grey and faint lines creased the corners of his mouth. That's what happened when a person was no longer bonded. I still didn't know why he hadn't taken another daēva, or how the first one had died, and I doubted he would ever tell me.

"Because I have a block, and the only way I can break through it is by practicing with Darius," I said. "I told you about it, remember?"

He grunted. "One hour a day. After evening chores."

"Thank you." I jumped to my feet and was almost at the door when the magus spoke.

"You feel his emotions very strongly, don't you?"

I froze. "Sometimes."

"Not all do. Some feel nothing at all, only the power. It's easier for them to maintain the necessary detachment. But your gift is strong. So is his. Mind what you do with it."

"Yes, magus."

I felt his eyes on my back as I walked out the door. On the way to the stables, I wondered if the magus had been one of those like me. I had a feeling he was, that he had been very close to his daēva. That he was still in mourning.

For the next hour, I helped Tommas muck out the stalls. Neither of us spoke much. I knew Tommas was in mourning too, for Abraxas. Ilyas had quickly reverted to usual self—cold and condescending—but Tommas never seemed to mind. His patience with Ilyas seemed boundless. I decided I would probably never understand the two of them.

And it didn't matter, because I had a hard enough time figuring out my own daēva.

He had to have known I was coming, but he still frowned when he saw me. Dark shadows made his eyes an even more vivid blue. It had been three days since the fall, three days since his spine had shattered, and yet he was half sitting up, propped on a mound of pillows.

"Nazafareen. What are you doing here?"

"I have permission," I said quickly.

"That's not what I asked."

"Don't be impertinent," I said.

Darius coughed to cover a smile. The movement made him wince.

"How is it?" I asked.

"Healing. Slower than I'd like."

And twenty times faster than I would, I thought, if I ever healed at all.

"Can I get you anything?" I asked him.

"I'm fine, thank you."

I stood there. An awkward silence ensued.

"I told the magus we should practice with your power," I said finally. "If you're able to."

Darius settled deeper into his pillows. "What's the point?"

I scowled. "Do you want me to apologize again?"

"No. But we both know that you're perfectly fine when you're feeling calm. It's when you're scared or angry that you lose your head. Practicing won't change that."

I knew he was right, that he'd cut to the heart of it. But I suddenly didn't want to leave just yet. I hated to admit it, but I missed him a little.

"We could do something else. Aren't you getting bored?"

He shrugged.

"I could tell you stories. I know some good ones."

He flung an arm over his face. "I'm too tired," he mumbled.

"Fine. I know how exhausting it is to lie around feeling sorry for yourself. I used to do it when I first got here. You can talk to the spiders. Or play shadow puppets on the wall. That's always entertaining."

I turned to go and heard the covers rustle.

"Hang on. What kind of stories?"

"Well...there's Prince Jamshid and the pomegranate seeds that turn into three beautiful maidens."

"I know that one. Doesn't it have an evil daēva that takes them captive?"

I winced a little. "Yes. Sorry, I forgot about that part."

There was a long pause as I tried and failed to think of a story without some kind of Druj in it. To my surprise, Darius rescued me.

"I have one," he said. "My amah used to tell it when I was a child. It's about a clever young girl and the wicked satrap who wedded her."

"What's an amah?"

"Like a nursemaid."

"Does it have a good ending?" I asked.

Darius shrugged. "I always hoped she'd kill the evil

73

bastard, but I suppose it's not a tragic end. She does outwit him and keep her head."

So I sat on the floor, resting my back against the side of the bed, while Darius started to speak. He had a pleasant voice, with a slight trace of the lilting western accent. And every day thereafter until he healed, my daēva told me stories. I enjoyed the one about the girl and the satrap because it had lots of stories *inside* the story, but the one I liked best was called *The Midnight Sea*.

It was about a general who had gone to war against Queen Neblis and had to sail home with his men through the wine-dark waters off of Bactria. They had many adventures along the way, but then their ship was battered by a storm and broken apart. The general tied himself to the mast, tossed in the roiling seas. All manner of Undead were closing in from the depths when the current swept him to an island.

It was paradise, with fruit trees and lovely maidens whose songs kept the Druj away. But he could never leave it, or he would die.

So the end was both happy and sad at the same time, which was my favorite kind.

AFTER THOSE FEW WEEKS TOGETHER, I NO LONGER fumbled with his power. I held it lightly, if I bothered to hold it at all. I didn't tell the magus this. He would have been very angry. Water Dogs were supposed to keep their daēvas in check at all times. To release them only when threatened. But I knew Darius wouldn't take advantage of my lenience, despite what he had said on the roof that night.

We patrolled in the northern reaches and we killed Druj together. Too many to count. Ilyas had been right when he said the border wasn't safe anymore. The satrap asked for reinforcements, but was refused. The Immortals and most of the Water Dogs had been sent to Persepolae to protect the capital. Eskander, the boy general who had sacked the Free Cities, now sat on the other side of the Hellespont, waiting for the spring thaw. It was a thousand leagues away, but the thought still made me uneasy.

And no matter how many Druj died at the end of my sword, I never found the peace I was looking for.

Once Darius healed, we went back to our old routine. But I found myself thinking of him at odd times. Figs, for example. I used to like them. But Darius despised them, and now I couldn't look at one without feeling ill.

One day I decided that since I had to endure the water blessing every morning at dawn, I might as well go perform it with him. So I went down to the river. As before, he was stripped to the waist. But this wasn't the boy I remembered. Darius was twenty now, lean and hard. I paused and prayed to the Holy Father that he had his walls up against me.

"Why aren't you at the fire temple?" he asked, setting his bowl down.

Because you can't go inside, I thought, although I didn't say it.

"My people did the water blessing too," I said. "I miss it."

He looked at me. I couldn't tell if he knew I was lying. His emotions were too jumbled up.

As were my own.

I filled the bowl with water and waited.

Darius hesitated. Then he dropped gracefully to his knees and I poured the water over his head. I watched it trickle through the curls at his neck and down the line of his back, as smooth and perfect as it was before the accident. His withered arm no longer repelled me. If anything, it made me feel more gentle toward him.

"Good thoughts, good words, good deeds. May the Holy Father guide and keep you."

He kept his head bowed for a moment. Then he rose and started to leave.

"Wait!" I said. "You have to do me now."

Darius looked scandalized. "I can't…"

"Yes, you can." I knelt before him. "Give me the blessing." I peeked up at him through my hair. "I insist and you have to obey me, don't you?"

Darius let out a long breath. I heard him fill the bowl.

"May the Holy Father guide and keep you," he said hoarsely, slowly pouring the water over my head.

I leapt to my feet. "That wasn't so hard, was it?"

"Don't tell the magus…"

"Bah! Why would I tell the magus anything?" I laughed and it felt good. It had been a long time since I'd laughed. "Besides, you're more devout than anyone I've ever met."

"That's because I have to be," Darius said quietly.

He was getting all sorrowful again and I didn't want that.

"Don't make me go eat some figs," I warned.

Darius gave a startled laugh. "You know about that?"

"Unfortunately, yes. I used to like them."

"Well, your nomad ways make me restless," he said with a straight face. "That's why I was outside that night. I don't like sleeping with a roof over my head anymore."

I filled a bowl from the river and threatened him with it.

"Go ahead," Darius grinned. "I'm already wet."

We both turned as Ilyas came running down the hillside. Darius grabbed his tunic and hastily yanked it over his head. I stepped away from him.

"What in the name of the Father is going on here?" Ilyas demanded.

"We were just performing the water blessing," I said, staring at the ground.

"That's not what it looked like."

"She didn't do—" Darius began.

"Shut up." Ilyas hadn't raised his voice, which somehow made it worse. "Back to barracks, both of you. I will not have fraternizing outside of practice and patrol, is that understood?"

We nodded. I could feel Darius's fear, thick and choking, like a cornered animal. What did he think Ilyas was going to do? Our captain demanded discipline, but his punishments were nothing out of the ordinary. When Tijah and I had snuck off into town to browse the bazaars and were late returning, Ilyas had made us carry rocks back and forth across the yard until well after dark, a backbreaking exercise made worse by its sheer pointlessness, but hardly torture. And the time he'd caught Myrri using the power to dry Tijah's hair on a cold morning, which seemed to me a more serious infraction, he'd simply made them wear the grey again for two weeks. Tijah had been mad as a kicked boar at the humiliation, but it could have been a lot worse.

I risked a glance at Ilyas now. The disappointment in his eyes cut me. As though I had betrayed him somehow.

"Nazafareen, you can stop at the fire temple first," he said. "Ask for forgiveness, and contemplate the righteous path. For if you stray from it…Well, the fall can be long and hard."

I DID AS HE COMMANDED, ALTHOUGH AS I STARED INTO THE brazier and mumbled the words of purification, I kept seeing Darius with his shirt off. This went on for an hour or so, despite my best efforts at piety, and I departed faintly surprised that I hadn't been dispatched to hell on the very spot.

Ilyas hadn't said that I was confined to barracks, so I

reported to the stables a few minutes earlier than usual that afternoon, thinking I would ask Tommas if Darius had ever spoken about his life before he came to Tel Khalujah. Every time I raised the subject, Darius brushed me off. But his reaction to Ilyas's displeasure had been so extreme, I couldn't help but wonder what his last bonded had been like. I knew he had trained with a contingent of Immortals in Karnopolis, but I had no clue what the upbringing of a daēva consisted of. I'd asked Tijah, but she didn't know either. Myrri had been raised with her in the household.

My steps slowed as I heard a familiar voice inside. Ilyas was there. I knew I should leave, but I couldn't resist lingering by one of the open stalls.

"...her. They are far too familiar with each other."

"It sounds innocent enough," Tommas said.

"That's how it begins." I heard Ilyas's boots, pacing up and down. "I want you to watch him. Tell me if you witness any improprieties."

"Improprieties?" Tommas laughed. "Such as what? They're bonded. It's only natural—"

My heart clenched as I heard the unmistakable sound of a palm striking flesh.

"It's not *natural*," Ilyas snarled. Then he kicked something. From the rolling clatter, it sounded like a wooden stool. "I'm sorry," he said in a softer voice. "Tommas. I'm sorry."

I had never heard my captain use such a tone. Almost pleading. Tommas didn't reply. An instant later, Ilyas grew brusque again.

"Just watch him," he said.

I pressed my back against the wall as Ilyas emerged suddenly from the stables. If he had so much as glanced to the right, he would have seen me. But he strode off in the direction of the gardens and didn't look back.

"Go on, come inside," Tommas said. "I know you're there."

I startled, although I should have guessed he'd sensed my presence. Daēvas had the hearing of bats.

"Are you all right?" I asked gently.

His right cheek and ear were an angry red, but he flashed me his crooked smile like nothing was wrong.

"I'm sorry," I said miserably. "This is my fault."

"No, it's his," Tommas said, and I didn't think he meant Darius. "But I'd take care if I were you. Don't give him any excuses." He sighed. "Ilyas...He means well. He's just afraid."

That threw me. "Afraid of what?"

"Of failing in his duty. I think he sees a lot of himself in you, Nazafareen. He cares for you very much."

I picked up a broom and started sweeping out the nearest stall to hide my confusion. Was it possible that Ilyas felt *jealous*? The thought had never occurred to me. He had always treated me as a sister. But I had been a child then, and now I was nearly nineteen. Ilyas was only a few years older. I had never seen him with a girl, although it wasn't forbidden. Water Dogs were not magi. They could do as they pleased, as long as they were reasonably discreet, didn't marry, and kept their hands off the harem.

The daēvas were different, of course. The magi had explained that they were not permitted to have sexual relationships because it could lead to offspring, and only the King decided how many new daēvas would be bred in a given year. It was all strictly controlled.

"I have nothing to hide," I said.

"And I believe you. Just make sure Ilyas does too."

"Would he harm Darius?" I asked. "If he thought...we were being *improper*?"

"I don't know. But if your daēva matters to you at all, you'll protect him by staying away."

I nodded, feeling unhappy but resigned. Shirtless fantasies aside, I knew the whole thing was ridiculous anyway. As for Ilyas, I felt flattered if he was interested in me, but I didn't return his sentiments.

It was time to go back to basics—nursing my vendetta against the Undead. Just because Ashraf had stopped showing up in my dreams didn't mean she'd forgotten about me. And frankly, *she's* the one I really didn't want to piss off again.

⚙️

"SO YOU'RE RENOUNCING MALES OF ALL SPECIES?" TIJAH asked when we were alone that night, and I'd filled her in on my day. "Sounds boring."

"Pretty much."

"Ilyas is a fuckshit," she said.

I laughed into my pillow. Tijah spoke Aramaic fluently, although it was her second language. But when she cursed, she tended to just string dirty words together with no concern for meaning or order.

"Tommas says he means well."

"Poor Tommas. Look at him. He's like an abused wife."

I stared into the darkness. "I know. It's not right."

"Someday, he's going to snap and rip Ilyas's head off. His balls too."

"I'm surprised he hasn't already."

"Fuckshit is lucky he's here instead of in Tel Rasul. Did you hear what happened?"

I rolled to my side so I could see her face in the moonlight. "No, what?"

"There was some kind of rebellion in the Water Dogs. They put it down, but two daēvas are dead, and one of their bonded."

"A rebellion?" I sat up. "What kind?"

"I'm not sure. Zohra says two of the Dogs were planning to run off, and tried to convince the others to come along. When they refused, there was fighting in the barracks. Finally, the satrap's soldiers set fire to the building."

"Holy Father."

"Zohra thinks they might have been trying to run to the barbarian king."

"But why would they do that?"

"You really don't know the answer? Come, Nazafareen. Do you think the daēvas enjoy their bondage? Would you, in their place?"

"I suppose not," I said uncomfortably.

"We use them because we must. There is no choice. The magi say it is the will of your Holy Father, but I think it is the will of the King. And that is the way of things, nomad girl. The victor makes the rules. But it doesn't mean they will last forever. Nothing ever does."

EXCEPT FOR THE TIMES WE WENT OUT ON PATROL, DARIUS and I saw little of each other after that. His chore was to work in the gardens, and I would see him from a distance sometimes, using a spade one-handed or pruning the rose-bushes. He must have sensed I was there, but he never looked over. Still, I knew when he was hungry or tired or restless. When he'd pricked his finger on a thorn, or taken a hard blow to the ribs in sparring practice.

I missed the sound of his voice. His rare smiles, which were nonexistent now. Would we live the rest of our impossibly long lives this way, privy to the most intimate, mundane details and yet hardly knowing anything that mattered? It was like the papyrus scrolls the magi kept in his study. I admired the graceful, flowing script, and suspected it held all sorts of fascinating secrets, but they were beyond my reach.

Ilyas settled down once he saw that Darius and I had learned our lesson, and if he still harbored any feelings for me —if he ever had—he showed no sign of it. In fact, on the King's birthday, Ilyas gave us all permission to play a game of chaugan in a dirt field some distance from the palace that the satrap kept for that purpose.

We hardly ever got a day off, but Artaxeros the Second's glorious entrance into the physical plane was a longstanding holiday throughout the empire. There would be a feast in the palace that night, and the servants had been dashing about for days, bringing in casks of fine Ramian wine and all manner of delicacies for the satrap's table. He had a sweet tooth, favoring dishes like stuffed and candied ostrich, which probably accounted for both his impressive girth and abundance of gold teeth.

I had watched matches between Jaagos's soldiers before, but never tried to play myself. It was a brutal sport, fast and lawless. Severe injuries were not uncommon. The King himself was an avid fan, and had even sent a taunting letter to Eskander suggesting he play chaugan instead of war-mongering. He had included the gift of a ball along with the message (a jab at the barbarian king's youth), to which Eskander supposedly replied that the sphere represented the earth, which he intended to hold in the palm of his hand.

Darius claimed that the sport had been invented by nomads, so I was feeling cocky when eight of us Water Dogs lined up on the field after breakfast. It was about three hundred feet long, with stone goalposts at each end, set eight feet apart. The teams consisted of Darius, myself, Tijah and Myrri, against Zohra and Behrouz, and their bonded. We all rode in the double saddle, and even the horses eyed each other warily as Tommas rolled the first ball between us.

Zohra's daēva was a whip-thin man with pretty black eyes named Cyrus. He was missing an ear, and kept his hair long to cover it. Behrouz's daēva, Rasam, had a twisted spine and wore a stiff leather girdle beneath his tunic. They were both very good, and soon Tijah was cursing foully under her breath as they shattered our defense and scored a series of goals.

I was an expert rider, but striking a little wooden ball with a mallet from horseback without whacking the horse or Darius turned out to be much harder than it looked.

"Can't you just give me a little help with air?" I muttered as I swung and missed the ball entirely. Again. The horse snorted, clearly unhappy with the how close the wooden stick had come to its muzzle.

"Are you suggesting that we cheat, Nazafareen?" he asked innocently.

"It's only cheating if you get caught."

Darius laughed. "Well, we would be. Daēvas can sense the power, whether they're wielding it themselves or not."

Darius himself was riding with only his knees to keep seated, since he carried the mallet in his right hand and his left was useless.

"Fine." I raised my eyes heavenward. "Holy Father, I know you're a firm believer in humiliation, but please don't let me permanently disfigure myself or others today. Especially the horse."

It had rained the night before, and within minutes, we wore a generous coating of mud. Tijah, who had a competitive streak, got so mad at one point that she rode straight into Behrouz and ended up flat on her back in the dirt. As for myself, once I accepted that defeat was inevitable, I decided to just enjoy the rare chance to spend time with my daēva. Darius was in a good mood for a change. We pounded up and down the field, screaming at small victories and howling when our opponents scored.

At the break, I was sharing a water skin with Darius, feeling giddy and flushed and happier than I'd been in a long time, when Ilyas galloped up. His grey eyes surveyed us with disapproval, and I was about to remind him that he had given us his express permission to be there. But his next words came as a surprise.

"A messenger just arrived," Ilyas said. "Half-dead, pursued by a pack of Druj to the very gates of the city. He came from Gorgon-e Gaz."

Something sparked in Darius at the name. I'd never heard it before, and I was fairly certain it wasn't on the map in the magus's study.

"What's Gorgon-e Gaz?" I asked.

Ilyas looked at Darius. "Tell her," he said.

Darius's expression didn't change but I sensed turmoil in him. "It's where they keep the old ones. The first to be leashed. Most of them have been there since the war. It's a prison, Nazafareen."

"Why?" I glanced from Ilyas to Darius. "I don't understand. Didn't they help beat back the Druj?"

"After fighting at their side," Ilyas spat. "The Prophet knew they couldn't be trusted. And he was right. There's been an escape. Six daēvas."

"That's not possible," Darius said.

"It is. Their bonded guards helped them. There was a massacre. More than a dozen are dead."

Darius and I looked at each other in shock.

"Where is this place?" I asked.

"Half a day's ride," Ilyas said. "Tell the others and get back to the barracks, we leave in an hour."

"So we're..." I trailed off, suddenly afraid.

Ilyas's face darkened. "Yes. We're catching them and bringing them back," he said.

❧ 9 ❧

I saw the first body the moment we emerged from the pass.

He lay on the rocks, arms carefully arranged at his sides. A young man with pale skin and black hair. The gulls had been at him. A cloud of them rose as we galloped down the hillside. I knew that this was how we said goodbye to our dead. Beneath the open sky. Only after his bones had been picked clean would he be ready for burial.

But the sight still unnerved me. I made the sign of the flame.

Good thoughts, good words, good deeds.
We are the light against the darkness.

The corpse we passed lay about five hundred yards from the outer curtain wall of Gorgon-e Gaz. It started at the foot of the cliffs and extended into the shallow water. Grey stone, weathered by centuries of storms blowing in from the Salenian Sea. Curved walls twenty feet thick, with slits for windows.

The breath tightened in my lungs and I unwound the *qarha* from my face. It caught the wind, streaming out like a scarlet banner. Darius sat behind me in the double saddle, and I didn't need to look at him to know his eyes were chips of blue ice. I sensed fury in him, and shame.

"Lord Father," I muttered as we pass two more broken bodies, both in the gold and white tunic of the guards.

Our horse was too well-trained to shy at the carnage—better trained than I was, apparently. I'd become used to killing Druj, but human bodies were another thing entirely. My stomach churned but I kept my face impassive. Only Darius knew how close I was to being sick.

"Hold," Ilyas barked.

Someone was coming out of the fortress.

I leaned back slightly and dropped the reins. To my right, Tijah and Myrri did the same. They both looked ready to kill anyone who came too close.

It was a man of middle years, with thick white hair and the neck of a bull. He ran up and I saw the badge on his chest, a roaring griffin in a circle—the King's emblem. This must be the warden.

"What took you so long?" he demanded. "And where are the rest?" He squinted at the six of us and didn't seem reassured by what he saw. "We need reinforcements—"

"You forget yourself," Ilyas said calmly. "When you speak to me, you speak to Satrap Jaagos, who has the unpleasant task of informing the King of this disaster. It is eight days ride to Persepolae. Pray hard we find the runners and bring them back before that time."

The warden paled.

"I need names, both daēva and bonded, including infirmities and whatever else you know about them," Ilyas said.

The man nodded. "Aren't you coming inside? I can show you what they did..."

"There's no time. You can explain to the satrap how they accomplished it. My task is only to catch them." Ilyas turned to me. "Find the trail while it's still warm. We've already lost too many hours crossing the mountains as it is."

"Where do you want to start?" I asked Darius.

"At the high tide line," he replied.

On our way to the prison, I'd learned a few things about Gorgon-e Gaz, the secret stronghold that wasn't on any maps.

It held one hundred and thirteen daēvas. One hundred and seven now. When the Prophet forged the cuffs during the war, he used the first daēvas he caught to capture the rest. Some died in the fighting. Those that remained after Queen Neblis was driven back across the mountains had been brought here.

They remembered what it was to be free—not like the Water Dog daēvas or the Immortals, who had all been bred in captivity and raised to follow the Way of the Flame. As a result, they couldn't be trusted outside these walls. But Ilyas told me that the daēvas in Gorgon-e Gaz still served a useful purpose. Their bloodlines were strong. So it was both a prison and a nursery. Before he was sent to the magi in Karnopolis, Darius had been born here.

I was still grappling to understand all this as we rode down to the water. I'd joined the Water Dogs to kill Druj—the Undead kind. I never expected to be hunting daēvas who were more than two centuries old and powerful enough to crack the hulking fortress of Gorgon-e Gaz in half.

Because now that we had reached the tide line, I could see the shards of stone on the seaward side, the waves washing through a jagged crevice that must be forty feet high.

Darius dismounted and laid his good hand on the broken bones of the prison, the sea lapping at his feet. We stared at it for a moment and I felt the first flutter of fear in him. What daēva could channel so much destructive power and survive it? Earth was one of the most violent elements, I'd learned. If Tommas had tried to do this, it would have shattered him. I didn't know if Darius had the strength. He might, but it would have cost him dearly. He'd snapped a rib just throwing a few rocks at the village of Ash Shiyda, and earth was his strongest element, just as air was Tommas's.

My daēva turned to me. Our eyes met and I felt a trickle of power flow through the bond. He cupped a handful of sand and let it slip between his fingers. I was glad this kind of *sensing* didn't hurt him. It was only when Darius used his will to affect an element that he paid a physical price.

I felt his mind quiet as he stared down the beach.

"They've gone west," he said. "Twelve riders. Half a day ahead."

When we told Ilyas, he seemed confident we would catch up to them in the rugged terrain of the mountains. After seeing the cracked fortress, I couldn't help but worry about what would happen when we did. But our captain had expected this—unless the runners took a ship, the only other escape route would cross the Khusk Range—and our saddle-bags held supplies for a journey of up to two weeks, including quilted jackets similar to the *arqalok* of the Four-Legs clan.

"Dismount for the blessing," Ilyas said, filling a bowl from the sea.

We knelt in a row on the sand, heads bowed, as Ilyas walked down the line. I shivered a little as the freezing water trickled through my *qarha* and down the back of my neck. Then my skin prickled a second time as Darius got doused.

"May the Holy Father guide and keep us. May our impurities be washed away." Ilyas tipped his face back and unflinchingly poured the last of the icy water over himself. He shook wet hair out of his eyes. It shone like burnished copper in the sun. "This world is the battleground and we are the warriors, Dogs. Not in the next life, but here. Now. We will bring these renegades back alive if we can, dead if we must. But we will bring them back. If we fail, it is not only the king's judgment we will suffer. It is the Holy Father's."

Ilyas made the sign of the flame.

Good thoughts, good words, good deeds.

I kept my head down for an extra moment, praying for courage. Just a few paces away, I could hear the buzz of flies.

"Nazafareen," Ilyas said.

I looked up.

You know these mountains, don't you?"

"Like my own mother's face," I said. "But only parts. It depends on which route they take."

"You'll be our guide then. Darius can track them, but we need to close the lead."

"I know some shortcuts." I held the bridle for Darius, then leaped into the forward saddle. Tommas hesitated for a moment, studying the horizon with a wistful expression. He was forever carving little shells and boats and fish, like the one he'd given me my first day in the stables. He said they kept his memories of the Middle Sea alive.

"It's been twelve years since I've seen the ocean," he said.

"And I doubt she's changed much," Ilyas replied, not unkindly. "Come, the trail follows the shore. You can look all you want, as long it's from a saddle."

Several of the guards came out of Gorgon-e Gaz to watch us leave as Tommas mounted in one graceful movement and spurred his horse to a walk.

"We'll pray for you," one of the guards called. "May the Prophet speed your journey."

I took a final look at the stronghold and tried to imagine the force it took to shatter it. Then I made myself see the dead. All fourteen of them, scattered along the beach, their limbs snapped like kindling. The sweet rot of the bodies mingled with the salt tang of the sea and my bile rose. Could Darius really protect us from that? Could Myrri and Tommas?

89

The other, more seasoned Water Dogs had all been out on patrol when the messenger arrived. We were here only because Tel Khalujah was the closest satrapy to Gorgon-e Gaz. The prison was a backwater in the western reaches of the empire, a thousand leagues from the capitals. Nothing ever happened here. Until now.

The horses' hooves kicked up clods of wet sand as we thundered down the beach. We passed a stand of boulders and I could see the tracks myself now. They could have ridden below the tide line but they didn't bother. No effort was made to conceal their trail. Perhaps they knew that we could follow them regardless, or perhaps they just didn't care.

Perhaps they didn't fear us at all.

My hair was still damp from the blessing. Overhead, gulls hovered in the wind, crying to each other. I closed my eyes for a moment and felt the holiness of this place of convergence, this place where the water met the land.

I realized that part of me had stopped thinking of the daēvas as Druj. Stopped believing that their fundamental nature was evil. I didn't know Myrri very well, but I knew Tommas. I knew Darius. They were Water Dogs. But what had happened at Gorgon-e Gaz seemed to confirm everything the magus had said. The daēvas had nearly destroyed us before we chained them. And if these broke free of their bonds, they would do it again.

I hadn't gripped Darius's power in a long time. I hadn't felt the need to.

But I did now.

I closed my fist on that shimmering tidal pool and felt him stiffen. It wounded him, my sudden lack of trust, but I had to do it. I kept seeing those bodies. That jagged crack.

We rode hard for an hour or so. The beach narrowed to a spit and the trail turned west into the Khusk range, just as Darius had predicted. The highest snow-clad peaks were still several days' journey ahead, but as soon as we entered the foothills, the temperature began to drop. I could feel the bite of the wind through my *qarha*. Tijah blew on her fingers, shivering. She was a child of Al Miraj, of the brutal Sayhad desert, and had no idea what true cold felt like. She would though, very soon.

We were entering the lands of the Four-Legs Clan. I hadn't been back this way since I had left my people to join the Water Dogs. The Khusk range lay south and east of Tel Khalujah. On the other side was the Great Salt Plain, and beyond that, the Royal Road to the summer capital of Persepolae. I wondered if that was the runners' destination, or if it was someplace else.

When we camped that night, Ilyas told us he thought they were probably planning to join Eskander.

"If they make it across the western border, he'll give them sanctuary. It's their only chance," Ilyas said. The cold hardly seemed to touch him as he pored over his maps, checking different routes, trying to predict exactly when and where we would catch our quarry, and what advantage we could wring from that knowledge.

The firelight softened his sharp cheekbones, his long, straight nose and thin mouth. Our captain wasn't handsome like Tommas, or even Darius, but he had a quiet intensity, a restless intelligence that made him interesting to watch. In the years I'd known him, I'd learned that his mood could change like quicksilver, especially where Tommas was concerned. Ilyas would be charming one instant, icily disdainful the next. But he was a good leader. I trusted his judgment. He never took risks that weren't carefully calculated. And his courage in combat was legendary among the Water Dogs. I'd seen it myself, many times.

"Victor is the one we should worry about," Ilyas muttered, tossing the calfskin maps aside. "The warden said he killed more Druj in the war than any other daēva. A bloodthirsty animal, by all accounts."

"What's his infirmity?" Tijah asked, breaking off a hunk of bread.

"Minor. Three missing fingers on the right hand. He's very strong in earth. I have no doubt that he's the one who broke the fortress."

"What about the others?" I asked.

Ilyas reeled off a list of names. They meant nothing to me.

"But they're all still bonded to their guards?" Tijah asked.

Ilyas scowled. "Yes. Which means that the guards collaborated in the escape. It couldn't be done any other way." He gave us a level look. "When we find them, stay focused on the humans. Don't try to engage the daēvas. Your job will be to keep the guards at bay while the demons fight each other. You are the iron. They are the power."

"But why did the guards turn?" I wondered. "One, I might understand. But six? All at the same time?"

Ilyas shook his head. I could see he was troubled. "I don't know. The warden didn't know either. He said they were all trusted. And the protocol was to rotate the cuffs so no attachments could form between daēva and bonded."

I gave up trying to make sense of it and fed another piece of wood to the fire. Darius had left the moment Tijah struck the flint. He feared fire—all the daēvas did. It drew them in, enticed them, but it couldn't be controlled. Fire was their single weakness.

And, since they looked exactly like us, the one infallible test.

All daēvas were cursed by the Holy Father with physical infirmities, but some of them were hidden. Like Myrri's missing tongue. And most were things that humans might have too—a blind eye, a club foot. The King needed a sure way to tell us apart. To ensure that no one tried to breed them illegally.

His answer was the Numerators. Thousands of them roamed the empire, their white robes bearing the royal seal. They could bang on any door at any time, including the satrap's own sleeping chambers, and none would dare refuse them entry. Officially, they were census-takers, counting people and livestock to assess the proper taxes. But everyone knew what they really were: daēva-hunters.

We all had tattoos from the Numerators on our palms. Mine was two triangles, one inside the other. Darius's was a triangle with a slash through it, marking him as daēva. It was a special kind of iridescent ink that couldn't be forged.

When the Numerators found anyone without the mark, they dragged that person to the nearest fire temple. Not to burn them. To see what would happen as they approached the braziers. Humans, of course, would be unaffected. But within six feet of the altar, daēvas would start to feel the pull. Three feet and they'd be fighting not to reach for the wild, ferocious power of the flames. Much closer than that and the blood would boil in their veins.

So Tommas and Myrri stood guard at the edge of the light while we curled up in our blankets. He was singing softly to her, a haunting, melancholy tune in a tongue unfamiliar to me. Most of the other daēvas at Tel Khalujah shunned Myrri. I think her muteness disturbed them. Tommas was the only one who sought her out. He didn't seem to care if she could talk or not. Perhaps silence was a relief after dealing with Ilyas all day.

Tommas knew how to whistle a hundred different bird-calls, and Myrri would make hand signs telling him which ones she wanted to hear. Other than Tijah, he was the only person who could make her smile.

As I drifted off, I could sense Darius out there somewhere

in the cold and dark, scouting the trail ahead. My daēva only slept two or three hours a night lately, if he bothered to at all. I wondered if he was thinking about the runners. About what would happen when we caught up with them. If he secretly pitied them.

He would have to kill these daēvas. All of them. I knew in my heart that we'd never take them alive. They were too fast. Too strong. In this way, they were like gods. A law unto themselves.

🦋 10 🦋

We rode the next day from first light until it was too dark to continue. Ilyas wanted to keep going. He didn't know these mountains, not like I did. I explained to him that there were hidden chasms, that I had seen men fall to their deaths from one step to the next and in broad daylight. That it was suicide to try to cross in darkness. Finally, Tommas said something to him in a low voice and he reluctantly agreed to stop, but there was a desperate light in his eyes. If Ilyas had been alone, I think he would have foregone sleep entirely. He would have kept riding until he caught them or the mountains killed him.

He said he didn't know why the guards had turned traitor, and maybe he didn't, but I kept thinking of those Water Dogs in Tel Rasul, only a few months past. They too had tried to run, although they hadn't made it out of the barracks. Was there some connection between the two events? I'd believed the cuffs were infallible, but of course they had an obvious weak point. The *human* bonded of the pair. And I think that troubled Ilyas more than anything else. That our own kind would betray us. As much as he wanted the daēvas, he wanted their guards even more.

On the fourth day, it started to snow. We were coming into the final, deadliest passes. The temperature, already freezing, dropped even lower. I showed Tijah how to wrap her hands to ward off frostbite. Gloves were no good. The fingers would stay warmer if they touched each other.

She had started complaining of a terrible headache that wouldn't go away. Now she doubled over in her saddle, coughing. I winced at the harsh, racking sound of it. Myrri patted her back, brown eyes bright with fear.

I knew Tijah was getting the mountain sickness. Her body just wasn't made to handle the thin air of the high cols. If we didn't get over them soon, she could die.

According to Darius, our quarry was still a half day ahead. But soon they would reach the plains, and our lead would vanish.

"Which way, Nazafareen?" Ilyas demanded.

I hesitated. I did know a way. The shortcut my people had taken for generations. But it was not a place I ever wanted to see again.

"Which way?" Ilyas repeated. His eyes were bloodshot. He'd barely slept in days and looked almost as bad as Tijah. Our captain had become a man possessed, by demons of his own making. I didn't know what it would do to him if we failed in this mission. Even Tommas, usually cheerful, had adopted his master's demeanor and slumped in the saddle, silent and careworn.

"Follow me," I said finally, leading them into a narrow crevice in the rock. We climbed a steep rise, the flurries coming thick and fast now.

To the others, I'm sure the trail looked no different than the one we'd been following. Barren and rocky, devoid of life. But in my mind's eye, I kept seeing a long train of people, driving their herds of sheep and goats onward to the grass-lands that lay in the foothills beyond. Each step was horribly familiar.

And then we came around a bend and I saw the exact spot where I had stopped walking all those years ago. Where I'd tried to take the puppy from Ashraf.

I'm as strong as you, Nazafareen.

I paused for a brief moment to pay my respects. The snow drifted sideways, stinging my eyes.

"What is it?" Ilyas called behind me.

"Nothing." I pressed my knees into the horse's flanks and started climbing again.

WHEN WE STOPPED THAT NIGHT, I WAITED FOR ILYAS TO fall asleep. Then I left the fire and went to sit with Darius. We were...well, not friends. There was no equality between us. But we had once enjoyed the other's company, and I thought we might do so again.

His *qarha* was wound tight, so all I could see were two blue eyes. Despite the bone-deep chill, my daēva was relaxed, arms propped on his knees. He controlled his body temperature by slowing everything down like a hibernating bear. I could feel his heart beating once every ten or fifteen seconds. My own wanted to keep pace with it but I'd learned long ago to crush that impulse. It would kill me if I let it.

I settled into the shelter of the rock. The weather had cleared and the stars looked close enough to touch, a spray of frozen dewdrops against the dark mantle of the sky.

"The Holy Father's army," I said, pointing to the heavens. "The magus says they're angels that will come down to earth when the final battle is fought against the Druj."

Darius looked at me. I sensed amusement. "Perhaps," he said.

"What?"

"Well, they may be angels, but they are also suns, like ours. Just very far away."

I frowned. "How could you possibly know that?"

"I know. I can feel what they're made of." He shifted uneasily. "A terrible fire."

"But they look cold," I protested.

"Trust me, they're not."

"You feel them through the...the nexus?"

"Yes."

"I still have no idea what that is," I confessed. "Both Tommas and magus tried to explain it, but I never truly understood."

He hesitated. "It's hard to describe in words. But there is a sameness to all things. An underlying order at the smallest level. It is in me, and you, and those stars. We call it the nexus."

"Why can't I feel it too?"

"I don't know. It's a sense you humans seem to lack, perhaps because you have to still yourself to notice it. Let go of who you are. Or who you *think* you are." He touched his chest. "My name is Darius. I am twenty years old, and I am a Water Dog. I am daēva." I felt him grin. "I hate figs. But to touch the nexus, I have to forget all of those things. I have to be nothing at all. And then I am everything. And it responds to my will. Do you see?"

"Not really. But I do sense it through the cuff. Is that where you used to go? When you sat beneath the pear tree?"

"You came there once."

"I was curious. But I didn't want to bother you."

"It's a peaceful place," he said, and I wasn't sure if he meant the orchard or the nexus or both. "More peaceful when I have no desire to use it for the power, but just to be quiet." Darius released a long breath, and it trailed from his mouth like smoke in the cold air. "What happened, Nazafareen?" he asked.

At first, I thought he meant the fact that I was gripping his power again. I searched for a way to explain it that wouldn't offend him. It wasn't personal. But I'd let myself forget the first rule of the Water Dogs: stay in control. Maybe something in the bond, some flaw we didn't know about, had allowed the daēvas to turn their guards. To corrupt them. I didn't believe Darius would do that to me, but I couldn't take the chance.

"Back there," he said. "When you stopped."

"Oh."

"You don't have to tell me."

I hugged my knees and the words tumbled out. "It was a long time ago. My sister was taken by a wight. I watched her die."

"I'm sorry."

And he was. But that didn't change matters.

"Do you remember Gorgon-e Gaz?" I asked, hoping to change the subject.

"Not really. I was only an infant when they took me to Karnopolis."

"What was it like, growing up with the magi?"

I felt his walls go up, pushing me away. "You may not have noticed, but your feet are frozen," Darius said. "If you don't warm them by the fire, they'll probably turn black and fall off, and then I'll have to carry you over these mountains, which sounds like a lot of trouble."

I smiled. "Goodnight then, Darius."

"Goodnight, Nazafareen."

I rolled up in my blankets and listened to the wind moaning in the high passes. The hiss of the flames as the fire burned low. We all had our ghosts, I thought. People we had loved—or hated—so much that they had become a part of us. No one's choices in this life were really their own. Even our brave captain was driven by desires and insecurities that had more to do with the accident of his birth than anything else.

But Darius said he lost himself when he touched the power. Became nothing. Just a thread in the great tapestry of the universe. And I wondered for the first time if being daēva was truly a curse, or a blessing in disguise.

ON THE FIFTH DAY, WE CAME THROUGH THE LAST OF THE high passes. It had snowed on and off all morning, but now the skies cleared and the sun shone bright. I could see green foothills and beyond them, the Great Salt Plain, stretching like a calm sea to the horizon. Not a single tree, not a blade of grass, broke that expanse of white.

The Four-Legs clan would winter at the edge of it, many leagues farther south from where we were now. But they never ventured far. The mountains might have been unforgiving, but the Great Salt Plain was death. It boiled in summer, turned to quicksand in spring, and was a parched wasteland the rest of the time.

"Hold," Ilyas called.

I reined up. Darius gazed across the landscape, the wind ruffling his hair. I freed his power, let him search for the trail. We all expected it to turn north, following the spine of the mountains toward the border with Bactria. They would either join Neblis, or continue west over land to Eskander's army.

"What is it?" Ilyas asked. "Where are they?"

Darius's eyes fixed on a distant point, deep in the Great Salt Plain. He held up his right hand.

"That way. Perhaps four hours ahead."

I thought Ilyas would be pleased that we had gained so much ground, but he was frowning.

"Are you sure?" he asked Darius.

"Yes."

Ilyas pulled a map from his saddlebags, shielding his eyes from the glare. We were still well above the snow line and the sun was dazzling. He traced a finger across the map. When he looked up, the blood had drained from his face.

"They're heading for the Barbican," Ilyas said. "It's the only thing out there."

I exchanged a look with Tijah. She seemed stronger, and I wondered if Myrri had used the bond to help her in some way.

"The Barbican?" Tijah said. "Isn't that where...?"

"They forge the cuffs," Ilyas said grimly.

The news shocked us all into silence. I didn't know much about the Barbican. Like Gorgon-e Gaz, it was isolated, in the middle of nowhere. The secret to the daēvas' enslavement was jealously guarded, but I knew it had something to do with the Holy Flame, a special kind of fire discovered by the Prophet two hundred years ago.

Darius shifted behind me. "But it's the most heavily fortified place in the empire outside the King's palace in Persepolae," he said.

"So was Gorgon-e Gaz," Ilyas pointed out. "And that didn't stop them."

"But what could they want there?" I wondered, looking out at the Great Salt Plain and the stronghold that lay somewhere over the horizon.

"There's only one possibility," Ilyas said. "To destroy it." He rubbed his jaw. "I can't see how though. They are daēva. The flames the Purified use at the Barbican are even holier and more powerful than a fire altar. They can't get near."

"They might not have to," Darius said quietly. "And don't

forget the humans who are helping them. The guards aren't bound by the same constraints."

Ilyas rolled up the map and shoved it into his saddlebag.

"Then we must catch them on the plain," he growled. "We must!"

Ilyas wheeled his mount toward the slope. I had just started to follow when Darius's head whipped around. He stared at a distant ridgeline. I squinted, but saw nothing.

"What is it?" I whispered.

"I don't know," he muttered. "Something living. Something powerful."

"One of the runners?" I scanned the ridgeline again and thought I glimpsed a tiny figure, just a dark speck against the snow. The hair on my arms rose.

Darius shook his head in frustration. "I can't tell. Ilyas! Tommas!"

They were already partway down the slope, Tijah and Myrri at their heels.

"We've got to—" Darius began, but he didn't get any further because at that moment, I heard a dull roaring sound from above. The snow around us started to crack, then break into great slabs. Our horse whinnied in terror as the snow-pack began to slide, slowly at first but gaining speed.

Darius reached for the power and I let it go, but it was too late. We were swept into the raging torrent. I tumbled from my saddle. The world hurtled past in dizzying flashes: sky, snow, sky, snow, and finally, eerie black silence, broken only by the sound of my own labored wheezing.

I couldn't move. Not an eyelash. The weight of it pressed down on me like a mountain. I felt my mind drifting away, unmoored. The only thing that tethered me to my body was the bond, and the demon on the other end of it. He would come for me.

The minutes passed, and my breath turned to a thin shell

of ice on my face. I tried to spit. It took a while to summon enough moisture, but I finally managed it. I discovered that I was more or less upright, one arm flung above my head. This was a lucky thing, because it had created an air pocket. Not a large one. Just a fist-sized gap. But it was enough to keep me going, for a little while at least.

On such small coincidences do our lives hinge sometimes.

As my limbs grew numb, and Darius didn't come, I had a thought that would have made me laugh if I'd had enough air in my lungs. Of all the Druj I'd fought, in the end, it would still be the damned mountains that killed me.

Of course, he did come, although it was almost too late. Darius had been swept far down the mountain and had to climb back up. He couldn't melt the snow. That would require working with heat. But he knew exactly where I was, and he could dig.

The first thing he found was my right hand. The one with the cuff. I remember a terrible pain, not my own but his, as his skin came into contact with it. But he didn't let go. Sunlight blinded my eyes, and then they filled with a deep blue that I thought was sky but turned out to be his tunic.

I distantly heard him saying my name. Pulling me out and into his arms. Tearing my soaked coat off and sliding his right hand under my tunic, to the small of my back, so he could pour his own warmth into me. I shook like a leaf in a windstorm, partly from the agony of blood returning to frozen limbs, but also from the sensation of his embrace. Never had we touched this way, pressed together head to toe with just a thin layer of fabric between, and it was like the night I took his hand but magnified a thousand times. I saw myself through his eyes, felt my own body through his hands. That was the nature of our bond.

It shattered my walls in an instant. There was nothing in the world but the raw intensity of that strange echo chamber, and the knowledge that he was as lost in it as I was.

I don't know how long we stood there, clinging to each other, his breath warm in my ear. It could have been one minute, or twenty. But eventually the others found us. Ilyas came first. He must have been running, because he was panting hard when his hands found my shoulders and wrenched us apart.

He didn't say a word. Just stood there. But his eyes blazed with a kind of sick fury. I had never seen him like this before. It scared me. His hand moved toward the hilt of his sword and I'm not sure what would have happened next if Tommas hadn't appeared with Tijah and Myrri.

"Thank the Holy Father," Tommas said. "We thought you were gone."

And just like that, Ilyas took a ragged breath and got ahold of himself. I saw the force of will it required, but our captain was nothing if not disciplined.

"The horses are below," he said flatly, turning away. "Tommas moved quickly and plucked them up with air."

I felt Darius slam his walls back into place. He stepped away from me. Neither of us could bear to look at each other. I still felt his hand on me and ducked my head to hide the heat in my cheeks.

"One of the daēvas must have brought the avalanche down on us," Darius said. "It's my fault. I sensed something, but it was too late. Whatever it was, they're gone now."

"Are you all right?" Tijah asked me. "Can you ride?"

I nodded, not trusting my own voice.

"Of course you can, nomad girl." She grinned. "I suppose you're used to these sorts of things. What did Darius call it?"

"An avalanche," I said.

"How lovely. And your people actually live here?"

I forced a smile.

"At home, I thought a scorpion in my slipper was a bad day." Tijah shook her braids in wonder. "Of course, we do have sandstorms. Those can be very annoying..."

She chattered on as we found our horses. Darius was careful not to touch me when he mounted, for which I was grateful. I knew he had just been trying to save my life, but I felt as though my world had shifted on its axis, exposing feelings I had struggled to ignore since I'd come to know him in those days we'd spent together in the daëva barracks. Beneath his cool exterior, Darius was very funny, in a bleak sort of way. A complex man, who could be indifferent, even harsh, one moment and kind the next. But unlike Ilyas, whose mood swings seemed beyond his control, Darius struck me as deliberate. He had long practice in keeping others at arm's length.

And yet when he had touched me, what I'd felt from him was far from indifference.

Our bond was stronger than most—I'd realized that at the village of Ash Shiyda when his power left me gasping on the floor. It was not the same for Tijah, nor for Ilyas. I knew because I'd asked them.

I wondered if they had given us defective cuffs, ones that somehow magnified the bond and made this whole impossible situation worse. The look on Ilyas's face when he saw us together had been nothing short of murderous. I felt his eyes on us now. Weighing, measuring. It was the law of the land that humans and daëvas could never lay together. The magus said the products of such forbidden unions were immediately killed as Druj spawn, and the parents given to the Numerators.

Well, we had hardly crossed *that* particular line, but Holy Father, part of me wanted to, which came as a shock. I had never been so fiercely attracted to someone, and so afraid of where that attraction could lead. Besides which, it seemed wrong somehow. The daēvas were slaves in all but name, and I was one of the masters.

So I stuffed Darius back into his box and resolved to keep him there. I couldn't escape him, but I could endure the exquisite torture of our bond if it kept him safe. There was no other choice, not for either of us. I had sacrificed everything to become a Water Dog. I'd abandoned my clan, foregone any chance to marry and have children. I had sworn to honor my sister by hunting her killers.

Ilyas could watch us all he wanted, but there was nothing to see and there never would be.

Just two Water Dogs, carrying out the King's justice.

THE MOUNTAINS DWINDLED BEHIND US AS WE RODE OUT onto the Great Salt Plain.

My clan called it the Dasht-e Kavir. In the springtime, when the earth became saturated with runoff from the snowmelt, we grazed our herds at the edges. After the seasonal marshes dried up, they left a residue of salt behind, and the sun baked the plain into fractured plates that looked like the scales of a lizard.

The temperatures in summer could kill a horse and rider within hours. Luckily for us, it was winter, so the day was remarkably pleasant. Soon we shed our quilted coats and were basking in the warmth, despite Ilyas's relentless pace.

Tijah seemed recovered from the brutal crossing of the Khusk range. She hadn't reacted at all when she saw me and Darius together, but Tijah had different views about daēvas, I knew—views that would be branded heresy if she had spoken them aloud.

Once we had come to trust each other, she told me that in Al Miraj, daēvas are not considered by most people to be inherently evil. Not Druj. They were still leashed because they were too powerful to be given free rein and the King insisted on it, but they were treated with greater respect. It was no shame to take a daēva as a lover even, which shocked me to my core. Tijah had just laughed and called me a prude.

But that wasn't it—or at least, it wasn't what Tijah thought. I didn't consider myself a prude. The Four-Legs clan was not especially modest on questions of sex or nudity or any normal bodily function. We lived in tents, very close to each other, and privacy was a scarce commodity. I'd seen animals mating, and on occasion, people. It was a natural part of life.

What disturbed me the most was the idea that if the daēvas were *not* evil, were not Druj, it was still morally acceptable to enslave them.

But that ran against everything the Prophet had taught us, not to mention the fact that daēvas had fought alongside the Druj in the war. And no one who had seen a wight or lich or Revenant would deny that those things were evil incarnate. Or that any creature that stood with them was the same.

I shoved the memory away. How had I gone from being glad that Tijah was recovered to doubting the entire foundation of my faith in thirty seconds flat? Because our minds are ridiculous, I decided. With nothing to do but stare at a blank horizon, they have to find a way to entertain themselves. Like a child chasing a butterfly, they skip from place to place, until suddenly they look up and find themselves lost in the wilderness.

All that mattered was this moment, and the confrontation that lay ahead. We had just gotten a taste of what our foes were capable of. Now they were racing to the holy fire, the very heart of the empire. The Father only knew what they had planned.

Or how many more would die if we didn't stop them.

I took a careful sip from my water skin. We had filled them to bursting at a spring I knew in the foothills, but it would be the last for hundreds of leagues. Or at least until we reached the Barbican, if it still stood.

My head jerked up as Tommas shouted something to Ilyas. They reined in their mounts.

I shaded my eyes. There was something on the plain ahead. A dust cloud.

"Riders," Darius said.

"How many?"

They were the first words we had exchanged in hours.

"Five."

"Are they the daēvas?"

"No." He was troubled. "Something else."

"Human? Druj?" I pressed.

"I don't know. Human, I think, but something is...*off* about them."

His tone discouraged any more questions. I think he felt as frustrated as I did.

"Form up!" Ilyas shouted.

Tijah loosened her scimitar and we rode up next to Ilyas and Tommas, our four horses forming a ragged line on the plain.

"They're coming from the Rig-e Jenn," I said.

"What's that?" Ilyas asked. Every line of his body was rigid with tension.

"It means the devil's dunes. A cursed place. The trade caravans all go around it."

As the riders came closer, I could see that their mounts were even larger than those bred for the Water Dogs. Great black beasts that made ours look like ponies. The reason for this became clear when they reined up a short distance away.

For each bore not one, but three riders. The ones that sat behind wore thick metal collars around their necks. Their clothes were nothing more than rags. I was just near enough to make out the perfectly blank expressions on their faces. As if they no longer saw anything that was happening around them.

They were a mix of men and women, even two or three children. But they all had a sameness, slack and wide-eyed, that made my skin crawl.

Chains ran from the collars to cuffs around the left arms of the riders in the front. Unlike their captives, these men wore long sleeveless tunics of pale leather. From where I sat, they looked human. Unremarkable, except for their odd attire. I saw no swords or spears or any other weapons. And yet there was something about them, an invisible aura, that made me want to strike them all dead on the spot.

Darius stiffened behind me. Our loathing was mutual.

"Necromancers," he spat.

Ilyas blinked. "It can't be. They haven't come so far south in centuries."

"He's right," Tommas said, his handsome face hard as stone. "They're linked to their human slaves. It's the source of their power."

Ilyas was silent for a moment. "What if we kill the slaves?" he asked quietly.

He was ruthless enough to do such a thing, I knew. He wouldn't take pleasure in it, quite the opposite, but if it was necessary, he would do it without hesitation. The thought sickened me.

"I'm not killing children," I said flatly. "Or adults, for that matter."

"It won't work anyway," Darius said. "For every linked

slave that dies, five Druj are born. It's something about the backwash of the dark magic. The warrior-magi in Karnopolis warned me about this. They keep extensive records from the war there. We would soon be facing fifty, rather than five."

"Use the power then."

"Theirs is equal, if not stronger."

"So how do we fight them?" Ilyas demanded.

"We don't," Darius said shortly. "Not unless we have to."

"But we can't just leave these people," I said, turning in my saddle to stare daggers at Darius.

"He's right," Ilyas interrupted. "We can't afford losses, not now. Our task is to catch the runners from Gorgon-e Gaz. Everything else is secondary."

"What?" I couldn't believe what I was hearing. "We're Water Dogs! What happened to protecting the powerless? Punishing the wicked?"

"Enough, Nazafareen," Ilyas growled.

"If you won't ride with me, I'll fight them myself," I said, knowing I was pushing him too far but unable to stop myself. "I won't sit back like a coward—"

"Enough!" Ilyas voice cracked like a whip. "Enough. I don't care if you like it or not. But you will follow my orders or you will no longer wear the red. Understood?"

I subsided, still raging inside. Tijah spat in the dirt and I knew she was just as disgusted as I was.

"Water Dogs!" The lead rider called across the plain.

"In the name of King Artaxeros the Second, dismount and release your captives," Ilyas yelled back.

The rider laughed. "But he's not our King! And you haven't heard my offer yet."

Tommas and Ilyas exchanged an unreadable look.

"What offer?" Ilyas called. "I don't make bargains with necromancers."

"We call ourselves Antimagi, Water Dog. But that is

neither here nor there." The rider seemed darkly amused. "I know our rulers aren't the closest of friends, but we have the same objective. For now, at least. To take the one named Victor."

To his credit, Ilyas's calm demeanor didn't alter, although he must have been surprised.

"I see. And what do you want with this Victor, assuming I even know who you're talking about?"

"Why, he's the most sought-after daēva in Bactria!" the rider replied, and they all laughed. "The queen has desired the pleasure of his company for many long years. She's most pleased that he managed to break free of the prison you locked him up in. She owes him a debt, you see. A great debt."

I suddenly remembered Ilyas's words as we sat around the fire.

He killed more Druj in the war than any other daēva. A blood-thirsty animal, by all accounts...

Ilyas ran a hand through his hair. "And if we give you Victor..."

"You may have the rest. Come now! We both know you're sorely outnumbered. Those daēvas will eat you pups alive. And Victor's of no use to you. Even if, by some miracle, you manage to capture him alive, he'll be going straight back to Gorgon-e Gaz. More likely, he'll kill you all. So I propose a temporary alliance, only until we find them." The rider grinned. Despite the noonday sun, his eyes were deep hollows in his face. "And then you're free to run me through with your fearsome sword!" He laid a mocking hand on his chest.

I stared at my captain. He couldn't actually be considering this unholy pact...

The silence on the plain seemed brittle as ice over running water. I slowly eased my sword from the scabbard, just an inch but enough to whip it free in a heartbeat. I would rather burn for all eternity than ride with these creatures and their human chattel. Darius gave the tiniest nod as I released my hold on the bond.

Maybe we'd even manage to kill one or two of them before we died.

Then Ilyas sat up straighter. He had reached a decision.

"Your offer is refused," he said in that ringing voice I remembered from the day we met.

I closed my eyes and let out a breath.

"The daēvas are the property of the King, not your Bactrian witch. Tell Queen Neblis that if we see any of her *Antimagi* in these lands again, we will return their heads and leave the corpses for the carrion birds." His lip curled. "If they're even willing to touch your debased flesh."

The rider laughed at this, but he no longer sounded amused. "It's a pity you have that one." He pointed a pale hand at Darius and the chain jerked tight, nearly dragging his slaves from the saddle, but their doll's eyes never changed. "The others would be easily disposed of and then I could find a place for you in my retinue." He stared at Ilyas. "I think you would last a long time. But alas! I don't wish to test that daēva of hers. He reminds me too much of the one we seek."

The necromancer must be referring to Darius's power, I thought. That he was as strong as the ancient ones. Nothing else. I refused to believe that my daēva was truly Druj.

They wheeled around and rode back the way they had come, into the shifting sands of the Rig-e Jenn. I watched them vanish over the horizon. I wondered if any of the slaves had been taken from the village of Ash Shiyda, and felt even sicker.

"How did that scum know of the escape?" Tijah asked. "Do you think they followed us?"

"The messenger from Gorgon-e Gaz," Tommas said

thoughtfully. "He was pursued by Druj. They must have reported back."

"Can they track like Darius?"

"Perhaps not. Their magic is focused on the dead, not the living. It would explain why they needed our help."

"Once we have these daēvas in hand, we will hunt them down and destroy them," Ilyas said. "You have my word."

He made the sign of the flame. Ilyas was calm again. In control. But he had not been himself these last days. I caught Tommas's eye and knew he was worried too. He would never say anything, but he felt it.

Something in our captain was very close to breaking.

❧ 1 2 ❧

We rode so hard I feared Ilyas would kill the horses, but we did not catch them on the plain. Nor did we see the necromancers again. So I was braced for the worst when we got our first glimpse of the Barbican some hours later.

I expected a pile of rubble. More broken bodies. But from all appearances, the fortress was untouched. It squatted on a lump of rock in the middle of a shallow lake. Fires burned all along the grey walls, spaced only a foot apart. Heavily armed soldiers guarded the entrance, and dozens more watched us ride up from atop the circular towers anchoring each corner. A wooden bridge arched over the water, leading to a pair of massive iron gates.

We reined up on the shore. The air had a strange smell to it, and I could feel Darius's discomfort.

"The final defense," he said quietly. "If the fortress is attacked, they have only to toss a torch into the lake and the water will burn. A combination of pine resin, naphtha, some other substances I don't recognize."

"But they didn't light it," I said.

"No, they didn't."

"Darius!" Ilyas called. "The runners. Did they come this way?"

"I..." Darius frowned and I felt power flow into the bond. "They passed a little ways south. But...I don't understand it..."

"What? Tell me!"

Darius shook his head. "They're gone, captain."

"What do you mean, they're gone?"

"I mean, I can't feel them anymore."

"Could they be dead?" Ilyas asked hopefully.

I knew what he was thinking. That the necromancers had caught them. Maybe both sides had massacred each other in the battle. Two birds with one stone.

"They could be," Darius said. But he doubted it. I did too.

Ilyas blew out a long breath. "Nazafareen, come with me. The rest of you wait here. Let's find out if they've seen anything."

I spurred my horse into a canter and we rode across the bridge, hoof beats echoing on the wooden planks. When we reached the gates, Ilyas made the sign of the flame and explained that we'd been sent by Satrap Jaagos, but he didn't elaborate further. The soldiers, all hard-faced men, opened the gates just wide enough for us to pass, then winched them shut again.

We entered a courtyard and then the fortress proper. Everywhere, torches burned, casting flickering light on the bare stone. No daēva could enter this place.

We dismounted and two magi in hooded robes of plain brown roughspun led the horses away. A third gestured for us to follow him. I couldn't see his face, but his hands bore a welter of scars, burns by the look of them.

"They call themselves Purified," Ilyas whispered to me as we followed the magus down a long corridor. "They welcome the pain of working with the holy fire. It's a badge of their devotion."

I nodded, wondering how far those scars extended under the robes. I was as pious as anyone, but the thought of burning my own body for the sake of the Holy Father made me a little ill.

"The High Magus," our escort said, throwing open a door.

A man stood before a small fire altar. He was stooped and white-haired—just as I had thought a magus should look when I was a little girl—but his black eyes were lit with the intensity of a true zealot. He wore a white robe with a gold faravahar embroidered on the breast. I noted the harsh set of his thin-lipped mouth, the gauntness of his face, and understood right away that this was a very different sort of man than the magus we had at home.

"Water Dogs from Tel Khalujah," the High Magus said. His voice was deep and rasping, as though he didn't use it often. "What is your business at the Barbican?"

Again, Ilyas made the sign of the flame before speaking. "A week ago, there was an escape from Gorgon-e Gaz. Six daēvas. We've pursued them across the mountains, and now the plain. The trail led here, but we...Well, we seem to have lost them."

The High Magus's expression didn't change, although his disapproval was clear. "I see. And why would you think to find them here?" He waved a hand at the altar, the multitude of torches burning in brackets on the walls. "We have no fear of *daēvas*." He spat the word, like it was a piece of rotten meat. "This fortress is impregnable."

"I'm well aware of that, High Magus," Ilyas said evenly. "But until a few minutes ago, they were heading directly for the Barbican. We feared an assault of some kind."

"Your fears are unfounded. All is well here."

"We also encountered necromancers on the plain," Ilyas

said. "They have human captives. If you can spare some soldiers—"

"I'm afraid I can't," the High Magus said. "Especially with dangerous daēvas on the loose. Now, if you'll excuse me, I have other matters to attend to."

He was turning away when I found myself speaking. I hadn't planned to, but a thought had just occurred to me. I didn't believe it was a coincidence that the runners had passed so near the Barbican. If what the necromancers said was true, they would have avoided Bactria at all costs. Queen Neblis clearly held a grudge. She wasn't their ally—quite the opposite. If she got hold of these daēvas, she would probably torture them to death.

Which left them two choices. Run south, toward the Sayhad desert and the satrapy of Al Miraj, or north for one of the coastal villages of the Midnight Sea, where a ship could bring them straight to Eskander's lines. That was the obvious choice. But they had done neither of those things. They had risked crossing the open plain, with Water Dogs in pursuit. Until we lost them, they had made a beeline for the Barbican. There had to be something here they wanted.

"Wait," I said.

Ilyas frowned and tried to take my arm but I shook him off. The High Magus stared at me.

"Speak, girl," he said impatiently.

I took a deep breath. If I was wrong, we'd be lucky to leave in one piece.

"At Gorgon-e Gaz, the guards aided in their escape." I paused, letting that fact sink in. "They had help on the inside."

The High Magus's predatory black eyes bored into me. "What exactly are you suggesting? That we have traitors here?"

"No, High Magus. I would never think such a thing. Only

that you may wish to find out if anyone has come or gone in the last several hours," I said. "Soldiers. Purified. Anyone at all."

I thought he might throw me onto the flames of the altar himself, but the High Magus froze. His eyes roved unseeing across the room. Ilyas and I stood very still.

"No, it's impossible," he said finally. "As you will see in a moment. The bridge is the only way in or out."

We followed as he strode out the door and back down the corridor, through the inner courtyard to the gates. The soldiers there snapped to attention when they saw him.

"Has anyone left this day?" the High Magus demanded. "Speak truth, or I'll know it!"

The soldiers looked confused.

"Well, yes," one of them said. "Two Purified passed through the gates not an hour ago. By your own orders, High Magus. I checked the papers myself. They bore your seal."

The High Magus's face seemed to collapse in on itself.

"A forgery," he whispered. "Treason has been committed here."

The soldiers looked terrified, and I felt sorry for them.

"Who was it? What were their names? Speak!"

"Magus Yari and Magus Mahvar," the guard stammered. "They carried a small urn with them. They said it was a gift for the King."

Whatever color remained in the High Magus's face drained away at these words. He raised a shaking hand to his forehead. "It cannot be...Never, in two hundred years..."

He suddenly looked frail and lost, just an old man in a fancy robe. Ilyas swore under his breath and stepped forward, taking the High Magus by the elbow.

"What did they steal?" he asked firmly. "The holy fire?"

The High Magus didn't respond.

"I can still get it back, but you must explain everything to me," Ilyas said. "Where was it kept?"

He looked on the verge of shaking the answer loose when the High Magus spoke, his voice barely a whisper. "I'll show you."

He led us to a chamber in the heart of the fortress. We passed several hooded Purified on the way, but the High Magus ignored them. I had expected an altar, but my first impression when we entered was of a blacksmith's forge. I saw an anvil and hammer and other tools, a vise gripping a set of half-finished cuffs. Trays of raw gold nuggets.

In the center of the room sat an empty pedestal.

"Holy Father, forgive me." The High Magus buried his face in his hands.

"Do you not keep it locked and guarded?" Ilyas asked in disbelief.

"It *was* guarded. The soldiers, the lake...I never..." He took a deep breath. "The brothers here served the flame. We always assumed that the threat lay outside these walls, not within."

"Why would they take it?" Ilyas muttered. "Why?" He stalked over and slapped his palm on the bare stone. "To forge new cuffs? But to what purpose?"

The High Magus looked up. "Not to forge new cuffs," he said in a dead voice. "To break them."

❧ 13 ❧

"The cuffs cannot be broken," Ilyas said, his jaw clenched. "The bond can be changed to another, yes. But not broken. Even if they are removed, the link remains. Everyone knows that."

"No." The words came out of the High Magus slowly, painfully. "When the cuff is given to the flames it was forged in, the bond will shatter. The daēva will be freed."

Ilyas slammed his fist down. His face flushed red with rage. "Why were we not told of this possibility?"

"It is kept secret," the High Magus said sharply. "For obvious reasons."

"We are Water Dogs!" Ilyas growled. "Bonded to these Druj. We were promised they could never turn on us. Never! And yet you allow two Purified to walk out the front door carrying the key to their cages." He paced up and down, then halted suddenly as the full impact of the High Magus's words hit him.

"The Immortals," Ilyas whispered. "There are five thousand bonded daēvas in Persepolae. *Five thousand*. What if Victor and the others mean to set them free?"

I suddenly remembered that first day with the magus at Tel Khalujah, his reassuring words to a frightened child.

All our daēva soldiers have been raised in the light. We've trained them to overcome their wicked natures...

But was it really true? And if it wasn't, what retribution would they exact for their enslavement? I knew what I would do if I was a daēva, offered a chance at freedom.

"There's something else," the High Magus said hollowly. "Once freed, it's likely they will no longer have infirmities."

"*What?*"

"The infirmity occurs during the bonding process. The cuff takes a piece of the daēva. Maims them. It's different for each one. We never know in advance what it will be. But I would imagine the reverse is true. If the bond is broken, the daēva will become whole."

I thought of Darius's withered arm and a wave of nausea rolled over me.

"But the Way of the Flame teaches that they were born that way," I said.

The High Magus pursed his thin lips and said nothing.

"You're liars," I spat. "The Holy Father didn't curse them. *You* did."

"They are Druj!" the High Magus thundered. "Everything we do here, we do out of necessity. Who are you to pass judgment?"

I wanted to stab the old man right there, but Ilyas stepped between us.

"What else?" he asked in a deadly tone. "Any other surprises?"

The High Magus gazed at him, black eyes as murderous as my own.

"None. I've told you everything. And now you must swear to keep what I have told you secret. If our enemies knew that the cuffs had a weakness..."

"I'm not—"

"Shut up, Nazafareen," Ilyas said calmly. "We swear it. Now, I need fresh horses and as many men as you can spare without leaving the fortress undefended."

The High Magus nodded curtly and swept from the chamber.

"Nothing has changed," Ilyas said. He seemed strangely detached. "They would have fought us regardless. We can't bring them back if the cuffs are broken, but we can still kill them. We can still catch them before they reach Persepolae. We must."

"Ilyas…"

"I will not be remembered as the man who brought down the empire, Nazafareen."

I stared into his grey eyes and felt a chill.

"But we have to tell—"

He pressed a finger to my lips. "No. We don't." Ilyas smiled coldly. "I've been lenient with you, but your tongue has grown very loose of late. I was the first to see your potential. I see it still. Do not press me on this. We are at the end now. The only question is *whose*."

He gave the pedestal a happy little slap. Like quicksilver, I thought.

"Good thoughts." His fingers drifted to my forehead. "Good deeds." Ilyas poked my chest. "Good words." He touched my mouth a final time. I wanted to bite him, but I managed to leash my temper.

"Remind me of the Water Dog loyalties, Nazafareen. I hope you still remember them."

"Holy Father," I said. "King, then satrap."

"Very good. Daēvas are not on the list, are they? Bonded or otherwise."

"No," I said quietly. "But they fight for us still."

"Because they have to. And without them…Well, our

borders would be worth nothing more than lines on a map."
He gazed into the space just above the pedestal, as though he
saw writhing flames there. "Even if they don't manage to free
the Immortals—which I'll admit wouldn't be a simple task,
nor a certain outcome—what do you think Eskander would
do with the holy fire? The power to both forge the cuffs and
break them at will? Or maybe they'll bring it to Neblis. How
does that sit with you, Nazafareen?"

"They won't bring the fire to Neblis," I said wearily.
"Weren't you listening? She wants those daēvas dead as much
as you do."

And it occurred to me then that the necromancer had
never actually said anything about the daēvas *changing sides* in
the war, only that their queen owed Victor a great debt.
Darius and Tommas despised the Druj Undead more than
anything on earth. So did Myrri. If the magi had lied about
the cuffs, what else had they lied about? It was all such a long
time ago. Who still lived that knew the truth? Not even the
magus at Tel Khalujah was so old. I could only think of six—
the daēvas we hunted—and Ilyas wanted to kill them all.

Clearly, I wasn't the only one harboring serious doubts.
This had gone beyond Gorgon-e Gaz now. Beyond a few rebel-
lious Water Dogs. Two *Purified*—the most devout and fanat-
ical sect in the empire—had just betrayed their faith, and they
weren't even bonded. There was no question that their actions
had been a deliberate choice, made of their own free will.

I felt the foundation of everything I believed start to
crumble beneath my feet. How did we know Neblis was a
daēva? And even if she was, did we have the right to punish
an entire race based on her actions?

I hate this thing. And sometimes I hate you...

Maybe Darius had every right to. Maybe we were no
better than those necromancers.

"Enough, Nazafareen," Ilyas said, and I wondered how much he had read in my face. "Every second they're getting farther away." He started to walk to the door, then turned back. "And if you tell your daēva what we learned here, I will have Tommas kill him on the spot."

We found six fresh horses waiting in the courtyard, along with two dozen mounted soldiers carrying lances. They wore egg-shaped felt caps and their tunics bore both the faravahar and the griffin.

"Captain Ilyas?" A man with a short beard and faint white scar across his chin rode forward. "I am Lieutenant Parshad. The High Magus says we are to accompany you in returning two Purified to the fortress."

Ilyas nodded. "Did he tell you who else we're hunting?"

The lieutenant swallowed. "Yes, Captain."

"Good. I plan to catch them on the Royal Road."

When the guards saw Ilyas's face, they winched the gates open without a word. I think they were just relieved we hadn't arrested them for treason.

As for myself, I didn't know who or what I believed anymore. But I still wore the scarlet tunic, and I didn't have a shred of doubt that Ilyas would carry out his threat. Which left me with very few choices, all of them bad.

The moment we passed over the bridge, Ilyas summoned the rest of the Water Dogs.

"Two Purified may have gone to join them," he said. "The High Magus graciously lent me some of his troops as reinforcements, but all is well in the Barbican."

I knew Darius sensed my turmoil. He couldn't miss it, especially since I made no effort to conceal how I felt. He looked at me, blue eyes questioning, but kept his face impassive. It was the only warning I could give him. I hoped it would be enough.

"We cannot allow them to reach Persepolae," Ilyas said. "So here's what we're going to do."

When he finished laying out his insane plan, no one spoke for a moment. Then Tommas nodded.

"It might be possible," he said.

"It is possible," Ilyas growled. "And you'll make it happen. Now! Or you'll learn what the bond can do to a daēva that disobeys its master."

Darius tensed, but Tommas only smiled. I marveled at his calm. I couldn't begin to imagine what it must be like to be yoked to Ilyas in his current state.

"Easy, Captain." Tommas turned to the other daēvas. "How strong are you with air?"

Myrri tilted her palm back and forth. *So-so.*

"Fairly strong," Darius said.

"Can you follow my lead?"

"I'll try."

Myrri nodded. Her skin was a lighter brown than Tijah's, almost the same color as my hair, and she had large, liquid eyes that always seemed to be slightly unfocused. I think she lived in that nothing place as much as possible, and I was starting to understand why.

Tijah made the hand sign that I had learned meant *Be careful.*

I looked at my sister in the Water Dogs and wondered what she would do if it came down to it. Where her own loyalty lay. And I knew in my heart it would be to Myrri.

The problem was, I also knew that Ilyas wasn't entirely wrong. No one could predict what freed daēvas would do. Most likely, it would be Gorgon-e Gaz on an unimaginable scale. Because even if they weren't evil before, two hundred years of servitude had made them into something twisted and vengeful.

I watched as Tommas, Darius and Myrri walked out onto

the plain. They stood facing west, their backs to the Barbican. Tommas took a deep breath. Beside him, Darius and Myrri did the same. I felt power surge through the bond. My daēva's shoulders heaved. His heart sped up until I feared it would burst in his chest. And then he drew still more power. The cuff seared my wrist, that familiar sensation of frozen fire. My own breath caught in my lungs as Darius's awareness dissolved into the air and began bending it to his will.

The soldiers had gathered in a tight knot around their lieutenant. Their eyes were wide with fear, and I wondered if they had even seen a daēva before. One of them pointed. An excited murmur erupted.

At the edge of the plain, just at the visible horizon, something was forming. A wall of dull grey. I blinked as it swallowed the sun.

Just when I was about to run over there and scream at the daēvas to stop before they killed themselves, Tommas fell to his hands and knees. "It's done," he gasped.

I seized the bridle of one of the fresh horses and led it to Darius.

"Tommas did most of it," he said hoarsely. "I've never seen anything like——"

"Mount up!" Ilyas shouted. "In the name of the Holy Father and King Artaxeros the Second, I pledge my sword to stem the tide of evil staining this land. Who shall join me?"

The soldiers from the Barbican roared their approval. Tijah waved her scimitar in the air. Darius bowed his head, muttering a prayer. I alone was silent, but Ilyas didn't notice. He was already digging his heels into the horse's flanks, the end of his *qarha* streaming behind him like a bloody banner.

I offered Tommas my hand. He looked utterly spent.

"Ilyas," I said, as Tommas staggered to his feet. "He's not..."

Sane? Trustworthy? The man I had once loved like a

brother? I was still deciding what I meant to say when Tommas hoisted himself into the saddle of the last horse. He had a quiet strength that was easy to overlook. His beauty was the first thing you noticed, but it was his character you remembered. Unfailingly decent to his friends, implacable to his enemies.

"Make sure you wind the *qarha* tightly, Nazafareen," Tommas said. He gave me a crooked smile.

And then he too was gone.

As we galloped toward the sandstorm, I looked back only once. An unnatural twilight had fallen across the plain, but I could see a red glow in the distance, glimmering like a fallen star.

The High Magus had set the lake on fire.

❦ 14 ❦

I f you are one of those fortunate people who have never faced a very large sandstorm approaching on an open plain, I can tell you that it is one of the most terrifying things in all of Nature.

That we were riding *toward* it rather than *away* from it made matters worse. The wind picked up, blowing a fine grit into our eyes. I could see the outer edge of the storm clearly now. A boiling wave that rolled across the earth, far taller than the highest towers of Tel Khalujah and as wide as the Midnight Sea.

At first, it seemed to be creeping like fog, but as we drew closer, I realized this thing they had conjured was racing along. The horses whinnied in fear.

"Stick close," Tommas called over his shoulder. "I'll try to make an air bubble once we enter."

Darius rode only a few feet away. It was strange not to feel him at my back, but we'd taken separate mounts from the Barbican. He clutched the reins with his right hand, his left hanging dead by his side. The weight of the cuff around my own wrist never seemed so heavy. *It takes a piece of the daēva. Maims them...*

Ilyas was far ahead, leading the vanguard. I could tell Darius the truth right now, tell him what we learned at the Barbican, and Ilyas would never know.

But in the time it took for me to consider this, we had closed the distance to the storm. I took a deep breath and reflexively made the sign of the flame. A moment later, the world turned to choking brown dust. It whipped my skin, howled in my ears like a chorus of Druj. I crouched in the saddle, head bowed, as the horses slowed to a walk.

They're mad, I thought. We can't fight in this. We can't even see. The poor horses will be blinded...

And then I felt a force open a small space in the maelstrom. Tommas had made good on his promise. I could still hear the roar of the wind, but it no longer touched me. I wondered what it was costing him to shield us, and how long he could keep it up for. Part of me hated Ilyas for pushing him so hard, but I had seen more than a hint of exhilaration in Tommas's eyes when he'd made the storm. He *enjoyed* working with air, and why wouldn't he? He was like a bird with clipped wings, suddenly able to fly again. And air didn't do the same damage as earth. It didn't break you. Just *used* you, like a blacksmith used a set of bellows to heat his forge.

We crept forward, passing a weathered stone marker that indicated we'd found the Royal Road to Persepolae. I drew my sword. The storm battered at Tommas's walls and I wondered what would happen if they collapsed completely. We would never find our way out, and the Holy Father only knew how long it would take for the sandstorm to subside.

Still, Ilyas led us deeper. The light dimmed, turned a strange shade of yellow. And then we stumbled out into clean air. And a scene from nightmare.

Bodies littered the ground. Some wore the white and gold

of the guards from Gorgon-e Gaz, but at least three were clad in tunics of light blue, a triangle with a slash through it embroidered on the breast. The same symbol that was tattooed on Darius's palm.

Daēvas.

They looked charred. Some were still smoking.

We were not out of the storm, not by any means, but someone had created a wide dome that held it back, a hundred times larger than the bubble Tommas had conjured. From the black lightning that flickered along its surface, I guessed it was the necromancers. The Antimagi.

Four of them were facing a knot of the surviving daēvas off to the left. They had added links to their chains and I saw one of the brown-robed Purified from the Barbican stumbling along, blank-faced, as his new master strode through the carnage, teeth bared in a savage grin.

"To me!" Ilyas screamed, galloping toward the necromancers.

Tommas and most of the soldiers followed him, but I wheeled my mount in the opposite direction, where the last living humans were about to be slaughtered by Druj. I counted nine Revenants on the battlefield, and several drifting shadows that could only be liches. Myrri ripped one apart with air, as Tijah raised her scimitar and rode at a Revenant, screaming her ululating Al Miraji battle cry.

I shook sand from my eyes and ducked under the whistling blade of one of those Undead warriors. The air reeked of blood and cooked meat. Then Darius was at my side. We were both mounted, but the thing still looked us in the eye. I parried another thrust, my teeth rattling in their sockets, as Darius crept around behind it. The Revenant was big but not very smart, and a moment later, its head was sailing through the air.

One of the guards from the Barbican screamed as a lich

wrapped him in its cold embrace. I watched in horror as his mouth worked silently, the veins on his face and neck turning black. Myrri tore it apart just as he bit through his own tongue. A second later, another rose up behind her, swaying like a cobra. I lunged, slashing wildly. My blade severed its inky substance, but the parts began to coalesce again immediately. Then Tijah emerged from the murk and we managed to hold it off long enough for Myrri to recover and destroy it.

But the tide of Druj seemed endless. The instant we killed one, another appeared to take its place. I swung my sword until my arms grew numb. We'd been lucky with the first Revenant, but the others were proving much harder to kill. I was bleeding in a dozen places where I had been too slow to escape those five-foot-long iron blades. Thanks to the strength I drew from our bond, none of the wounds were life-threatening, but I was starting to feel foggy, disconnected from my body.

Across the dome, I caught a glimpse of Ilyas and his scarlet *qarha* hacking a path through the Druj like a scythe through ripe wheat. One of the necromancers seemed to be down, but so were most of the soldiers from the Barbican. Tijah and Myrri had been swept away from me. Dust swirled in the orange half-light, although the barrier seemed to be holding for the moment.

I blinked sweat from my eyes as a tremor shook the ground, followed by a hail of rocks and dirt aimed at the necromancers. Someone very powerful was working with earth and it wasn't Darius. I would have known.

"Nazafareen!" My daēva rode over. He too was streaked with blood, some of it his own, some of it the foul black ichor of the Revenants. He had saved me more times than I could count this day, leaving my side only to rescue the last Purified from certain death at the hands of a Revenant, whose head he now flung to the ground.

I unwound my *qarha*. "There's something I need to tell you," I said. "About the daēvas. Ilyas—"

I saw his eyes widen and looked over my shoulder just in time to see a necromancer striding out of the gloom, chains clanking. His captives seemed wholly attuned to their master's movements, limp as dolls but never hindering him. Their hair was dry as winter grass, their gums stretched over skeletal teeth, even as blood and life flushed the necromancer's ruddy cheeks. He held something silvery in his hand. It looked like an orb.

My horse reared up at the sight of him, whinnying in terror. I was thrown from the saddle, striking the ground with a bone-jarring thud as the necromancer hurled the orb toward us. I rolled and it exploded a few yards to my left. Thin lines of flame shot out in all directions. I felt Darius's fury as he was driven back. Of course they would use fire, I thought dimly. Those charred bodies should have been warning enough. I realized that I had no idea how to fight this creature.

The necromancer walked straight through the dancing flames as though they didn't exist. His captives shambled along behind him and I could smell them now. Shit and piss and the stink of human misery. I turned and retched on the barren earth.

I thought it was the necromancer who had entreated us to join them on the plain. The leader of their little band of Antimagi. He looked like a normal man. If you saw him in a crowd, your gaze would pass right over him. He had shoulder-length brown hair, held back by a golden circlet. Sharp cheekbones and a long, slightly crooked nose. As he drew closer, I noticed that his tunic had a fringe on the bottom, and that fringe looked like human hair. *Pale, soft leather...*

I scrambled to my sword and picked it up, heart thumping.

He stopped a few feet away and looked me over. Then he smiled. Without breaking eye contact, the necromancer yanked one of his captives forward, a black-haired boy, and slashed a knife across his throat. The boy sagged against the necromancer's chest, his feet kicking feebly. He couldn't have been more than eight years old. A skinny little thing, all knees and elbows. Shock gripped me as the boy's life ran out of him in a red tide.

A mercy, a mercy, it's a mercy, I thought, tears blurring my vision. He'll rest with the Holy Father now.

I started to raise my sword, but had no time to use it before the ground at my feet began to crumble and gape open. Hands thrust out, the nails black and ragged. Then five swords erupted, ringing me in rusty iron.

"My children!" the necromancer cried. "Witness their birth, Water Dog!"

I knew I would have only one chance to kill the Revenants before they emerged fully so I didn't waste my breath cursing him. I just started hacking. My blade bit through putrid flesh, through bones as old and hard as fossils. I screamed my sister's name, let my hatred of the Druj lend strength to my failing body. Always, I had relied on Darius. We fought as a pair, each watching the other's back. No matter how bad things got, I knew my daēva would save me.

Not today. But I was still a Water Dog. The light against the darkness. And I still believed that, despite the magi's lies. I was born to kill Druj. If not for the King and Satrap Jaagos, then for myself. For the cause of right.

It almost worked, this little speech I gave myself.

I managed to behead four of them, but then a pair of arms like iron bands wrapped around me and lifted me off the ground from behind. They reeked of the grave. My breath came in harsh gasps as it squeezed me tighter. Stars exploded behind my eyes.

The necromancer's face swam in front of me. I saw him open a hidden catch in the dead boy's collar and let the corpse fall to the ground.

"I've always wanted a Water Dog," he said, in the same way a child might say they had always wanted a kitten to play with.

I struggled and kicked as he came forward, the open collar in his hands. It was a loathsome thing, caked with gore and what smelled like dried vomit. I screamed and the Revenant clamped a hand over my mouth.

"Shhhh," the necromancer whispered, as he fitted the collar around my throat. The metal was ice cold. "We'll have fun, you and I." He trailed his fingers across my breast. "It's a long journey to Bactria. But you're young and strong. I'll be careful not to use you up too quickly." My knees buckled as the collar snapped shut.

"Release her," he told the Revenant.

I felt his mind, dark and crawling like a rotten stump. Firelight flickered red on the chains, reflected back from the mirrors of his eyes.

"On your knees," the necromancer commanded.

I sank down. My sword lay at his feet, but he had no concern for it. He owned me now.

"I think I shall name you Lea," he said musingly. "It was my mother's name. You have the same color hair. Like sun-warmed honey."

The look on his face when I seized the hilt and drove it into his belly was priceless.

"I'm already bonded, you fool," I said, giving the blade a vicious twist and then sweeping it out in an arc that severed his hand at the wrist. The chain hadn't yet struck the ground when I took the Revenant's head on the backswing.

For in the moment that the collar snapped shut around my neck, I felt my daēva drive him back. My true bond, that preceded all others. A shining wall around my mind and soul that the necromancer's scrabbling fingers could not breach. For some reason, he couldn't sense it. The power of the nexus, of the living world, was beyond him.

The instant the necromancer lost his slaves, the flames winked out. He shrieked in pain and rage. I still wore the collar, the end of the chain trailing in the dirt with his severed hand twitching inside the cuff like some loathsome pale spider, and I wanted it off more than I have ever wanted anything in my life. How many people had this creature tortured and killed over the years? He looked at me, still clutching his belly, and *smiled*.

I brought my boot back to kick him in the face. He would not die fast, I decided. Not at all. And then a shadow detached from his body and solidified into a *second* Antimagus, and I realized with something close to despair that this fight was not over.

The gut wound should have been a mortal one, had he been truly human. But he was something more, even without the poor creatures whose lives he had fed on. Thank the Father, the others were still alive. A woman and one of the Purified from the Barbican. They curled on the ground, trembling. I was glad they had survived because there had already been too much death today, but also because the thought of facing ten more Revenants made me want to curl up beside them.

I felt Darius at my back an instant before he pushed me aside and faced the twin necromancers. Each had seized a blade from the Revenants I'd slain, and they whirled them one-handed in blurring arcs.

"Thank you," I whispered.

Darius glanced at me, and for a wonder, his lips quirked in a smile.

"I think you would have been tough meat for him to chew, bond or no," he said.

I felt the coating of blood and sand on my face crack as I grinned.

"Oh, you silver-tongued flatterer," I said, and then we were both fighting for our lives again.

Parry, thrust, stab, block. The necromancers were skilled with a sword, but Darius and I were better. Again and again, we dealt them blows that should have been fatal. Each time, they healed within seconds. Exhaustion washed over me as I spun to the side and narrowly avoided an overhand strike to my face. But the necromancers showed no signs of tiring. Mirror images of each other, one was missing its left hand, the other its right. If we did manage to kill one somehow, would it too split in half? The thought chilled me to the bone.

Darius staggered as the necromancer he fought slammed the flat of his blade into Darius's withered arm. He sank to one knee, getting his own sword back up just in time to avoid a killing stroke. The tide was turning in their favor, I realized with a sickening dread.

And then I heard the sound of hoof beats.

"The heart!" Ilyas screamed. "Through the heart!"

"I already tried that!" I yelled back through gritted teeth. "It doesn't—"

"At the same time! Both of them at the same time!"

Darius leapt to his feet and I felt a final burst of shared energy through the bond. We pressed our backs together. I caught a flash of golden hair, a familiar rolling gait, as Tommas came, followed by Tijah and Myrri. The necromancers howled as they were lifted in bonds of air. When they floated directly over our sword points, the daēvas let them go.

Darius grunted under the weight of the Antimagi as it was

impaled on his sword, but the angle was true—straight through the heart. At first, I thought I had miscalculated with mine. It fell onto the blade but the substance of it was like air. Then I realized that I must have been fighting the shadow twin, whatever that was. The thing's soul, perhaps, if it still had one. Either way, our enemy was finally dead.

I threw my sword down for what seemed the first time in hours and groped frantically along the inner rim of the collar. Suddenly, I couldn't bear to feel that repulsive metal against my skin for another second.

"Let me," Darius said quietly, and I stilled, pulse racing, as his fingers brushed the nape of my neck. The collar clicked open and he flung it to the ground. Then he spat on it, and I felt like kissing him, strange as that sounds.

"How did you figure it out?" I asked Tommas. He looked terrible, but then we all did.

"The hard way," he said. "We finally got lucky."

"Not luck," Ilyas growled, making the sign of the flame. "The will of the Holy Father."

Tommas nodded, his eyes wary. "Of course," he said.

"The soldiers from the Barbican?" Darius asked.

"All dead," Ilyas said shortly.

"And the daēvas?"

"Five bodies wearing the blue accounted for. But we need to make a formal tally. Of the Antimagi too." His eyes roved across the dome. I wondered if he had found the fire. But I knew that if he did, it would be in his hands. It was too dangerous to leave lying around.

"Well, let us do it fast, because I think the ceiling is about to fall down," Tijah observed dryly.

I looked up and saw she was right. Whether it had been constructed by the daēvas or the necromancers, they were dead now, and the sandstorm—whose fury hadn't abated—

was starting to billow inward. The magical defense was ebbing.

"I might be able to hold it—" Tommas started to say.

I frowned as he turned and looked behind him. The boy stood there. It was the one the necromancer had killed. His eyes were hard black almonds in his face, and he held the same knife that had taken his own life. I opened my mouth to scream as he plunged the blade deep into Tommas's thigh.

The daēva's emerald eyes flew wide with shock. He staggered but didn't fall.

"Wight!" The voice was high, cracked, and it took me a moment to realize it was my own.

An instant later, the boy's head was gone. Ilyas threw his sword down and just managed to catch Tommas as his legs failed beneath him.

"All right, all right," Ilyas said soothingly, cradling Tommas in his arms. "Let's see what we're dealing with." He lifted the tunic and his face froze.

"He'll heal, won't he?" I said, dropping to my knees beside them. Tijah, Myrri and Darius all crowded round. It hadn't seemed such a serious wound. Not a stab to the heart or neck or any other vital organ.

But I could see the spreading pool of blood in the dirt. Ilyas ripped his *qarba* off and wound it tightly around Tommas's thigh.

"Tijah, Myrri, go behead the rest of the dead," Ilyas barked. "Now!"

Tijah nodded, her face tight with worry, and they ran off.

"Darius, Nazafareen, help me..." He looked lost suddenly. Blood was pumping through the tourniquet, and I realized that the knife had pierced the large vein in Tommas's leg. "Push it back into him. Use the power!" Ilyas screamed at Darius.

"I...I'll try," Darius said. "But I don't know how to work with living tissue. It's too delicate..."

"Just do something!"

I pulled off my own *qarha* and wrapped it over Ilyas's. Darius stared at the wound and I felt a delicate flow of power through the bond. Still, the pool grew larger. Finally, I felt him let the power go. He looked at me and shook his head slightly.

Then Tommas's eyes fluttered open. "Ilyas?"

"Yes, yes, I'm here." Ilyas took his daēva's hand, cupping it gently.

"I...I would like to go to the sea. Once more."

"The sea?" Ilyas blinked in confusion.

"The Middle Sea. I've missed it...all these years."

Ilyas's face crumpled. "Please don't go," he whispered. "I'll take you there, I swear it. Just...don't leave me."

It took Tommas another six minutes to die. He was unconscious for most of it. No more words were spoken between them. But I suddenly understood what had been obvious all along, if I had only seen it.

Ilyas loved his daēva more than anything in the world. Loved him deeply and passionately. And hated himself for it. Hated them both.

It wasn't because Tommas was male. There was no shame in a man loving another man. But Tommas wasn't a man. And that was the heart of the matter.

I wept for Tommas, because I had loved him too. And I wept for Ilyas. But I also wept for the rest of us, who were still alive. Because the last thing that had made our captain human was now gone.

I lyas sat with the body for a long time, not moving or speaking or crying, just rubbing the cuff around his wrist. Compulsively, as if doing so would somehow bring his daēva back to life. He seemed to have forgotten that anyone else was there.

Myrri and Darius took turns holding the dome in place while Tijah and I dragged the Revenants into a pile. It was disgusting work, but I needed to do something that didn't require thought. I felt utterly empty, weightless. Like I would blow away if I stepped through those invisible walls into the storm.

The moment she saw Tommas's body, Myrri had gone to that nothing place of the nexus. Other than Tijah, Tommas had been her only real friend. I knew she would have to face her grief eventually. It would wait for her like a spurned lover, demanding to be heard. But I couldn't blame her for choosing numbness right now. I wanted the same thing.

Tijah said a quiet prayer for him in the language of her own gods, then got to work. None of us was strong enough to leave until the storm abated. We would have to stay here until the dawn, which meant clearing a campsite that didn't reek of death.

The soldiers from the Barbican had been killed to a man. We laid them out in rows, far from the Druj. Then we did the same for the guards from Gorgon-e Gaz. I thought they should rest with the daēvas they had sacrificed everything for, and Tijah agreed. But we only found five corpses wearing the blue. All were charred beyond recognition.

Likewise, we only found four dead necromancers.

A daēva and an Antimagus were missing, and so was the holy fire.

But I didn't want to think about any of that.

I used my sword to sever the hands of every necromancer, and removed each collar from their victims. We placed the bodies with the soldiers from Barbican.

All told, thirty-nine humans had been killed by the Druj, and five daēvas. Six, counting Tommas.

The only survivors were the woman and the Purified I had freed when I cut the necromancer's hand off. The woman was in a similar state to Ilyas. There, but not there. She looked like a grandmother, with pure white hair that hung down her bony back. I was surprised the necromancer had chosen someone so old as a slave, but maybe a person's strength didn't depend on their age. I knew women in the Four-Legs Clan who made the trek over the mountains long past their seventieth year and were still as spry and nimble as the herds.

Or perhaps she had been young when he'd taken her. The necromancers were like ticks, feeding on their captives through the chains until their bodies were empty husks. I hoped this woman would recover in time, but for now she sat staring into space. Tijah had tried to give her water. It dribbled past her lips and down the front of her stained tunic, and she gave no sign that she even knew Tijah was there.

The Purified was in better shape, mentally at least. He

had only been enslaved for a short time. When he saw what we were doing with the bodies, he came and started to help without a word. He was the younger of the pair from the Barbican, with dark hair shaved to short stubble and a narrow, fine-boned face. I wasn't sure what we were supposed to do with him and Ilyas wasn't giving any orders. I knew this man was a traitor, but I didn't have the energy to care. In truth, I was just glad for the extra pair of hands.

"What's your name?" I asked him.

"Yari," he said.

"I'm Nazafareen."

He nodded warily. His hands only bore a few burn scars, not like the other Purified I had seen at the Barbican. Yari must have been fairly new to the robes.

"Tend to the horses," I said. "The ones you can find that are still living. Put any that are badly injured out of their misery."

"Have you seen my brother magus?" he asked plaintively. "His name is Mahvar."

"I really don't know," I replied, and I didn't. I'd been dealing with corpses for the last hour straight, and I could no longer remember much besides blood and gore and my own horror. One thought kept running through my mind. Tommas, and the fact that we hadn't cut his head off. I knew Ilyas would never let us do it, and I didn't want to, but if he came back as a wight, I thought my mind would snap. I didn't want to remember him that way. Like I remembered Ashraf.

I tried to push the worry from my mind, but to be ready if it happened.

When we were done with our grim task, I went and sat down next to Darius. He'd thrown his walls up again, but it was clear he felt guilty that he'd been unable to stanch the bleeding. It wasn't his fault. When the large vein of the leg is opened, death comes too swiftly for anyone to stop it.

"Why are you smiling?" he asked me.

I looked at him and felt a rush of very strong emotion that he was still alive. I didn't know what I would do if I lost him. Once, I had hated his presence in my mind. He was so strong, I'd been afraid I would lose myself. Now that strength was a comfort. Yes, he had darkness in him, but it no longer frightened me. Because he also had light, and goodness, even if he refused to see it.

"I just remembered something. The first morning after I came to Tel Khalujah, Tommas found me washing up in the horse trough. I didn't know about the bath houses. I'd never seen plumbing before."

"What did he do?"

"You know Tommas. He didn't want to embarrass me. So he joined in. You should have seen Ilyas's face when he found us."

Darius laughed. And we started swapping our memories of Tommas. We laughed and we cried, and for a little while, our friend came back to us. Tijah came over, and Myrri when her turn to hold the barrier was over. Her fog seemed to lift a little as she listened to us talk, pointy chin propped on one hand, her eyes dark and luminous in the twilight.

"What about you?" I said to her. "I think of all of us, you knew him best."

Myrri thought for a moment, and then her hands started to flash. Tijah translated, pausing every few moments to find the right words.

"She says there is a story Tommas used to tell her. His first master was one of the richest merchants in the empire, with influence at court, which is why he had been given a daēva by the King. He had a large fleet of ships. They sailed not only the Middle Sea, but the southern gulf as well. When Tommas was a boy, he served this man by calling the wind, but also as a diver. He could sense the pearls hiding in their secret beds. With practice, he learned to go deeper and deeper on a single breath. The human divers could not follow him, and he would explore the depths alone. His master didn't mind because he always brought back the largest and finest pearls.

"One day, Tommas swam through a canyon and discovered a city, sunk beneath the waves. It had marble palaces and gardens of coral, but whoever had dwelt there was long gone. The seabed was littered with fragments of statues, their empty eyes staring into the gloom with only fish for company."

I listened to Tijah's words, but it was Myrri's face and hands I watched. She performed an eerie pantomime of Tommas treading water with an expression of fear and wonder, and for an instant, I could see it myself, this drowned city. The crabs scuttling along the bottom of cracked fountains. The domes and towers coated green with algae.

"Tommas thought that perhaps it was the place the daēvas came from, but they had angered the Holy Father and he had taken away their gills so they could never return." Myrri shook her head and made a sign I recognized as *wrong*, one palm pressed down flat against the other.

"I told him I did not believe it. We are not fish, although it sounds pleasant under the sea. There is no fire to worry about. But the daēvas have three talents—air, earth, water— for a reason. We do have a home, but I think it must be someplace far from here." She smiled and pursed her lips. Then she made a circle with thumb and forefinger and held it up. Tijah's eyes shone with unshed tears as she translated.

"Perhaps Tommas walks there now, whistling in the moonlight."

We sat quietly for a while after that. Ilyas never stirred from his daēva's side. He still held Tommas's hand in his own, although it had grown cold. Sometimes it is those who appear the hardest that are the most brittle underneath. I thought, somewhat bitterly, that Ilyas did not care to join us because he had so few glad memories to share, but this wasn't entirely true. Other than that single slap in the stables, I had never seen him physically abuse his daēva. In fact, if Tommas took an injury, even a minor one, Ilyas would fuss over him like a nursemaid.

I remembered how he would watch from the window of his room as Tommas sparred in the courtyard, and yet when we were all together, he almost never even looked at him. And now I understood what he meant when he said he fought a war inside himself. It was not general sin he was speaking of, but a very specific one.

He sees much of himself in you, Tommas had told me.

Not that Ilyas desired me, as I had so foolishly believed. He recognized my feelings for Darius, because he had the same ones for Tommas.

I thought of this as Darius rinsed and bound my wounds. Then I did the same for him, although his were already scabbing over. I tried to control my reaction when he touched me. I knew what to expect now. But it still burned me, flushing my skin and making my heart skip. Here I sat, surrounded by death, aching all over and one of the few people I loved in the world gone, and Darius could still make me want him. Desperately.

For that's what it was. I couldn't pretend otherwise any longer. Against my will, I saw him as he stood that day by the river, the clean lines of his body as he performed the water blessing. The way the early morning sun lit his eyes, making them glow like sapphires. And then I remembered his palm sliding under my tunic. The intense heat coming off him in waves, and most of all, the way I could feel his desire as he touched me.

I could count on one hand the number of times Darius had allowed the leash on himself to slip. That moment on the mountain was one of them.

And I wondered what it would be like with nothing between us at all. Just skin, and his mouth on mine.

I almost laughed, and not from joy. As if I didn't have enough problems already. We needed to get to Persepolae, and I dreaded giving the King the news we brought.

I was just about to check on Ilyas when a man walked out of the storm.

Straight through the barrier, as if it wasn't there. He had thick black hair, cropped short, and the shoulders of a bull. A darkly handsome man, with a square jaw and sensuous mouth. He wore a light blue tunic. Beneath the bloodstains, I could just make out a triangle and slash embroidered on the breast.

He looked us over. I'm sure we appeared a sorry bunch. "Where is it?" he asked flatly.

The sight of him roused Ilyas from his stupor. He growled and launched himself at the man, and was instantly thrown back, as if he'd struck an invisible wall.

I reached for my sword, eyes scanning his hands. Victor's infirmity was three missing fingers. But this man appeared normal. Then I remembered what the High Magus said. When the bond was broken, the daēva would become whole.

I couldn't be sure it was Victor, but some part of me knew.

"Where is it?" he asked again, more harshly. "I could kill you all where you stand right now, in a heartbeat. But all I want is the urn. Give it to me and I'll spare your lives. If only for killing the Antimagi that hunted me."

Ilyas tried to rise, was batted back again with air, like swatting a fly.

"Take him!" Ilyas screamed, his face twisted in rage.

Victor ignored Ilyas completely, his gaze now fixed on Darius. I felt my daēva reach for the power.

"Don't," Victor said in a dead voice.

I saw Darius notice his lack of a cuff, felt his shock, and I realized that in my grief over Tommas, I had forgotten to tell him about the fire. To tell any of them. Tijah had her scimitar in her hand, but she wasn't moving. Neither was I. We both knew this wasn't our fight. The Purified just watched, his face unreadable.

"The holy fire was stolen from the Barbican," I said, loud enough for all to hear. "It doesn't just forge the cuffs. It breaks them. The daēvas had it, but it seems they lost it."

Ilyas shot me a furious glare, which I returned calmly. Even he had to see it was too late for secrets now.

"*Where is the fire?*" Victor roared, and then all hell broke loose as Darius hurled him back and they started to duel. The earth cracked beneath our feet, wind and sand whipped our faces. I managed to crawl a little ways away, ducking as one of the Revenants' huge swords hurtled over my head and planted itself in a rock like a knife slicing through butter.

Myrri couldn't help. She was keeping the barrier in place, although I wondered how long it would hold under the onslaught of magic inside the dome. I made the sign of the flame, fear gripping my heart that Darius had finally met his match.

The Purified—whose name I had already forgotten— dragged the old woman away and sheltered her with his body. Tijah lay next to me, eyes squeezed shut. I looked for Ilyas, hoping he wasn't crazy enough to get between them. I wouldn't put it past him to try to stab Victor himself. But he was sprawled on his back next to Tommas, unmoving. I didn't see any injuries and assumed he had been knocked out.

The wind reached a fever pitch, tearing at my hair. And

then it died as suddenly as it had started. The dust cleared. I lifted my face and saw Victor pinned in the air, feet dangling, as the storm raged just inches behind him.

Darius stood with his head lowered, jaw clenched tight with effort. A thin line of blood ran from his nose. I could feel the damage he'd done to himself. It was a wonder he was still conscious.

Victor coughed. He too was bleeding inside, for it stained his lips red.

"You're strong," he whispered. And he smiled, a crooked, bitter smile.

Darius swayed on his feet. I knew what it was costing him to hold this daēva. The man who had cracked Gorgon-e Gaz in half. Who was no longer cuffed and we had no means of controlling. No means of bringing back. Darius knew it. He started to squeeze tighter.

Victor coughed again. His teeth were scarlet when he spoke, the words coming out in harsh gasps.

"Would you kill your own father, Water Dog?" he whispered. "Have you sunk so low?"

"Liar," Darius spat, but I felt the power waver.

"Why did I let you track me? Do you really believe I couldn't have hidden our passage from a pup like you?"

Darius said nothing, but his face was white as the fur of a snow cat.

"I brought you to the Barbican, Water Dog. I intended to free you. To free all of you." Victor closed his eyes. Even hanging in the air like a puppet, he gave off a raw, overwhelming magnetism and I wondered what being bonded to such a man would be like.

Perhaps something like being bonded to his son. Because I could see it now. The undeniable resemblance. In the mouth, and especially the eyes, although Victor's were nearly black. Not the color so much as a shared ferocity that masked deep, half-healed wounds.

"I don't wish to be free," Darius growled. "And you're not my...not my father! How could you know?" His last words almost sounded like a plea.

Victor stared at him, at his claw hand. "They forced me to sire many, many children in that rathole, Water Dog, but I still remember the day you were born. Perfect in every respect. You had your mother's eyes. She tried to smother you before they could get the cuff on, but the guards dragged her away."

Darius blinked, emotions spinning out of control, and I felt his connection to the nexus snap. A moment later, Victor flew backwards into the storm and was gone.

❧ 16 ❧

"How could you not tell me they were unchained?"

Darius paced up and down, his right hand clenched in a fist. I had never seen him so angry.

"I'm sorry. Ilyas said he would kill you if I did."

A small lie, but I didn't want him to know that Ilyas had threatened to make Tommas do it. The knowledge would tarnish Darius's memory of him, even if we never knew what Tommas would have done.

My daēva's eyes were blue ice, but underneath simmered a white-hot rage. I took an involuntary step back.

The problem with not allowing yourself to feel anything is that it all builds and builds like flotsam, and when the spring melt comes, the banks can't hold the torrent. Darius was a river in flood, ready to burst. I knew I needed to be very careful.

"Tell me now then," he said in a deadly voice.

"The Purified stole the holy fire from the Barbican," I said quickly. "It can break the bond. Victor and others must have done it, but they lost the urn in the fight."

"It's gone?"

"Yes. The necromancer who escaped must have it." I paused. "Victor was whole because the cuff causes the infirmity. The magi lied when they said it was a curse."

Something in him flickered. That darkness. "Did you know? About Victor?"

"Of course not! I never would have kept that from you." I looked at him, the blood on his face, and felt an aching sadness. "You're hurt. Let me help..."

"Don't touch me, Nazafareen," Darius said coldly.

"It doesn't change anything," I said.

"Doesn't it? My father is a murderer. I meant it when I said I didn't wish to be free." His eyes gathered the light and threw it back. "It's not safe. I'm not safe."

"Stop it," I said. "You're talking nonsense, Darius."

"I'd give anything to be like you," he said. "To be good. But I'm Druj. And I wish you'd stop pretending otherwise."

"They're liars!" I yelled, not caring who heard me. "Maybe they lied about other things too. Maybe they lied about all of it!"

"Don't. I know what I am. Take the power, Nazafareen! I don't want it."

"No."

"Take it!"

I sighed and closed my fist on the bond. Darius raised a shaky hand to his face. The fight was ebbing out of him. It was a wonder he was still standing.

"This isn't done," I said to him.

If Victor was his father, I wondered who his mother had been. If her burned remains lay with the other daēvas, or if she had stayed behind at the Barbican. Victor said she had tried to kill her own child rather than see him bonded. The thought made me sick. I had always accepted that the daēvas were our enemies, that they had brought their slavery on themselves.

They were cursed. They were Druj. They rejected the holy fire because their natures were evil. But were any of those things actually true? I knew for a fact that the first wasn't. Darius had been born looking like any other healthy child. What must the shock of being bonded, being *maimed*, been like for an infant?

King Xeros had banned human slavery when he took power. His reign was a period of enlightenment, tolerance, prosperity. The empire was civilized, and our foes were barbarians.

But what were we really?

I had joined the Water Dogs to serve the light. I believed with all my heart in the way of the flame. And it was very possible that I had spent the last four years of my life helping enforce a system of cruelty and oppression on a scale that boggled the mind.

If it hadn't been for Ilyas, I might have walked away right then. I don't know if Darius would have gone with me. I do know the choice would have torn him apart.

But I looked over at my captain, covered in his daēva's blood, and knew I couldn't leave him. Not now.

His eyes were open, staring unseeing into the storm. I didn't know how much he had heard. But I was fairly certain he had been unconscious at the end.

"We're not telling Ilyas any of this," I said to Darius in a low voice. "Victor broke free and disappeared. That's all."

Darius didn't reply.

"You didn't see him at the Barbican. He was unstable even then. With Tommas..." I trailed off. "Please trust me on this. We can't tell him the rest of it."

Darius gave a short nod, then stalked away. Tijah was over by Myrri. She'd made a quick retreat when she saw the look on Darius's face. I knew she would keep his secret if I asked.

"Ilyas." I dropped down beside him. "Are you all right?"

A stupid question. He was very far from all right.

Ilyas's left hand found the cuff, started rubbing it again. He had aged in the last hour, not from losing the bond but from grief. It pulled the corners of his mouth down, stretched the skin tight around his grey eyes. When they finally turned on me, I found I couldn't read them at all.

"I'm terribly sorry about Tommas," I said. "We all loved him. If there's anything..." I cleared my throat. "Anything you need. Anything I can do. Just speak the words."

I looked at Tommas, so pale in death, like a marble statue. Thank the Holy Father he hadn't risen again.

"A wight took my sister," I said. "A year before you came. It's why I joined the Water Dogs."

Ilyas nodded thoughtfully, as though I had just told him it would rain tomorrow.

I sighed and took a breath. "Victor is gone. Darius couldn't hold him. But we know he doesn't have the holy fire. So it must be the last necromancer. He's probably heading for Bactria. What would you have us do?"

"We ride for Persepolae," Ilyas said brusquely, pushing to his feet. "If I'm correct about our location, it's less than a day's ride."

"Yes, captain," I said, ignoring the uneasy feeling in the pit of my stomach.

He crouched down and laid his scarlet *qarha* over Tommas's face. Ilyas's shoulders hitched as he whispered a prayer. When he stood, his face was empty again. A mask.

"Why is the prisoner not bound?" he demanded.

"What?" His shifting moods threw me off balance.

"The Purified. He's a traitor. Tie him up!"

"He hasn't shown any sign of trying to run away," Tijah pointed out. She'd walked over to join us.

"I don't care," Ilyas seethed. "He's part of this conspiracy. Bind him."

She shrugged and did as Ilyas asked, using rope from the saddlebags.

"Please don't tell him about Victor," I whispered, as I held the Purified's hands together. Ilyas had gone to round up the remaining horses.

She raised an eyebrow. "That he's Darius's daddy?"

I scowled. "Yes."

"Poor thing," she said, and I didn't know whether she meant Darius, or Ilyas, or both of them.

"I'm serious, Tijah."

"Just like you didn't tell me about the fire?" she asked.

"That's different! I had no choice. And I was going to anyway. But I never got the chance."

She cinched the ropes tight and stood back. The Purified kept his head down, but I knew he was listening to every word.

"You keep your mouth shut too," I hissed in his ear. "Or you may not live long enough to see the King's dungeons."

"I am loyal to the Prophet, Water Dog," he said calmly. "Your threats mean nothing to me."

"The Prophet?" I laughed. "Whether or not your cause is just, I doubt very much if he'd approve of what you've done. Queen Neblis will thank you though, I'm sure."

"Neblis?" His delicate, boyish features sagged.

"Yes. That's who has it now, or will soon enough." I felt eyes on my back and saw Ilyas staring at us from across the dome. "Just keep quiet about Victor. If you're an ally of his, which you seem to be, he'd want you to protect his son, wouldn't he?"

The Purified swallowed like he had a rock wedged in his throat.

"Tijah?"

She returned my gaze, tilted eyes steady. "Of course. You're my sister."

I blinked back sudden tears. It was a miracle any of us were still alive. I could have lost so much more this day. I could be Ilyas. Half my heart ripped out, mourning something that never was. For it's not the loss that undoes us in the end, I realized. It's the regret, for words unspoken, small kindnesses withheld.

If Ilyas was not the satrap's bastard, if he didn't look like a barbarian, would he still be such a hard man? Maybe not, maybe so.

And what was I? Was I Four-Legs Clan? A Water Dog? A heretic? I still didn't know.

"Why did you help them?" I asked the Purified. "Tell me why. Please."

"It is the will of the Holy Father," he said simply. "He wants his children to be free."

🙚🙘

DAWN BROKE AS WE RODE OUT ONTO THE PLAIN. IT WAS A red dawn, the sun refracting through the settling dust until it seemed the whole world was on fire. I'd snatched a few hours' sleep curled against Tijah's back amid the wreckage of the battlefield. Somehow, her hair still smelled nice, like the lavender-scented soap she used at home.

Ilyas refused to leave Tommas behind, so we wrapped his body in blankets and slung it over the back of Ilyas's horse. I wondered if he planned to take him all the way to the Middle Sea when this was done. Perhaps carrying out Tommas's last wishes would give him some measure of peace. But the haunted, blank look had not left his eyes, and I doubted it would for a very long time.

We found the Royal Road, heading almost due north to Persepolae. After several hours, the desert gave way to rolling hills, then grasslands. We stopped at a river and filled our water skins. I took the chance to wash, scrubbing the sand and blood —a foul mix of human, daēva and Druj—from my tender skin.

Darius rode apart, lost in dark thoughts. His walls were back but I had no wish to intrude on his emotions. Just as Ilyas clutched the cuff, Darius clutched the faravahar he wore on a chain around his neck, so hard it left a deep mark in his palm.

The woman sat behind me, swaying silently in the saddle. I had tried speaking to her several times and finally given up. We would hand her over to the magi. Perhaps they could discover where she came from and return her to her family, if any of them still lived.

The Royal Road switched from dirt to paved stone. We came over a rise and I saw the southern wall of the capital, set against a dramatic backdrop of sheer cliffs. It was pierced by two gates. Burning braziers flanked the first, but not the second. A steady stream of people moved in and out, mostly through the first gate. The handful of travelers using the second all wore shades of blue.

"Darius and Myrri must pass through the daēva gate," Ilyas said. "We'll split up and meet on the other side."

Persepolae was built on a terrace, with the palace complex at the top. The Royal Road wound through a bustling unforti-fied town of mud-brick houses where the servants and arti-sans lived. A few noble mansions were also scattered through the valley outside the gates, but only the royal family, their attendants and the garrison of Immortals were allowed to reside within the walls of Persepolae itself.

"What's your business here, Water Dogs?" the gate captain asked warily, eyeing the body draped over Ilyas's saddle and the bound Purified.

I noticed that the burning braziers had been placed so

that anyone wishing to pass through the gate would be forced to ride directly past them.

"I carry an urgent message for the King," Ilyas responded. "We come from Tel Khalujah."

"Then I shall escort you myself," the captain said. "Dismount. My men will see to your horses." He paused. "And their burden. Who is it?"

"His bonded," I said.

The gate captain did not wear a cuff himself, but he immediately understood and his stern features softened a bit. "We'll bring him to the daëva garrison. You can collect him after the audience."

Ilyas looked at Tommas's body and hesitated, biting his lower lip. He ran a hand through the tangled red-gold mess of his hair and gripped a chunk of it in his fist.

"I'll stay with him," Tijah said.

Ilyas finally nodded. "Swear to me you won't leave his side," he said. "I won't have him touched."

"I swear it."

I watched Darius and Myrri ride up to the second gate. The guards roughly seized their arms and held them up to scrutinize the cuffs, then waved them through.

"We'll take charge of the prisoner," the captain said.

"Bring him along," Ilyas said. "The King will want to question this one himself."

Once we reached the other side, our cuffs were matched to our daëvas. The old woman was given into the care of two servants. Myrri went with Tijah and the horses. It was better for them to stay away from the palace anyway, I thought. Tel Khalujah was a backwater, but this was the summer capital of the empire. It was more than possible that Tijah's father had sent men here looking for her. Almost five years had passed since she'd fled Al Miraj, but someone could easily remember her description.

Darius fell into step beside me as the gate captain led us down a long, straight boulevard to the first set of stairs leading to the enormous platform of the palace complex. One side was open, but the other had been carved to depict a procession of people from all parts of the empire, bearing gifts as tribute to their ruler.

Ilyas walked with his back straight and his eyes fixed on the gate captain. I imagined he was thinking about what he would tell the King.

I had never seen Artaxeros the Second, of course, but I'd heard he had the gift, as did his father and grandfather before him. We'd only had three rulers since the founding of the empire two centuries before. Xeros the Great was thrown from his horse shortly after the construction of Persepolae. Artaxeros I reigned for the next one hundred and fifty-seven years, until he too died suddenly, of a mysterious wasting illness that even the stamina bestowed by the bond couldn't save him from. There were whispers that he'd been poisoned, but no one dared to voice them publicly since the prime suspect was the new King, his son, Artaxeros II.

He'd taken the throne a little over a decade ago. The magus at Tel Khalujah said he was a just man, if not the brilliant strategist his father had been. I clung to this hope as we approached the palace. That the King would not blame Ilyas for all that had happened.

I knew he already judged himself more harshly than anyone. But Ilyas had done everything humanly possible to fulfill his duty. Even his refusal to engage the necromancers on the plain had been logical. He couldn't be faulted for losing the fire in the bloody chaos of that dome.

I will not be remembered as the man who brought down the empire, Nazafareen.

I studied the ranks of Immortals lining the stairs to the royal palace. They stood at attention, their scaled armor alternating crimson and sky blue, spears as tall as a Revenant gleaming in the sun. They appeared well-fed and disciplined. Most had been trained from birth for this, human and daēva alike. Seeing them made me doubt that their loyalty to the King could be shaken so easily, even by the promise of freedom.

They were bonded, just like me and Darius. I knew he would never turn on me. He didn't even want to be released. My anxiety eased a bit until we passed a rectangular building that could only be the Hall of the Numerators. A cluster of them stood on the steps, watching us go by with impassive faces. Daēva hunters. They wore pristine white robes with red hems. In contrast to their plain, even austere attire, these men oozed arrogance, and my unease returned.

The Purified walked with his head down next to me, but we both craned our neck at a statue of the Prophet, some forty feet tall. He had a long beard and flames danced over his open, upraised palm. A male daēva knelt at his side, head bowed as though to receive a blessing. The sculptor had diplomatically chosen not to give the daēva a visible infirmity, but he skillfully captured the ethereal, animal-like grace in the smooth muscles of his body.

I glanced at Darius. I knew he hadn't forgiven me for lying to him. I also knew his anger was directed at Victor as much as me. He had been burdened with knowledge he didn't want, couldn't reconcile.

What Darius needed was rest, I decided. By all rights, he should be in a sickbed, recovering from the injuries he'd inflicted on himself using the power. With any luck, the audience would be a short one. I would tend to him myself afterwards, whether he wanted me to or not.

We ascended the final flight of stairs, past two colossal stone bulls and more bas-reliefs of the King battling lions and other fantastic beasts I had no names for.

"The Hall of a Hundred Columns," the gate captain said, leading us into an enormous space that reminded me of a stone forest, its tall fluted pillars crowned by animal-headed capitals.

At least fifty Immortals stood in ranks around a throne at the far end of the great hall, along with assorted nobles, magi and advisors. We walked between the center columns, our footsteps echoing on the marble. My palms started to sweat. When we were twenty feet from the throne, the gate captain halted. I lowered my gaze, but I caught a quick glimpse of the King. He was a burly man with a short black beard. A woman stood behind him wearing the flimsy gown of the harem. She had a long, melancholy face, not beautiful in the classic sense but still riveting somehow. One of her eyes was a dead, milky white, the other sapphire blue. She raised a hand to tuck a strand of long hair behind her ear, and I saw a gold cuff around her slender wrist.

The captain shoved the captive Purified to the ground and pressed his forehead to the stone. Ilyas, Darius and I hastily followed suit.

I was whispering a prayer to the Holy Father that the King would go easy on Ilyas when he jumped to his feet. An agitated murmur erupted among the court.

"On your knees, Water Dog!" A magus thundered, stepping forward. "The King will tell you when to rise."

"I beg forgiveness," Ilyas said humbly. Then he stood back and pointed to Darius. "But this daēva is a traitor, conspiring to overthrow the King! Arrest him!"

My heart stopped. I instantly released the power and reached for my sword, then remembered they had taken it from me at the gate. The Immortals surged forward, a wall of blue and red surrounding Darius.

"No!" I screamed, as my arms were seized. "It's not true!" I turned to Ilyas. He refused to meet my eye. "Tell them! We fought necromancers together! Druj! He's loyal! He's done nothing!"

"He is the son of Victor, one of the old daēvas," Ilyas said in a loud voice. "A group of them broke free from Gorgon-e Gaz and stole the holy fire from the Barbican. He pretended to lose their trail. But then I myself witnessed this daēva allowing Victor to escape. They are clearly conspirators. The Purified will confirm it. He is in league with them."

I thrashed and spat at the Immortals and waited for Darius to seize the power, to wreak havoc. I felt his shock at Ilyas's betrayal. But he didn't fight back or say a word in his own defense. He just stood there as the soldiers chained him.

"The holy fire has been stolen?" The King stood. "Where is it?"

"Taken by Neblis's witches," Ilyas said. "The other daēvas are all dead. I would have ridden for Bactria to pursue the urn, but I knew I must tell my King what had transpired." Ilyas dropped to one knee, and I wanted to kick him in the face. "This daēva is very dangerous. I couldn't arrest him myself. But I'm sure you will see justice is done."

The King studied him. "What of his Water Dog bonded? Is she a traitor too?"

"No, my King. She is innocent."

"Then why does she struggle?"

Ilyas did look at me then. I bared my teeth at him. "She is surprised. I couldn't explain my intention to her lest he discover it and try to run. The bond runs deep, but I believe she can be redeemed. Perhaps if you confine her to barracks?"

"You bastard," I hissed at him. "You filthy, treacherous bastard. I'll see you dead—"

"Remove her from my presence." The King waved a hand.

As they dragged me past Darius, I called out his name. "I won't let them," I said. "I won't—" And then an elbow jabbed into my gut, expertly freezing the muscles that let me breathe. Someone grabbed my hair and yanked my head back. My last view as they carried me out was of a beautiful timber ceiling worked with a thousand faravahars, each feather rendered in lifelike detail.

Flee this place, Darius, I thought, as blackness took me. *If you were Victor, you'd kill them all.*

❧ 17 ❧

Ilyas was waiting when I clawed my way back to consciousness. I opened my eyes and saw him sitting there at the foot of the bed, leaning on one hand like he'd just popped in for a casual visit. My hands and feet were tied with heavy rope that had been looped around my back, but still I wriggled and twisted in a pointless attempt to kick him.

"Calm yourself, Nazafareen," Ilyas said.

I shook the hair from my face and glanced around. We were in a small room in the Immortals barracks, by the sound of swords ringing outside the window. The sun cast long shadows across the stone floor. Late afternoon then. A whole day had passed. I reached for Darius through the bond and nearly wept. He was still there. Still alive.

"Why, Ilyas?" I demanded, sitting up as far as my restraints would allow. "Why are you doing this? It's insanity!"

He studied me. "Did you truly believe I didn't know? I saw everything. Saw that demon claim him as its unholy offspring. Saw Darius set him free. I knew then why our journey seemed cursed." Ilyas rubbed his thumb across his own cuff, making tiny circles on the gold. "I thought the Holy Father had turned his face away from me. That I had done something to offend him. But after the plain, it all became clear. Your daēva had somehow conspired with the very same Druj we were chasing."

"You've lost your mind," I said flatly. "Victor said those things to knock Darius off balance, make him lose his connection to the power. I felt it! Victor broke free on his own, Ilyas. No other daēva besides Darius could have even held him that long. You saw what he did at Gorgon-e Gaz! How can you doubt it?"

Ilyas shook his head sadly. "The bond has tainted you, Nazafareen. The Druj are evil. You cannot see it."

I stared at him. "If you do not renounce your accusations, I swear before the Holy Father, I will see you burn. I will hunt you to the end of my days—"

Ilyas was at my side in two steps, and the open-handed blow he delivered across my jaw made my head spin.

"That's enough," he said mildly. "The King will pass judgment on him tomorrow."

Several of Tijah's filthiest curses sprang to mind, but I knew Ilyas would just hit me again. And I needed to keep my wits. Pushing him over the edge wouldn't help Darius.

"I want to speak on his behalf," I said, tasting blood. "And I want to see Tijah."

"No."

"To which?"

"To both. But I do have an offer for you." Ilyas sat down again and rested his arms on his knees. I had seen him do this many times, a familiar gesture. It made the hair on my neck rise.

He still looked like Ilyas, moved like him, but the man before me now was a stranger.

"The King, and the Numerators, would prefer that Darius confess his transgressions."

"He won't do it," I said immediately.

"Likely not," Ilyas agreed. "Which means that he will be executed. That is the penalty for treason. To be given to the fire."

Pain flared behind my eyes. My breath grew shallow, panicked. This couldn't actually be happening. Oh Father, they were going to kill him...

"I'll speak with Darius," I heard myself whisper.

Ilyas smiled. "Good. If he admits his crimes publicly, the King might consider a lesser punishment. A prolonged stay in the dungeon, perhaps. But, Nazafareen..."

I looked up, into his grey eyes. They were the same color as the stone walls and had as much sympathy.

"If you let go of his leash, or if either of you tries to flee, you'll burn together."

⚜

TEN IMMORTALS LED ME DOWN INTO THE CELLS BENEATH the palace. Their leader was a man named Lieutenant Kamdin. He looked a bit like my uncle, with a thick mustache and cleft chin. He was neither friendly nor hostile, just briskly efficient.

They flanked me five to a side, humans on my left and daēvas on my right. All were impressive specimens and the top of my head barely reached their shoulders.

I was relieved to see the dungeons were well-kept, if chilly. Most of the cells were empty. A few ragged souls huddled in the darkness, calling out softly as we passed, but it was otherwise silent. We turned a corner and Lieutenant Kamdin stopped. A dozen Immortals, all wearing the blue, sat on wooden chairs staring through the bars of a cell. I realized they would never leave a daēva prisoner unattended like the others.

"You have five minutes," he said, opening the cell door with a large iron key.

I stepped inside and it clanged shut behind me. The floor was bare stone, lacking even straw bedding. I saw no food, no water. Only Darius. He stood up when I entered.

"You shouldn't have come," he said.

"Don't be stupid," I replied, closing the distance between us.

They hadn't been gentle with him. I saw a fresh bruise on his cheek. Blood matted his dark hair. And he was still beautiful to me. More now than ever. Tears blurred my eyes as I reached out to touch his swollen mouth.

Darius grabbed my wrist by the cuff, gritting his teeth at the pain. He almost seemed to welcome it.

I yanked my hand away. "All right," I said, stung. "I won't touch you, then." I leaned in close. "But I want you to listen to me. They're going to kill you. Ilyas is a monster. He'll never recant. He's our captain. Even if Tijah or me deny the charges, no one will care what we say. It's Ilyas's word against ours. All they want is a scapegoat now. Do you understand?"

Something in his eyes seemed to recede, like a turtle pulling into its shell. "Has he threatened you? Are they saying you're a part of it too?"

"Not really. He's perverse. Some part of him still wants to protect me."

Darius sighed. "Thank the Father."

I wanted to shake him. "It's not myself I'm worried about!"

His lips quirked in an almost smile. "Then one of us has to."

I forced myself to take a breath. My usual style was to blurt whatever came to mind and worry about the consequences later. I was not accustomed to biting my tongue, and here I was, doing it twice in one day. But I knew that I had only one chance to convince him of what had to be done. I glanced at the guards. I didn't think they could hear us, but our time was almost over.

"Darius, please. I'm begging you," I whispered. "You could blow the doors off this cell before they know what's happening. I'll get one of their swords and we'll—"

He pressed his thumb to my lips. As always, the contact undid me, setting every nerve on fire, weakening my knees.

"No," he said, although I could feel his own pulse racing. "I am not my father. I will not take lives to spare my own."

"Then you're a fool," I said bitterly, turning my head away. "And so am I, for caring what happens to you."

Pain creased his features, as though I had dealt him a physical blow. He was so hard to understand sometimes.

"Do you remember the last thing I said to you on the roof that night? After Ash Shiyda?" Darius's body was rigid with tension, but he didn't pull away.

"Yes."

I'd never forgotten a word of it. My reckless needling. His sudden fury. The rain dripping from his hair as he caught my arm and stopped me from falling.

He'd told me that he hated the cuff. Hated *me*.

Darius was so close now I had to tilt my chin up to meet his gaze. I used to think he was made of ice. Cold, unfeeling. But that wasn't it. He was just protecting himself, and he'd done it for so long, he didn't know how to stop.

"I meant the first part," Darius said. "Not the second."

We looked at each other for a long moment. I wanted him to throw his arm around me, to kiss me hard, to do *something*.

But he seemed frozen, still stubbornly clinging to those walls, and before I could do it for him, the cell door was banging open and Lieutenant Kamdin had taken my arm.

"Darius!" I cried, suddenly terrified I would never speak to him again.

"Goodbye, Nazafareen," he said.

And then he turned his back to me.

I shook Kamdin's hand off, anger and despair turning my heart to a hard lump in my chest. I hated Darius in that moment. Hated his refusal to see the good in himself. To fight back. He probably thought he deserved this somehow.

What had been done to him by those magi in Karnopolis? Those pious old men?

I scrubbed a fist across my eyes, unwilling to let the Immortals see me weep. Lieutenant Kamdin kept his gaze straight head. He struck me as a decent sort.

"Where is the Purified we came with?" I asked him as we walked down the corridor. "I need to see him. Only for a moment."

Kamdin hesitated. "He's here, in one of the eastern cells."

"Please. It could save a man's life. I don't even have to go inside."

He sucked his teeth, the mustache wiggling up and down. "I don't suppose it would do any harm." He eyed me sideways. "I heard you killed a necromancer."

"Together with my daēva. I couldn't have done it alone."

Kamdin's brows drew down. "Dark times are upon us. The King's eyes are on the western front, on Eskander and his Companions, but I wonder if the worse threat isn't at our backs to the north."

"Neblis."

"The Bactrian witch has been quiet for too long," he growled. "Some say your daēva is in league with her too."

"What? That doesn't even make sense. We fought a hundred Druj to get here!"

"I didn't say I believed it," Kamdin said gruffly. "But his fate is for the King to decide."

He escorted me to a cell four turnings from Darius's. The Purified had slightly better conditions, I saw. He knelt on a threadbare blanket, eyes closed and mouth moving in prayer.

I floundered for his name but couldn't remember it. "Magus?" I whispered through the bars.

He looked over. Holy Father, he was young. His cheeks were still smooth as a boy's, without a trace of beard.

"I need to know. Will you tell the truth tomorrow? When the King passes judgment?"

The Purified looked confused.

"About my daēva. Darius. You know he had nothing to do with stealing the fire, don't you?"

"It is an evil to lie," he said, making the sign of the flame.

I returned the gesture.

"Fear not, child. My soul is bare to the Holy Father. He knows I am clean of sin. That I only carried out his will."

"Yes, I know," I said impatiently. "But you must tell them that Darius is innocent."

He considered this. "None of us are innocent. But I will tell the truth."

I nodded. It was the best I was going to get.

When they brought me back to my quarters, Ilyas was waiting. I wondered if he had sat there the entire time.

"Well?" he asked.

"I assume you made the offer yourself," I said. "Before you asked me to."

He stared at me. "Yes."

"Then the answer is still no. Because if you think I'm going to beg him to confess to something he didn't do, then you don't know me at all. And if you think Darius would do it, then you don't know him either."

Ilyas gave a strange, shuddering twitch. Revulsion contorted his features into a grimace, there and gone in an instant. Then he rose and left without another word. I heard the door lock behind him.

I was still sitting on my bed, staring into space, when an Immortal brought a plate of food several hours later. Just looking at it turned my stomach.

Who could help me? The answer was no one. I was a stranger here. Kamdin had treated me decently, but he could hardly be counted as an ally. I had hoped Tijah would come, but so far I hadn't seen her since we'd entered the gates. Either Ilyas wasn't allowing her to visit, or she thought Darius was guilty. It had to be the first. I didn't believe Tijah would turn her back on me if she had any choice.

At least they hadn't tried to break our bond. They couldn't, not without the key to the cuffs, which was with the magus in Tel Khalujah. That meant that when they carried out the execution, I would feel every moment of Darius's agony when they gave him to the fire...

I pushed this thought away, but it kept returning. How had everything gone so terribly wrong? I used to look up to Ilyas. He was my mentor. Brave, selfless, loyal. I had trusted him with my life.

But there had always been a hidden fault line in him. Buried deep, invisible to the eye, like the crevasses in the mountains I'd known as a child. Bring the right pressure to bear on precisely the right spot, and he would shatter.

First the escape, then the Barbican, then Tommas. He might have held together if not for the last. I knew that losing his daēva had been by far the hardest blow.

I didn't want to end up like Ilyas. Tortured, despising myself for loving a demon. But Darius wasn't a demon. He was worth a thousand of these supposedly good men. These men who claimed to walk in the light even as they grew rich and powerful on the backs of the daēvas. It was all one big, unforgiveable lie.

If only I could make Darius see it too. For I knew in my heart that he was the only one who could help himself.

🦋 18 🦋

Darius's trial was held the next morning in the Hall of a Hundred Columns. I'd been afraid Ilyas would prevent me from attending, but it seemed the King had insisted I be present. Most likely to keep my daēva under control when the judgment was passed.

I had thought all night, trying to foresee every outcome, looking for chinks in Ilyas's claims. Of course, they were a complete fabrication. He had no real evidence, other than what Victor had said. But I knew Ilyas believed it and his words would carry the weight of conviction. He needed someone to blame. Someone to punish. The real culprits—Victor, the necromancer, even Queen Neblis herself—were out of his reach. That left Darius.

As I walked with my escort of Immortals to the audience chamber, I tried to keep calm, despite the dryness of my mouth. I had a strange floating feeling, from lack of sleep and, let's face it, sheer terror. But I would need to choose my words carefully. If I offended the King, it was over.

The chamber was packed to bursting with Immortals, Numerators, magi and the King's retinue of richly dressed nobles. The King himself sat stone-faced on the throne. A staff rested across his knees and he wore a crown of solid gold, adorned with jewels and serrations on top that looked like tiny towers.

I nearly wept with relief when I saw Tijah. She was standing next to Ilyas on the other side of the chamber. I moved to join them but one of my Immortal guards clamped a hand on my arm.

"Bring out the accused," the King said.

A hush fell on the Hall as Darius was led out and shoved to his knees. My breath caught at the sight of him. I tried to send comfort through the bond, but he was oddly calm. As if he already accepted what was about to happen.

No one moved, except for the woman I had seen standing behind the throne the day before. She brought a hand to her mouth, as though stifling a cry. The King stared at her for a long moment, eyes narrowed. Then he motioned her to sit at his feet. She dropped the hand, her expression perfectly neutral, and sank to the ground, sheer gown puddling around her. The way her limbs flowed with an otherworldly grace confirmed my suspicions that she was a daēva. The King's bonded. Her good eye, that astonishing blue, fixed on Darius as she drew her long legs to her chin.

"Captain Ilyas," the King said. "You say this daēva committed an act of treason. Is that correct?"

"Yes, King of Kings," Ilyas said, stepping forward. "We set out from Tel Khalujah eight days ago. A messenger had come from Gorgon-e Gaz, reporting the escape of six daēvas and their guards. They massacred fourteen good men and fled into the Khusk Range. We rode in pursuit. That daēva"—he pointed to Darius —"was our tracker. Someone, perhaps he himself, brought an avalanche down on us as we came out of the mountains. But we survived it and continued onto the

Great Salt Plain, where the trail appeared to lead to the Barbican."

I'd hoped Ilyas would appear as unhinged and delusional as I knew him to be, but his tone was mild, almost regretful, and my heart sank.

"We encountered a group of necromancers on the plain, King of Kings. He advised against engaging with them, as we were too evenly matched, and I agreed. The first priority was to ensure the security of the Barbican."

I gritted my teeth as the King nodded. Not exactly a lie, but not the whole truth either. It had been Ilyas's decision to let the necromancers go. And Darius had probably been correct in his assessment. They were more dangerous than I'd imagined. If the other daēvas hadn't already killed two of them, we'd all be dead right now.

"Shortly after, he claimed to lose the trail of the runners. It made no sense. He had been tracking them since Tel Khalujah. Suddenly, they disappear? The Barbican appeared unmolested, but I thought it prudent to consult with the High Magus. It was he who confirmed that the holy fire had been stolen by two Purified not an hour before. Undoubtedly, Darius was in league with them."

"I understand you managed to bring one back," the King said. "Where is he? I would hear in his own words what transpired, and what drove him to commit this act of heresy."

I pressed my lips together to stifle a smile. The Purified was our best hope. I just prayed he would keep his word. I thought he would. He feared the judgment of the Holy Father far more than these men.

Then Lieutenant Kamdin strode forward, his face grim. He prostrated himself before the King.

"Speak."

"King of Kings," Kamdin said. "I am afraid the Purified has taken his own life. One of the Immortals just informed me that they discovered his body hanging from the cell bars. It must have happened sometime in the night. He used the sash from his robes."

Excited whispering broke out in the Hall.

"A pity," the King said, cutting through the babble. "But a sure sign of a guilty heart."

I raised a shaking hand to my forehead. It took every ounce of control I could muster not to point a finger at Ilyas and scream, "Murderer!" For that's what he was. I had no doubts.

"Continue, Captain Ilyas," the King said, as if the man's death was a trifling matter.

Ilyas paused to gather his thoughts. "When I learned that the fire had been taken, I ordered our daēvas to send a sandstorm, hoping to slow them down."

"A clever strategy," the King said approvingly.

"It worked. We caught them shortly afterwards, but the necromancers had found them first. We arrived in the middle of a heated battle between the two sides. I have been told that Darius engaged the Druj, although I was otherwise occupied with slaying one of the necromancers and their unholy minions, so I can't verify this myself."

I stared at Ilyas. He knew Darius had almost lost his life a dozen times in that fight. And it wasn't because he had no choice. He was a warrior. And no matter what they did to him, no matter how badly they treated him, he would choose the light. He had done it again and again. And now he would die for it, at the hands of the very people he had tried to save.

If I could have seized the power myself in that moment, I would have. I would have levelled that palace and everyone in it, even if it killed me. I reached for it through the cuff, as futile as the gesture was, and thought that half-seen star glowed brighter for a second. I tried to still my thoughts, as Darius stilled his, and delve deeper into my body. My blood surged, and the power seemed to pulse in time with my heart. It felt so close...

And then Ilyas's voice dragged me back. It had taken on a hard edge. He was about to deliver the most damning evidence of all.

"The fight appeared to be over. We had slain our enemies, but the holy fire was gone. My daēva..." Ilyas cleared his throat. "My daēva, Tommas, succumbed to a wight. I was still reeling from the loss when one of the daēvas from Gorgon-e Gaz came back. The only survivor of their group. Victor."

The woman at the King's feet stirred at this. Some strong emotion seemed to flow through the bond between them, for he shifted in the throne, gripping his staff with white knuckles.

"I commanded Darius to slay him. Victor had used the fire to break the cuffs and there was no way to bring him to justice. They pretended to fight, but at the very moment that Darius had the upper hand, he allowed Victor to break free." Ilyas paused for dramatic effect. "Perhaps not surprising, since Victor is his father. I heard Victor claim him myself."

Several of the nobles gasped at this revelation, but the Numerators flanking the throne and the King himself seemed unmoved. Of course, they knew already. The entire audience was just a show, I realized with disgust.

"Did anyone else hear it?" the King asked.

"Yes, King of Kings. Nazafareen, his bonded. And Tijah, the third of the Water Dogs from Tel Khalujah."

"Where are they?" the King's eyes roved through the Hall.

"I am Nazafareen," I said, heart thumping in my ears.

"Come forward." His gaze settled on Tijah, whom Ilyas was whispering to. "You also."

I walked to Darius and knelt at his side. His hands and feet were chained together. Blood oozed from cuts in his skin where the manacles had bitten deep. I caught his eye for only an instant before his gaze flicked away.

Tijah's steps dragged as she approached the king and paid obeisance. Her expression was a picture of misery.

"Let's start with you," the King said to Tijah. "Did the rogue daēva named Victor claim Darius as his son in your presence?"

She licked her lips. "Yes, but—"

"And did he say that he intended to free Darius and the other daēvas with the Prophet's fire?"

Now I knew for certain that Ilyas had briefed the King privately, for he hadn't even mentioned this part.

"That wasn't Darius's fault, he didn't know—"

"Did he say it?" the King thundered.

Tijah's shoulders slumped. "Yes."

The King turned to me. "Two witnesses have confirmed the collusion between these daēvas. Do you dare deny it?"

I took a slow breath, the stares of the entire court boring into me. The faces of the nobles bore thinly veiled contempt. No matter what color tunic I wore, they saw only a dirty, backwards nomad girl. The King himself seemed impatient to conclude the proceedings.

Tread carefully, Nazafareen, I thought. *Do not anger this man more.*

"King of Kings, I would never deny the obvious truth. But I can tell you as his bonded that he did everything in his power to hold Victor. Ilyas did not mention that Victor is one of the strongest daēvas in the empire. That he cracked the stone fortress of Gorgon-e Gaz in half."

Astonished murmurs greeted this statement. The magi and Numerators looked at each other in alarm.

"Darius sustained severe injuries fighting the Druj, and then his own father. If you examine him, you will see for yourself that it is true. These are not the actions of a traitor, but of a daēva loyal heart and soul to the empire. When Victor told us his plans, Darius said he didn't wish to be free. Those were his exact words."

Tijah nodded. Ilyas scowled deeply, but he didn't deny it.

"Darius was raised by the magi in Karnopolis," I said. "He is the most devout person I have ever met. He even wears the faravahar around his neck, as a symbol of his faith. We've only been bonded for two years, but in that time I have seen him kill hundreds of Druj." I raised my arm and held the cuff high so everyone could see it. "The bond does not lie. It would have been impossible for him to conceal his true intentions from me. I can attest that his heart is pure."

Some of the Immortals nodded at this. The King just watched me, his expression unreadable. But he himself was bonded. He had to know that my words rang true.

"I think that my captain is a good man"—those words almost choked me, but they had to be uttered—"who has suffered an unimaginable loss. He sees snakes in the grass where there are none to be found. With all due respect, Queen Neblis is the true enemy. It is she who sent her necromancers across our borders, she who now has possession of the Prophet's holy fire. The threat lies to the north, not in this chamber. And we will need to stand together if we hope to defeat her. We will need every soldier, every daēva." I pointed to Darius. "He is your weapon, King of Kings. He lives only to kill Druj, and he is very good at it. Do not throw him away on the false claims of a man who himself has failed you."

Ilyas stared daggers at me for that last bit, but I sensed that the mood in the Hall had subtly shifted. The Numerators didn't look pleased but they were a sour bunch, concerned mainly with hoarding their own power. The magi were already nervous, since two of their own had been certain conspirators. But many of the Immortals wore thoughtful expressions. They would be the ones called on if another war broke out. They understood the need for unity.

I caught Lieutenant Kamdin's eye and he gave me the barest nod.

The King tapped his fingers on the staff.

"Darius," he said. "Do you also refute these charges?"

"I do," Darius said in a soft voice. "Victor may be my father, but I am a loyal son of the empire."

"Lies—" Ilyas hissed.

"Silence!" The King stood. He surveyed the room, then fixed his gaze on Darius. "In the name of the Holy Father, my judgment is thus." The entire Hall seemed to hold its breath. "The Water Dog daēva is a traitor and will be given to the Numerators. They will see him burn." His gaze landed on me. "His bonded is also guilty by default. Take her to the cells. I will determine her punishment at a later date."

My knees buckled as a phalanx of Immortals swept over and grabbed me and Darius. He was shouting my innocence, finally roused from his apathy, but it was too late. A breeze swept the chamber as dozens of daēvas summoned their power to hold him in check.

As they dragged me out for the second time in as many days, I saw Tijah's horrified face, Ilyas's smug grin, and lastly, the King's own daēva. She was staring at me intensely, and I had the odd sensation that her dead, milky eye was not blind after all.

All the way to the dungeons, Darius screamed my name. Screamed until he was hoarse. I knew he hadn't meant for this to happen. It was Ilyas's fault. Ilyas and the King.

They put us too far apart to hear each other. As I curled up on the cold stone floor, all I could think of was the fact that I never kissed him. Not even once. Of all the regrets in my life, and I had many, that was the biggest.

The Numerators came the next day. At least, I think it was the next day. There was no way to judge the passage of time in the dungeons. I had slept, and woken, and slept some more. It was my only escape. I welcomed the darkness, even if it was plagued by nightmares of Darius on a fire altar, that huge statue of the Prophet looming over him as faceless men prayed for his soul.

But I couldn't sleep forever. And when they brought me a bowl of slops, I drank every drop. There was no point in starving myself to death. I doubted I'd even have time to.

I was cautiously probing the various cuts and bruises on my body when I saw the flickering light of a torch coming down the passage. That told me right away it wasn't the Immortals. They always stayed in bonded pairs, and the daēvas would be unable to tolerate the fire.

I'd thought I was past fear since the worst had already happened, but as soon as I saw those pure white robes, my gut tightened.

There were six of them. Five kept their faces cloaked in shadow, but the last produced a key and entered my cell. He looked like a kindly grandfather. Thick silver hair, twinkling blue eyes, skin glowing with good health, although it sagged around his jowls a bit.

"Nazafareen," he said, smiling. His voice was rich, silky, like a purring cat, but it held an edge of authority. Besides the red embroidery at the hem, his robe bore the symbol of an eye with a dancing flame where the pupil should be. I had no idea what it meant, only that this man held some kind of special rank within their order.

I pressed my back against the wall and said nothing.

"I understand you come from the Four-Legs Clan," he said. "Mountain people. I wouldn't have expected a nomad to speak so eloquently." He chuckled. "I hope that doesn't offend you. It was meant as a compliment. I suppose you were educated by the magus in Tel Khalujah?"

His lips thinned at my continued silence.

"We haven't paid a visit to the Khusk Range in far too long," he mused. "Not that I doubt your people's loyalty. But I've found that even those in the farthest reaches of the empire need a reminder, from time to time."

"What do you want?"

"Straight to the point, eh? I'll dispense with the pleasantries then. Your daēva will be put to death in five days' time. He's a traitor. This is clear. And yet the King feels it would be prudent if he confessed his sins. Thanks to your pretty speech, some seem to think he might be innocent."

I guessed he was talking about the Immortals.

"It's a small matter, but we would like to lay those rumors to rest."

"Darius will never do it," I said. "Never."

The Numerator studied me. "How well do you understand the bond?"

"Enough."

"Are you aware that it can be used to...coerce?"

I suddenly remembered Ilyas's words to Tommas on the plain, right before he summoned the sandstorm.

You'll make it happen. Now! Or you'll learn what the bond can do to a daēva that disobeys its master...

"You want me to torture him," I said flatly. "With the cuff."

The Numerator's eyes glittered. "Torture is a strong word. The process leaves no physical mark. But yes, pain can be caused. Mortal agony, even."

I wondered if I could manage to snap his neck before the others got inside the cell. The odds seemed decent.

"If he confesses, his sentence will be commuted. As will yours. Not a full pardon, of course. But he'll escape the flames. Think on it, Nazafareen. You hold his life in your hands." He made a fluttering motion with his fingers. "Don't worry, they tend to break very quickly. I can teach you the most efficient techniques."

I stared at him, and wondered how I could ever have been a part of this. They were monsters. All of them.

"Would you like to hear something very interesting?" I said.

"What?" He leaned forward eagerly.

"Did you know that the stars are actually suns? Hot, burning orbs in the heavens?"

The Numerator frowned in confusion.

"Yes, it's true," I said. "My daēva told me. Another thing: mountains dream. But a single dream may last a thousand years."

"Have you lost your wits?" he snapped.

"Oh, and if you're very still, you can hear the forest breathing." I smiled. "It's all in a place called the nexus. A pity you're too stupid to notice it."

The Numerator's face darkened. His blue eyes no longer twinkled.

"I will see you're kept alive to feel him burn," he said. "And then I'll make sure your clan is wiped off the face of the earth."

I did attack him then, but the others were on me in a heartbeat, kicking and stomping until blood splattered their white robes. When they were done, and the cell door clanged shut again, I curled on the floor in a ball. I thought of my mother and father, my brother Kian, my uncles and aunts and cousins. And I wept, for them, for myself, for Darius.

I didn't move for a long time. Everything hurt. I had no energy left. They'd probably go ahead and torture him anyway, but I wouldn't help them do it.

Time passed. Distant voices approached, receded.

I may have slept a little more. I could still feel Darius, although his state of mind was as bleak as my own. I found his heartbeat, and focused on that, letting my own fall into rhythm with it. The next best thing to having him with me.

I tried reaching for the power again, as I had in the Hall of a Hundred Columns, but I was too numb, too exhausted. I could sense it though, swirling through the stones of the prison, the dank air that filled my lungs. It was everywhere, in everything. I knew Darius would seize it if he could. They must have been blocking him somehow.

Three days. I had three days to think of something. But my mind was blank. There was no way out of this place, not alive at any rate.

※

DIM DAYLIGHT FILTERED DOWN THE CORRIDOR. I SAT UP, wincing in pain. Footsteps, soft and stealthy. My heart lifted, hoping it might be Tijah. I pictured her with her scimitar drawn, wet with the blood of the guards, Myrri at her side.

Then I saw it was Ilyas. His eyes looked like black holes

in his face, like he hadn't slept in days.

"We need to talk," he said, stopping in front of my cell. "I didn't mean for this to happen."

I surprised myself by laughing, although it stabbed my ribs like a knife. "You didn't?"

"No. Not you. I didn't think they would arrest *you*."

"Take it all back then," I said, although I knew it was already too late for that.

"Save yourself," Ilyas urged. "Please. Renounce him. Say you know he's a demon. That he corrupted you, but you walk in the light now. The Numerators will go easier on you. I can bring you home to Tel Khalujah. The satrap will—"

"No."

"Why not?" He smashed a fist against the bars. "Why do you insist on defending him?"

I held his gaze. "Because I won't be like you, Ilyas."

He froze. "What do you mean?"

"You know what I mean."

"No," he said in a deadly tone. "I don't."

"You loved Tommas," I said. "Just as I love Darius." As I spoke the words, I knew they were true. "But instead of accepting it, you let it poison you."

Ilyas shook his head, his red-gold curls flying.

"No, no..."

"Tommas must have known. Of course he knew. I don't know whether he loved you back, but he put up with you all those years with more grace and patience than I would have." I knew I was pushing him too hard, but I no longer cared. "Maybe he did love you. Maybe he did. You should have been better to him, Ilyas! He wasn't Druj. None of them are Druj! It's all lies. And I won't be a part of it anymore."

"*Your daēva let him die!*" Ilyas raged, and I suddenly realized we had reached the heart of the matter. "He could have saved him, but he didn't. He let his blood pour out..." Ilyas's hand clamped down on the cuff. "I can still feel him. Feel him rotting. The bond is still there, Nazafareen. It never goes away! And I can't get it off." He broke into a sob.

I took a step forward. As much as I hated him, I wouldn't wish this on anyone. It chilled me to the bone.

"Ilyas—" I said. And his hand shot out, grabbing my wrist and dragging me hard against the bars.

"You have the taint too," he whispered, his breath hot in my ear. "I saw it that day down by the river, and again in the mountains. It's filthy. Unholy. There's a reason human-daēva offspring aren't permitted to live. They're an abomination. I won't let it happen to you, Nazafareen. I won't."

"Let go of me!" I screamed, but my face was pressed against the cell bars and his grip on my right arm was like iron.

"You're like a sister. It's my duty to protect you. Protect you from yourself." He pulled a long knife from a sheath at his waist. "Don't fight, Nazafareen. It will just make it worse."

"Ilyas, please...please don't..."

I did beg then. Begged and screamed and cried. Promised to do whatever he asked of me. But a strange calm had descended on him and I knew with a thrill of perfect terror that he had planned this all along, if things didn't go his way.

"Guards!" I yelled, my voice high and cracked. "Help me! Somebody help me!"

But nobody did. Nobody came. Ilyas twisted my arm so the elbow was locked down tight. I struggled. Oh, how I struggled. When the blade bit into the soft flesh above the cuff, I saw starbursts explode in front of my eyes. And when it caught in the bone, and he started sawing, I wished for death.

But the very worst part was the end. As I slipped into blackness, I felt an empty hole where Darius used to live. Our bond had been broken. My daēva was gone.

❧ 20 ❧

The next days passed like a fever dream. I fell in and out of consciousness. Magi came, holding me down while they cauterized the stump with hot wax. I saw Ilyas's face, swimming in the background, watching but not speaking. He looked sorrowful, but then he had looked the same while he cut my hand off.

They covered me with a blanket and still I shivered uncontrollably, teeth chattering. The pain was something to hold onto. A distraction from the loneliness and the fear of what was being done to Darius. For the first time in two years, I didn't know.

I didn't know.

Didn't know if he was dead or alive. Where he was. *How* he was. Because he was bonded to Ilyas now. The cuff had only to be touching skin. Ilyas wore it on a chain around his neck.

I wished they would just kill me and get it over with. But I knew he didn't want me dead. Just broken, like him.

Sometimes I still felt my hand. I would try to bring it to my face, to push the hair from my eyes, and I would see the stump, the circle of bone and scarred flesh. The skin at the edge was a lighter color, where it had been shielded from the sun. The sight made me retch.

They came and checked it twice each day, for infection, and I was too tired to fight them. So my mind settled into its own delirious routine. Fantasizing about what I would do to Ilyas if I ever managed to get out of here. And thinking of Darius—not the things we did as Water Dogs, but the time we spent when he was recovering in his bed. All the stories he told me. The late afternoon sun pooling on the wood floor, the soft rustle of the sheets as he shifted his weight.

That was when he told the bit about the mountains dreaming. I had laughed then, thinking he was teasing me, but his face was serious.

Darius closed the book. He took my hand, brought it to his lips, his eyes lit with an inner fire.

"You are my island in the Midnight Sea, Nazafareen," he said, pulling me into his bed...

Well, he didn't really say that. But it's how I liked to remember it.

I dreamed about Tommas too. His easy smile. The way he sang to Myrri. If he hadn't killed those Druj, he never would have been sold to the Water Dogs. He still would have been a slave, but he could have lived out his days on the merchant traders, filling their sails with wind.

If the Druj hadn't killed my sister, I wouldn't be here either.

Always the Druj.

My one consolation was that the Numerator was wrong when he said he would wipe my clan off the face of the earth. He had no idea who he was dealing with. At the first sign of danger, they would melt into the mountains and disappear. The Four-Legs Clan submitted to the King's authority because they needed to trade with Tel Khalujah, but no ruler had ever subjugated my people by force.

They had tried, of course. For a thousand years. And none of those soldiers had left the Khusk Range alive. Warfare in high mountain passes is a very different beast from large armies clashing on an open plain, or siege tactics, as the Immortals were trained for.

And when one side is defending their homeland, their wives and children, it doesn't matter how many armored bodies you throw at them. You will lose.

I knew this, and yet my heart grew cold when I thought of what was coming. How many would die before they realized they were under attack? The Four-Legs had been virtually left alone for two hundred years. When they saw the King's soldiers, they would have no reason to view them as a threat. Until the spears started to fly...

Lying in that cell, I felt like a flea in the belly of an aurochs. Like I had been swallowed by some enormous animal that was slowly digesting me, even as it moved on to seek out its next meal. For I was just a speck, hardly worth the effort it took to devour.

What had Tommas given his life for? The satrap? The Prophet? The King? This great empire, tottering under the weight of its own corruption? We should have run after the massacre in the dome. I had been a blind fool to believe that Ilyas could come back from the dark place he'd gone to. That the King could somehow set things to rights. And that belief had killed us.

Funny how we don't miss something until it's gone. A stupid yet universal truth. I'd taken my sister Ashraf for granted, and I'd taken Darius for granted. How many times had I longed for peace? Raged against the fact that I couldn't be rid of him, not waking or sleeping? There were times—

many times—when I would have given anything to have him out of my head for a single hour.

And now that he *was* gone—irrevocably, utterly gone—every minute seemed an eternity of emptiness. It almost made me understand what had driven Ilyas into the abyss. Almost. For now I would do anything to have Darius back.

Keys clanking. Cell door opening.

I turned my face from the light. If Ilyas was with the magi, I would get to him somehow. I only had one hand, but I could still rip his throat out with my teeth, if I could coax him near enough.

A hooded form bent over me. Soft hands touched my forehead. The smell of her, exotic, feminine. My eyes widened in surprise.

She pushed her hood back and I saw it was the King's daēva.

She leaned in until that witchy eye was inches from mine. I tried to focus on the other, which was a clear, pure blue. Taken separately, her features were all too long or too sharp to be considered pretty. But when she turned her head suddenly, at some noise too faint for me to hear, her profile coalesced into something striking. Elegant.

"My name is Delilah," she whispered. "I can get you out of here, but only if you take Darius with you. That is my offer."

I sat up. The action made my head spin. "He's alive?"

I didn't even know how many days had passed. It could have been five, or six, or ten.

"Until tomorrow morning," she said grimly. "Swear it. That you won't leave him behind. He must be re-bonded, or they will track him through the cuff."

"I swear. I would rather die." My heart pounded. I felt an unfamiliar sensation in my chest, like a slowly expanding bubble. It took me a moment to realize what it was: hope.

She nodded once. "Come, we haven't any time. The Water Dog captain is in his cell now. Can you walk?"

Ilyas. The thought of him with Darius dragged me to my feet. Too fast. A sickening wave of vertigo washed over me. I felt my knees buckling and thoughtlessly reached out to steady myself. My stump banged into the stone wall and I stifled a scream.

"Why are you doing this?" I panted.

"He is my son," she said, wrapping an arm around my shoulders.

I should have guessed. She and Darius looked nothing alike, but that blue eye...

"Does the King know?"

Delilah's mouth twisted. "Why do you think he sentenced him to burn? He knew my feelings when I first saw Darius, though I tried to hide them. It has been twenty years since they took him from me, but I recognized him at once."

"And the King would deliberately murder your child?" I asked, horrified.

"Darius has much of his father in him. It reminds Artaxeros of what he can never have. That while he may own my body, my heart belongs to another." Delilah paused. "You saw Victor?"

"I saw him."

"He was well?" Her voice caught.

"As well as you might expect," I said carefully. "He got away from us."

She closed her good eye. The other stared into the distance. Then her head jerked around, although again I heard nothing. "There is no time! Listen to me. Once we have him, you must go to a fishing village called Karon Komai. It is two days' walk north of here, on the shores of the Midnight Sea. Victor arranged for a ship, the *Amestris*. Go find it. The captain will take you to Eskander."

"How do you know this?" I demanded.

"He sent a message with the Purified. Victor had planned to come to Persepolae, to take me with him, but without the fire to break my bond with the King, I cannot leave. If you find him, tell him...Tell him I am fine."

I nodded, thinking *Eskander? The young wolf?* I'd heard he was a bloodthirsty beast, a slaver and conqueror. But what choice did we have?

"I will carry your message if you carry mine," I said. "To the Four-Legs Clan of the Khusk Range. Tell them war is coming. They must call in the khans and send the women and children to safety. Artaxeros the Second is no longer their King, but their enemy."

"It will be done," Delilah said without hesitation.

"What about the Immortals?" I whispered as we started down the corridor. My legs were still unsteady, but the thought of freedom gave me strength. "How do we get past them?"

"Leave that to me," Delilah said.

We crept through the dungeons. My nerves sang with tension, and not only from fear of the guards. This was the woman who had tried to kill Darius as an infant rather than see him cuffed. Whose son had become her worst nightmare. A hunter of his own kind. And yet still she would risk everything to help him.

I knew I was only here because she needed someone to break the bond with Ilyas. If not for that, she would have left me to rot. And perhaps I deserved to.

Then we rounded a corner and I heard faint screams. Darius's screams.

I bit back a cry and lurched forward. Delilah pushed me hard against the wall. She was slender as a willow, but she had no trouble holding me. Holy Father, I was weak.

"Not yet," she hissed. "Follow at a short distance. Stay to the shadows."

And then she was gone, walking swiftly toward the cell where Darius was being tortured.

I cursed under my breath and staggered after her. Even if I'd had my sword, I doubt I could have lifted it. The King must be holding her power. And if he was paying attention, he would know exactly where she was headed. What did this madwoman have in mind?

She paused ahead of me, taking out a small knife and slashing her palm open. Then she rubbed the blood over her face and neck, wiping red handprints on her sheer gown.

She rounded the corner and disappeared. A moment later I heard a shout.

I peeked around the corner. The twelve Immortals, all daēvas, still sat in their chairs. But there was a Numerator with them, the one who had come to my cell. And Ilyas. He had a sick look on his face, of guilt and pleasure and rage all mixed together. His fingers were twined through Darius's cuff. *My cuff.*

"The King is under siege in the audience chamber!" Delilah screamed. "There has been an attack on the palace! It's overrun with Druj!"

The Immortals stirred like a kicked anthill, leaping to their feet.

"Go! Hurry!" Delilah screamed. "The King of Kings needs you!"

Ten of them dashed off the opposite way down the corridor, followed by the Numerator. But Ilyas remained. As did two of the Immortals.

My heart sank. Of course they were too disciplined to leave the prisoner completely unattended. And two might as well have been twenty. They were daēva. I couldn't beat them on my best day, whole and rested, let alone in the condition I was now. Her ruse had failed.

But I wouldn't let Ilyas have Darius either. Even if the Immortals cut me down, I would see him dead first.

I ran forward with my teeth bared. Ilyas turned, his face a picture of astonishment when he saw me. But he recovered quickly. Ilyas hadn't survived so many battles because he was soft or hesitant. He pulled the knife from his belt, the one he had used on me, his heavy shoulders squaring.

"Seize her!" he yelled at the guards.

I looked into the cell and saw Darius. He was lying on the floor, soaked in sweat. From the pitch of his screams, I had expected the walls to be red with blood. But he seemed untouched, if a deathly grey color.

The sight drove me to new heights of rage. My vision narrowed to a tunnel, with only Ilyas at the end of it. I dimly saw one of the Immortals move to block my way and snarled like an animal. But it wasn't me he grabbed.

It was Ilyas.

"The cuff!" Delilah cried.

The Immortal nodded curtly and ripped the chain from Ilyas's neck in one movement. Then he tossed it to me.

I watched the cuff spin through the air, end over end. Without conscious thought, my left hand shot out and caught it. Pain lanced through my arm, searing through my shoulder and out the top of my head like a lightning bolt as I forced it onto the stump. My legs buckled again. From the metal circling my bruised flesh, but also from the sensation of Darius flooding back into me. A kind of bitter ecstasy.

Darius's eyes flew open and locked with mine. He pushed himself up.

"Get back," he grated.

Delilah grabbed me under the arms and dragged me down the corridor. The Immortals exchanged a glance and leapt out of the way. Ilyas stood frozen in front of the cell, his mouth working silently.

I felt power explode through the bond. The cell door groaned. Then it blew off its hinges, slamming Ilyas into the wall and pinning him underneath.

"Hurry!" Delilah yelled at Darius.

We could hear shouts, still distant but coming closer. It hadn't taken the other Immortals long to figure out they'd been tricked. Darius looked longingly at Ilyas and I knew he wanted to lift the bars and kill him.

"There's no time!" Delilah ran over. "She needs you! We must leave now, before they come!"

Darius's head snapped around, his eyes running over me. When he saw the stump, they went dead. He strode over to me and lifted me in his right arm like I weighed no more than a kitten.

"Nazafareen," he whispered.

I pressed my hand to his mouth. "Run," I said.

"This way!"

Delilah dashed off down the corridor. Behind us, I could hear the clanking of spears, the thunder of dozens of boots on stone. The two Immortals who had helped us drew their swords, standing with their feet spread wide in a fighting stance, huge muscles flexed. I knew they would be cut down. That they were giving their lives so we could escape.

I started to make the sign of the flame, to pray to the Holy Father that he would speed their souls to the afterlife. But the gesture seemed empty. False. I let my hand fall, wrapping it around Darius's neck instead. Feeling the damp, silky curls between my fingers.

I wondered if their human bonded were part of this resistance too. First the guards at Gorgon-e Gaz, then the Purified, now the Immortals. It must only be a small number or they would be in open rebellion. I wondered if Victor was their leader, or if it was someone else. I had so many questions for Delilah, questions that would probably never be answered.

She led us through the dungeons to a storeroom with wicker shields stacked against one wall. It had no windows, no way out, and I felt like a rat in a trap. Surely they would find us here in minutes ...

Then she lifted the corner of a faded tapestry, ironically depicting the king in full regalia, to reveal a hidden door.

"A daēva architect designed the palace," she said with a small smile. "It has many secret passageways, commissioned by Xeros the Great to sneak concubines into his chambers. The Queen was a jealous woman."

"Where does it lead?" Darius asked.

He hadn't asked her who she was, or why she was helping us. I wondered if he was afraid of the answer. If some part of him suspected.

"You can get nearly anywhere in the palace from here, but you'll want the sewers that run under the baths. They will take you beyond the palace walls." She studied him intently. "You are a tracker, are you not?"

"Yes."

"Then you can find your own way out."

She unlocked the secret door and turned to go.

"Wait," Darius said.

Delilah paused in the archway. With her bloodstained gown and long, tangled black hair, she did look like a witch. Not Druj, but not human either.

"Come with us," Darius said. "The King will know you betrayed him. He'll kill you."

Her mouth twisted in a bitter smile. "Yes, he will know. But he will not kill me. He hasn't the courage." She made a shooing motion. "Go! Will you have your cousins' sacrifice be for nothing?"

Darius tore his eyes from Delilah and kicked the door open. Cool air brushed my skin. The narrow space beyond was pitch black. Darius strode inside, the tapestry falling into place behind him. He eased the door closed. I heard the lock turn on the other side.

His warm breath stirred my hair. It was the first time we had been truly alone since leaving Tel Khalujah.

"When the bond broke, I thought..." His voice was rough. "I thought I'd lost you forever."

"Ilyas cut it off." Memories flashed in the darkness. My own screams. The cracking of bone. The sudden void in my heart. I shuddered and pushed them back down.

Darius made a terrible sound, half growl, half moan. I felt the force of his anger and guilt, so strong it threatened to sweep him away.

"It's not your fault," I said firmly. "Just find us a way out of here. And you can put me down now. I can walk."

He released a long breath. "Ilyas, I will chop into little tiny pieces, which I will feed to the buzzards. By the time I am done with him, he will curse the day Satrap Jaagos laid eyes on his barbarian mother. And if I ever find Victor again, I swear on all that is holy, I will make him pay too."

I was starting to think Delilah was the only person in the entire empire, plus Bactria, who didn't want Victor dead. Maybe it was best not to tell Darius that we needed him as an ally just yet.

"Add that Numerator to your list while you're at it," I said. "Can we go now?"

I held onto the back of his tunic as he led us through a series of twisting passageways, some so narrow we were forced to turn sideways to get through them. Cobwebs tickled my cheeks. From time to time, we heard voices on the other side of the wall. They sounded urgent, angry. I imagined the Immortals were tearing the palace apart looking for us.

Eventually, the way led down a steep flight of stairs. Rushing water echoed in the blackness.

"Can you swim?" Darius asked.

"No. Is there another way?"

"I don't think so. There's an aqueduct. It's only half full."

"Oh, that's a relief," I snapped. "It will take me only twice the time to drown."

I heard a strange sound. A sort of muffled wheezing.

"Are you laughing at me, Darius?" I demanded.

"Never. I'm just glad you're the same sweet, docile creature you used to be."

"Ilyas took my hand, not my wits."

"Well, we're a matched pair now," Darius said. "I suppose arm wrestling is out of the question?"

I'd forgotten what a black sense of humor he had. It was one of the ways he coped. That, and excessive praying—a habit I planned to break him of at the earliest opportunity.

"I'm afraid so. Regular wrestling though…"

My breath caught as he cupped my face with his right hand.

"Even if I could be free, I would choose you," he whispered.

Something inside me loosened. I'd been so afraid he would see me as I saw myself: maimed, broken. A creature worthy of pity, nothing more. But he still wanted me, very much. I could feel it.

I softened my lips for a kiss. The kiss I'd waited so long for. Instead, I was hoisted up like a sack of barley.

"Darius? What are you—"

"Hold me tight, Nazafareen. Don't let go."

I was opening my mouth to object when it filled with cold water. I spluttered and gasped as we were swept into the current. Darius pulled me against his chest. I disliked small spaces, and I disliked small spaces that were dark even more, and I *especially* disliked small spaces that were dark and filled nearly to the brim with icy water.

So every time I managed to suck in a breath, I used it to curse him as we rode the torrent that passed beneath the palace. The royal complex perched atop a high hill. I'm not sure how they managed to bring the water up, but gravity did the work in the other direction. The stone pipe twisted and turned. I was terrified that we would run into a grating or some other obstacle. Darius could break through it, but the Immortals would feel him working the power. It would be like lighting a signal beacon.

Finally, we popped out at the bank of a river. Darius helped me wade to shore. At least the dunking had washed some of my own filth away. I'd stopped smelling myself days ago, but I knew it couldn't have been pleasant.

As we wrung out our clothes, I repeated what Delilah had told me about finding the ship. I would have to tell him who she was at some point. My daēva did not react well to keeping secrets. But I understood why she had left that burden to me. If Darius had known, he would never have left her behind, even if it cost him his own life.

We'd made it past the walls, but I could see the palace complex looming less than a league away. We had to keep moving. And the last thing I needed was for Darius to come unglued again.

"Victor?" he snarled, slicking a hand through his hair. "We're supposed to meet *Victor*?"

"Yes," I said. "If you have a better idea, spit it out."

The sky in the east was starting to lighten. I felt dizzy for a moment. Partly because the ordeal of being swept through the aqueduct had used up the last of my strength. I'd still been recovering from the battle with the Druj when the Numerators gave me their beating, and then Ilyas...I had lost a lot of blood. The shock to my body—and mind—was severe. Only a few days had passed since he'd taken my hand. Days spent lying on a cold stone floor.

But that's not what shook me the most. It was the thought that if Delilah hadn't come, the Numerators would be leading Darius from his cell at this very moment. Leading him to their fire altar...

"How far is this village?" Darius demanded. "What's the name?"

"Two days," I said wearily. "It's called Karon Komai. She said it's on the shores of the Midnight Sea."

"I'll find it." He looked me over. "Are you sure you can walk?"

"Yes," I said, as my legs trembled and gave way, treacherous things.

Darius caught me and lifted me in his arms. I marveled at his strength. He too had been through terrible things in the dungeons, even if his torture had been inflicted with the cuff instead of knives and hot irons. But he had the ability to lock away his feelings and it served him now.

We headed north. The land beyond the river was forested with beech and oak, although their branches were bare. Darius ran in perfect silence, like a wraith. Through drowsy eyes I saw the red flash of a waxwing in the trees, heard the sweet warble of a wren. The winter woods seemed a peaceful place.

But I knew the Immortals would have trackers like Darius. Daëvas able to sense their quarry from a distance. And they would be mounted. Darius might be able to outrun a horse for a short sprint, but he couldn't keep it up forever.

They were called the Immortals not because they lived a long time. Very few soldiers in the empire had the chance to grow old and fat, even with the bond. They were called the Immortals because their number was always exactly ten thousand. When one fell, he—for they were all male—was immediately replaced with another. Unlike the Water Dogs, their cuffs were made to be torn off in battle so that a daëva could be bonded again on the spot if the human of the pair was killed. In this way had Xeros and his line forged the largest empire the world had ever seen.

At midday, we stumbled across a road. It led north and would have made for much easier walking than the forest, but we couldn't risk it. They had to realize we had escaped the palace by now. And Delilah knew exactly where we were going. She claimed that the King wouldn't kill her, but would he torture her, as Ilyas had tortured Darius? The Numerator said most daēvas broke quickly.

I glanced at Darius. He had put me down to rest for a few minutes. His handsome face was tight with exhaustion. How long had Ilyas been going at him before we arrived? I couldn't bring myself to ask. I knew he could go without food or sleep for days, but he had his limits, just like anyone.

"Show me your arm," Darius said.

I pulled it tighter against my body. I didn't like him looking at it.

"You can't hide it from me, Nazafareen," he said gently. "I know it pains you. We need to make sure it heals right."

"There's nothing you can do."

"Just let me see."

I showed him. His breath hissed through his teeth. Red lines were starting to radiate up my forearm. It throbbed against the cuff with every heartbeat.

"You need a magus," he said.

I remembered the magi holding me down while they thrust my limb into a pot of hot wax.

"If a magus ever touches me again, I'll kill him."

"A midwife then. Someone who knows the healing arts." He pounded a fist against his thigh. "I wish I knew how to help. There must be a way to use earth to knit the flesh, water to cleanse the blood...But they taught me only to destroy with it."

"I'm fine for now," I lied. "We just need to get to Karon Komai."

Sun slanted through the trees, warming the carpet of pine needles. It wasn't nearly as cold as the mountains, although that would change when night fell.

"Even if we do find this ship and it takes us across the Hellespont, do you really think we can trust Eskander?" he asked. "I have a bad feeling about this, Nazafareen."

"I don't know," I said honestly. "But the enemy of one's enemy..."

"Can turn out to be even worse," Darius finished. He clutched his faravahar, thumb absently stroking the eagle wings. The gesture reminded me too much of Ilyas with Tommas's cuff. I looked away.

"Eskander seeks to topple the empire," he said.

"And would that truly be such a bad thing?"

"It depends on what he plans to replace it with."

"He offers sanctuary to escaped daēvas," I pointed out.

"But for what purpose?" Darius said, voicing my own doubts.

"It's in his interest to divide us...them. Unless he breaks the Immortals, his cause is lost. Victor seems to trust him." As soon as the words left my mouth, I knew they were a mistake. So much for the new, discreet Nazafareen.

"And why should we trust Victor?" Darius demanded. "He and the other daēvas slaughtered those guards at the Barbican. You saw the bodies!"

I shrugged. "Every war has casualties."

"And you used to fight for the other side."

I stared at him. "What are you saying, Darius?"

He sighed. "Nothing. Only that we must be careful." His eyes bored into me, that unsettling daēva gaze, like the eyes of a panther. "I trust you. No one else."

I sighed and drew my knees to my chest. "Eskander holds

Macydon and the Free Cities. The only other *north* is Neblis. We could try for the southern border, but the only thing on the other side of *that* is the Sayhad, and we'd have to cross the Salt Plain to get there. But if that is where you wish to go, I'll follow."

He was quiet for a moment. "The Sayhad. Isn't that where Tijah comes from?"

"Yes." It hurt to think of her.

"Did you see her...after?"

"No." I felt an urge to defend my friend. "I'm sure Ilyas prevented her from visiting the cells. There's nothing she could have done."

Darius didn't bother to deny this. But it did trouble me that Tijah had never come, if only to say goodbye. If it had been the other way around, no one could have stopped me. But she had her own ghosts to worry about, I reminded myself. Men just as evil as Ilyas.

Darius picked up a stick and started snapping it into tiny pieces. "If Victor hadn't come back...hadn't said those things—"

"Ilyas would have found another excuse to punish us. He was mad with grief."

"Well, if Victor thinks to claim me, he can go to hell. I want nothing to do with him." He hurled the stick into the undergrowth. "Nothing!"

"All right. But aren't you the least bit curious? He must be very old, Darius. He knows the truth of what you are—"

"I already know."

"I don't think you do."

His eyes narrowed. "Don't press me on this, Nazafareen."

"Those necromancers on the plain. They never actually said—"

Suddenly, Darius's pupils dilated. We had paused in a stand of evergreens, a short distance from the road. In an instant, he'd gone animal on me. If Darius had hackles, they would have risen.

"Get on my back!" he whispered. "Hurry!"

I wrapped my right arm around his neck as he leapt up and caught a low branch. In moments, we were halfway up a spruce tree, nestled in the crook of its branches. Darius rested against the trunk, his arm curled around my waist. I leaned into him, heart pounding.

"Still your mind," he said in my ear. "Find the bond and hold it. Only the bond, nothing else. Can you do that?"

"I think so." I repeated what I had done in the Hall of a Hundred Columns, except that instead of trying to reach for the power, I just watched it, pulsing in the corner of my eye. Colors flowed through it, streaks of blue and purple and green. It was beautiful, mesmerizing. My heart slowed, matching his. I was no longer separate from him, or the woods, or the air. Everything was one.

Even the pounding of hooves on the road. The smell of many horses and the cold, sharp tang of iron. I was one with those too. They washed over me, through me. Not the enemy. Not anything to worry about. Just threads in the tapestry. When they slowed, shouted in consternation, and a small part of my mind began screaming in panic, Darius's calm flowed into me, gentle but firm, and my thoughts stilled again.

The power seemed to glow brighter as the riders milled about on the road. It dimmed as they moved on.

Long minutes passed. I didn't want to leave that place. The nexus. It soothed my pain.

Then Darius's voice dragged me back. "We must go now, Nazafareen," he whispered. "The *Amestris* awaits."

❦ 22 ❦

We pushed on past dark. I would walk until I couldn't any longer, and then Darius would carry me. The woods grew thicker. Branches tore at my hair and face. I felt boiling hot one moment, freezing cold the next. I understood that this was a bad sign.

Several times, he had sensed soldiers in the forest. Not as close as before, but still we would have to stop and hide ourselves in the bond. This made the going even slower. When it started to snow, Darius insisted that we halt for the night.

"How much farther to the coast?" I asked him.

"A day, at least." He broke off several pine boughs and made a pile of them on the ground. I sank down, more tired than I'd ever been in my life. A chill wracked my body, causing every muscle to tense. Darius pulled me into his arms. It was the first time I had ever been so close to him without feeling any desire whatsoever. I truly was at death's door.

"I'm sorry," I whispered. The ground spun in a lazy circle.

"For what?"

"For thinking you were Druj. For treating you...badly."

He barked a short laugh. "You never treated me badly, Nazafareen."

"Yes, I did. I helped them chain you."

"That wasn't you."

"Ilyas...the way he used the bond...that wasn't the first time, was it?"

He stiffened behind me.

"I'm so sorry," I mumbled.

"Shhhh." He brushed snow from my hair. "Sleep now."

And I did, but I woke many times, my own screams ringing in my ears. Monsters stalked my dreams, monsters with human faces. They scared me worse than any Druj. By morning, my fever was an inferno. I ached with thirst. Darius fed me snow, but his face looked strange. Everything looked strange, distorted, like objects glimpsed at the bottom of a river bed.

He picked me up and ran. The world moved past in flashes as I slid in and out of consciousness. I heard a harsh rasping sound, like someone sawing logs, and realized it was his breath. Off in the distance, a hound bayed, deep and excited.

Darius stumbled, caught himself. Ran on. Frost coated his hair and eyelashes. My own chills had stopped. I was beyond cold. Beyond feeling anything at all except a vague sort of regret. Somewhere, a ship waited. But we would never reach it.

He crashed through a frozen stream and fell to his knees. I looked at him blearily. His eyes had gone flat, empty.

"They're closing in," he gasped. "I can't..."

"I know," I croaked.

"If I draw too much of the power while you touch the bond, we will both die," he said, so close I could feel the warmth of his breath on my lips.

"Do it then."

Darius met my steady gaze and some of the frightening deadness lifted from his eyes. He tangled his icy fingers in my hair. The hounds bayed again, more insistently. I felt the cuff start to heat. Wind ruffled his tunic, and power surged through the bond. First air, then earth. My teeth ached from it, my bones seemed to vibrate, as a ripple swept across the snow, coming from deep in the ground.

So much still unsaid, yet words had become irrelevant. Neither of us was very good with them anyway. I raised my hand to his cheek and let my eyes drift shut. From far away, I heard the cracking of branches, the heavy groan of rock and dirt stirring in its bed. Darius drew deeper and the ache sharpened to pain.

"More," I urged softly.

He shuddered and pulled me closer. I filled my lungs for the last time with the smell of him, which is hard to describe but always reminded me of the clean salt wind of the sea.

"Wait for me behind the veil, Nazafareen," he murmured. "Promise you'll wait for me."

I tried to answer, to swear I would find him, but the vise of power held me fast. And then I heard the crunch of footsteps on snow behind us.

Do it, I thought, sudden terror nearly exploding my heart. *Please, oh please, don't let them take us again.*

A sandaled foot kicked Darius off me. My first thought, absurdly, was: *Sandals, in the snow?* The power winked out. And I was being lifted again, by someone even bigger and stronger than my daēva.

"Put her down," Darius raged, jumping to his feet.

A voice, deep and rough. "Follow or die here. The choice is yours, Water Dog."

I knew that voice. It belonged to Victor.

23

I recall little of our flight through the woods. Only that without the burden of carrying me, Darius managed to keep up with Victor's relentless pace. My thoughts weren't very lucid. Who were we running from again? Necromancers? Ilyas? Immortals with the black eyes of wights? Sometimes I thought I was back in the dome. That Victor was Darius. But he didn't smell right. And he was too big.

The hot tangle of my daēva's emotions swirled through my brain. Anger, relief, frustration, fear. Finally, I closed my eyes and let the darkness take me.

SEAGULLS.

Their rusty-hinge cries were the first thing I heard.

I cracked my eyelids open, then shut them again immediately. Mistake. I felt worse than the time Tijah and I had drunk two jugs of wine on my eighteenth birthday. We'd laughed late into the night, arguing over which of the Water

Dogs had the largest...sword. Her money was on the giant Behrouz who always seemed to get extra rations from the serving girls.

Not the dungeons. Not with the feel of soft linen against my skin. I burrowed deeper under the covers, the last two days coming back in small revelations. Victor. We'd been saved by Victor. Darius wouldn't like that one bit.

Gulls...The *Amestris*...Had we made it to the ship? I was too fuzzy to tell if the whole bed was moving, or just me.

I peeked out, suddenly burning with thirst, and saw a window overlooking a harbor. Fishing boats bobbed on a white-capped sea.

"She's awake."

Then Darius's bright blue eyes were peering into mine. His face cracked into a smile.

"Water," I whispered.

He helped me lift my head to drink. I guzzled a whole cup, then fell back on the pillows.

"Where are we?"

"You're in the home of a friend," the first voice said. A moment later, Victor was looming over me too. I studied his strong, masculine features. Wavy hair like Darius but a shade darker, also cropped short. Beard stubble roughened his jaw. He looked no more than thirty years old, but I knew he'd fought in the war. Two centuries ago.

Darius ignored him. "We're safe," he said. "For now."

"How long?"

"Have you been out? Two days."

"My arm..." I realized that the terrible throbbing had ceased. I still felt weak, terribly weak, but that poisonous burning sensation was gone.

"Victor healed it." He paused. "Your hand, it's still...He can't regenerate—"

"I know." I looked at Victor again. "Thank you."

The daēva nodded. His expression was guarded. I wondered what the two of them had been talking about for the last two days. The atmosphere in the room was as charged as the air before a thunderstorm. Perhaps they had been sitting there in brittle silence the entire time.

I took a deep breath and threw the covers aside. I wore only a thin shift that came down to my thighs. Darius immediately found something fascinating to stare at on the ceiling. I suppressed a grin. If he'd been raised in the Four-Legs Clan, instead of by dried up old magi, he wouldn't have minded at all.

"Where are my clothes?"

"You need to stay in bed," Darius informed a spider web in the corner.

"And we need to go to that ship. I won't hold you up any longer." I placed a foot on the floor, steadying myself with my right hand. My muscles felt like water.

"It's not here yet," Victor said, gently pushing me down with one huge hand.

I heaved a sigh and let him manhandle me back under the blankets. As much as I was desperate to get across the borders of the empire, the news came as a relief. I already felt like going to sleep again.

"When?"

"Four or five days," Victor said. "The *Amestris* was delayed by a storm. But I've been assured she'll arrive in less than a week."

"*Five days?*"

"Rest easy, Nazafareen," Darius said. "The Immortals have already come and gone. They searched the town, questioned everyone. The man who owns this house is a merchant. He is also the owner of the *Amestris*. He keeps a hidden room in the attic for...people like us."

"Why? Why is he helping?"

"You can ask him that yourself," Victor said. "Once you're better." He stood. "I'll see some soup is sent up from the kitchens."

I stayed awake long enough to eat a few mouthfuls. My stomach clenched with each swallow, as though it didn't recognize this strange substance I was inflicting on it. How long since I'd eaten? Days, even if you counted the slop they'd given me in the dungeons as food.

"Tell me a story," I said drowsily, pushing the spoon aside.

"If that is what you wish," Darius replied. He settled into a chair with one leg hooked over the side and started to relate the story of Pantea, wife of King Xeros's greatest general, who was so beautiful that she had to keep her face veiled at all times, or men would fall hopelessly in love with her. When her husband was killed in a battle with the Druj, King Xeros came to give her the news personally. Of course, he immediately desired Pantea for his own. He wished her to marry him, but her heart was broken.

"This doesn't end well, does it?" I said, annoyed with him for choosing a tragedy. "She probably killed herself rather than wed the King. Now she and her true love are buried next to each other on a hill covered with wildflowers. Blah, blah, blah."

"No, he gave her command of the Immortals," Darius said, lips curving in that subtle smile of his. "She took over her dead husband's bond and led them to victory."

"Oh." I closed my eyes as the sun came out from behind a cloud, flooding the room with warm light as the gulls squabbled over scraps on the street below. "Carry on, then."

When I woke the next day, I felt stronger. Strong

enough to eat a whole bowl of soup and ask about a hot bath. The maid, a pretty girl with thick eyebrows and an enviable figure, offered to help me, but I didn't want her seeing my body. I could count my ribs. The bruises and cuts had vanished thanks to Victor, but my arm...I hated it. Hated the way it looked. How useless it was to me. I stared at the snarling lion on the cuff, despising what it stood for, although it was my link to Darius.

Had he really meant what he said, just before we leapt into the aqueduct?

Even if I could be free, I would choose you...

Why would he? Victor's missing fingers had been returned to him when the bond was broken. Darius too could be whole again, if we ever found the fire. Take the power whenever he wanted it, not only when I allowed him to. Maybe there were other things free daēvas could do.

They were easy words to utter, but how would he feel if the choice were not abstract?

And what if it were me? Would I trade him for my hand?

I sank into the hot water. It turned grey immediately. Disgusting. I was disgusting. I felt a surge of rage at Ilyas. I never should have left him alive. At that moment, if I could have tortured him the way he'd tortured Darius, had him writhing on the floor slick with sweat, screaming, I would have done it.

I fumbled with the soap, repeatedly dropping it. It took two hands to get a proper lather. I reminded myself that at least I still had my sword arm. I planned to use it if I ever saw Ilyas again.

But it was the hundreds of mundane tasks, things I hadn't dealt with lying in the dungeons and then running with Darius, that now reminded me every moment of my loss. Washing my hair. Drying off. Getting dressed. I had to relearn everything, like a clumsy child. Braiding was obviously out of the question so I let my hair hang free down my back. It nearly brushed my bottom, and I finally relented and asked the maid to help me comb out the tangles.

In the afternoon, Darius came. I pretended to be asleep. He stood over the bed for a long while, just looking down at me. I knew *he knew* I was faking. I could feel his hurt, but I didn't want to face him right now. Jokes about arm wrestling aside, I had no idea what we were to each other anymore. Not Water Dogs. It was the first time in nearly five years that I wasn't wearing the scarlet tunic.

The maid had asked me what I wanted to do with my old one. I told her to burn it.

I ate more soup, plus bread, and fell asleep for a time. When I woke, it was dark out. A single candle burned in the corner. I stretched my arms over my head, letting my fingers trail across the stump. I had avoided touching it as much as possible, but now I felt curious. It was covered with smooth skin. Like nothing had ever been attached to it at all.

"You saw Delilah."

I startled. Victor was sitting in the chair Darius had occupied, although he had pushed it back into the shadows, well out of the candlelight. He wore a white tunic that left his calves bare and the sandals I remembered from the woods.

"Yes."

"How...Did she say anything to you?"

There was a desperate edge to his voice, although I could tell he was trying to control it.

"She asked after you. She wanted me to tell you she's well."

He shifted his weight. The chair creaked alarmingly. It hadn't been so long since I was terrified of this man. Of what he could do. I had been the hunter and he the prey, although if we had caught him before the necromancers did, those roles would have reversed in a heartbeat. I knew neither of us had forgotten that fact.

"She helped you escape the palace."

"Yes."

"So I think it's safe to assume she is no longer *well*," Victor snarled.

"I...she said the King wouldn't kill her."

He took a deep breath through his nose. Exhaled slowly.

"Did you tell Darius?" I asked. "That she's his mother?"

Victor frowned. "He doesn't know?"

"I sort of hoped you'd taken care of that."

A bitter laugh. "The boy is lost to me. A Water Dog through and through. We have nothing to say to each other."

"Why did you save us then?" I demanded.

"I happened to be passing by."

I couldn't help it. I rolled my eyes. Victor shrugged carelessly.

"I thought you'd go after the necromancer," I said. "The one who took the fire."

His face darkened. "I did. Just when I was about to take him, he met eight others. They rode north, into Bactria. It was pointless to follow."

"We saw the necromancers on the plain, just before we reached the Barbican. They told us Queen Neblis owed you a great debt. They wanted an alliance. To capture *you*."

Victor studied me. I held my breath, hoping I hadn't gone too far. Perhaps I shouldn't have reminded him of our former status.

"Are you asking why she sent her Antimagi a thousand leagues south? After one crippled daēva?"

I looked at his powerful shoulders, his brawler's hands and bullish neck. Even when he was cuffed, this man was never a cripple. Not like me.

"Well, they did seem awfully eager for your head," I said lightly.

"It's not my head she wants." Victor gave me a wolfish smile. "Though she might settle for it."

A bloodthirsty animal...one of the first to be leashed...breaker of Gorgon-e Gaz...

Whatever Victor was, I needed answers, and he had them. He was the only person I knew who had lived through all of it. Who knew the truth.

"Just tell me one thing. Did the daēvas fight for her in the war? Before they were turned?"

"Is that what they taught you?"

I nodded.

"Gods, no, though we held ourselves apart at first. Stayed on the sidelines. I argued against it. But there were few enough of us." His lip curled. "Far fewer than there are now, with the King's *breeding program*."

"But how do they..." I trailed off. "Against your will."

"Pleasure can be induced through the bond, as well as pain," Victor said shortly.

I felt my cheeks warming. "Oh. I didn't know."

He paced to the window, looking out over the darkened harbor. A full moon cast its silvery light on his profile. Darius had the same aquiline nose.

"We're solitary beings by nature," Victor said. "Staying out of each other's affairs, and the affairs of humans. We hated the Druj, killed them on sight, but they'd never troubled us before. Not in any numbers."

"So you lived within the borders of the empire?"

"Yes. Not the cities though. The wild places."

I knew nothing about the daēvas, what they were *before*. I found I was intensely curious.

"What happened?"

"I finally called a gathering of all the daēvas I could find. About a hundred. Xeros wanted us to fight for him. He wasn't King yet. Just one warlord out of many. My people refused. They were blind to the danger." He paused. "So I went to see Zarathustra."

"You knew the *Prophet?*"

"Yes. We were old friends. He was High Magus of Karnopolis then."

I tried to picture Victor chatting with the Prophet over cups of Ramian wine, but the image was too surreal.

"He told me he'd found a way to join humans and daēvas, so we could fight Neblis and her demons together. Some fey alchemy that let both wield the power. By this time, her Druj hordes had overrun most of the lands north of the desert. I thought the daēvas might see reason. If we didn't join the fray, we'd all die."

I pulled the covers to my chin, feeling almost like I did as a little girl when my father told us ghost stories. Wide-eyed and hanging on every word, yet safe in his presence. Victor was silent for so long that I thought he'd decided against telling me the rest. Then he sighed and returned to the chair.

"Zarathustra asked if he could test it on me. I agreed."

"Wait...you said fight *together?* Sharing the power?"

"Had it been master and slave, do you think I would have volunteered?" Victor growled.

"I...no."

"Needless to say, there was a flaw. The power only flowed one way."

"So he betrayed you?"

"Not him. Zarathustra was horrified at what he'd created." Victor held up his hand, the one that used to have missing fingers. "When he saw what the cuffs did, he wanted to give them back to the fire. Xeros stopped him. I tried to remove it myself and felt pain as I had never known before." His voice roughened. "Xeros wanted to use me to catch the others. When Zarathustra objected, they dragged him away." He looked at me defiantly. "I never would have done it. I would have taken whatever torment they dealt to me. But then they found Delilah. Used her as a hostage."

I didn't know what to say. If Victor was telling the truth—and I saw no reason he would lie—a staggering evil had been done. I'd always thought Xeros the Great was our savior, the greatest general ever born, and perhaps he was, but at a terrible price.

"A few managed to flee, but not many. Xeros bonded us to his army. Thus began the Immortals."

"I didn't know...not any of it. Nor does Darius. The magi say you fought with the Druj. That you *are* Druj." I paused. "Is Neblis truly a daēva?"

"She was. What she is now...I'm not sure."

"What do you mean?"

He sighed. "I can't say where the Druj come from, but she's the one who made them. She dabbles in powers beyond my understanding."

"But where do the daēvas come from originally? How old *are* you?"

Victor stared at me for a long moment. "I don't know, and that is the truth, Water Dog. I remember nothing beyond a decade or so before they cuffed me. It is the same for all of us." Wood cracked as he gripped the armrest. "Xeros could have freed us after we won his war, but he was afraid, and rightfully so. I've waited two hundred years for my revenge. I'm only sorry Xeros is no longer alive to see his works turned to dust and ashes!"

"Yes," I said uneasily. "I can't really blame you."

Victor looked down and blinked at the chunk of carved cedar in his hand. He carefully placed it on the floor. "I've noticed how the boy looks at you." He'd never used Darius's name in my presence, not once. "Tell me, why did you join the Water Dogs?"

His tone bore no malice, but still I felt ashamed. "To kill Druj," I said. "That's all."

"You hate them. I see it in your eyes. That's good. Hatred will keep you going when you have nothing else."

"What about love?" I said softly.

His black eyes flickered. "That too." Then he abruptly stood and walked to the door.

"Victor!"

He turned back.

"What is the nexus?"

He seemed surprised by the question. Then he laughed in amusement. "What do *you* think it is?"

"I have no idea."

"Nor do I. And maybe that's the point."

I LAY THERE FOR A LONG TIME AFTER HE LEFT, THINKING on all Victor had said. Some of it I had started to suspect. Other parts, like the Prophet's refusal to sanction his creation, came as a shock. He had been a friend to the daēvas. The Way of the Flame...was that just propaganda to make us believe they were devils because they couldn't tolerate fire?

There was nothing inherently wrong in most of the teachings, I decided. *Good thoughts, good words, good deeds.* I still believed that part. It was the way the King and the magi practiced them here on earth I objected to.

Darius needed to know. Even if he never accepted Victor, he needed to understand his true nature. For the magi had twisted him. Just as Ilyas was twisted, by his birth, his pride, and finally, his inability to accept the truth. In the end, it had taken his sanity. I prayed Darius was stronger than that. I also knew the simmering tension between them would come to a boil eventually.

And we needed to be well away from this place before it did.

❧ 24 ❧

By the fourth day, I started to feel restless. I dressed and sat at the window, watching for the sails of the *Amestris*. Karon Komai was built into the rugged cliffs above the sea. Its conical houses were made of mudbrick, and each had a walled garden with orange and pomegranate trees. A young boy drove a herd of goats down the winding road to the harbor. I stared out at the cobalt water. It was flat as a pond today. Small fishing boats plied the waters near to shore, but the horizon stayed empty.

I longed to wander into the town, to get some exercise and breathe the fresh sea air. To get out of this manor house. It was starting to feel like a gilded cage.

I idly flipped through the stack of books Darius had found. Their scribbles made my eyes swim. Finally, I decided to go see if any word had come about our ship. I was just approaching the door when Darius gave a tentative knock.

"It's open," I said.

He wore a belted white tunic identical to Victor's, with pants and short boots. His walls were up, but I could read him nonetheless. He thought I was angry at him.

"I'm sorry to disturb you," he said.

"You're not. I was just coming down."

"I have something for you." Darius held out his hand. Nestled in his palm was a gold pin with a tiny bird on the end. "Give me your sleeve."

I held my right arm out. He tucked my hem under the stump and pinned it in place.

"Thank you." I frowned, and he looked at me anxiously. "I was using it to wipe my nose, but..."

"Savage nomad." Darius grinned. It was so good to see him smile.

I examined the pin. "It's pretty. Where did it come from?"

"Our host. He should be returning any moment. Come, let's wait for him."

Darius led me downstairs to an airy room furnished with more of the beautiful, ornately carved pieces I'd seen throughout the upper floor of the manor. I took an orange from a bowl and peeled it with my teeth. Now that I was no longer ill, my appetite seemed bottomless.

"Who is he?" I asked, offering Darius a sticky wedge. The fruit smelled heavenly.

"His name is Kayan Zaaykar. He's a Follower of the Prophet."

"What does that mean?"

"A splinter sect, apparently." Darius seemed uneasy. "They claim the Prophet opposes the bonding of daēvas. That it's a mortal sin."

"Victor told me the same thing last night. He came to my room."

Darius's eyes fixed on me. "Why?" he asked in a neutral tone.

"Only to ask about your...Delilah." I paused. "Has he spoken of her?"

"We've hardly exchanged two words. I am a *Water Dog*."

"Was."

"It makes no difference to him."

I sensed thin ice and started paddling for shore. "What else do you know about the...Followers of the Prophet? How many are there?"

"I'm not sure. They've existed in secret since the war. They claim to have infiltrated every corner of the empire, except for the Numerators."

"The guards from the Barbican. And the Purified...I suppose they were part of this sect?" I grabbed another orange. "The one they murdered in his cell told me he was loyal to the Prophet. That by stealing the fire and giving it to Victor, he was carrying out the will of the Holy Father. I thought he was mad."

"Whether they're mad or not, they see Eskander as their chance to strike," Darius said. "Do you remember the men we tracked in Tel Khalujah?"

I remembered. It seemed a hundred years ago.

"They were part of it," Darius said.

"Well, now I feel bad."

"Me too."

Voices in the courtyard made us turn. A moment later, Victor entered with a stocky, red-faced man of middle years. They were deep in conversation.

I jumped to my feet, surreptitiously wiping juice from my lips. When he saw me, Kayan Zaaykar gave a formal bow.

"Welcome," he said. "My heart is glad to see you recovered from the grievous injury you suffered in the King's dungeons, may the Holy Father curse him and his offspring for ten generations." He pressed a hand to his substantial belly. "My home is but a poor hovel, but I hope you have wanted for nothing."

"Thank you, Kayan Zaaykar," I said, returning the bow. "I could not have wished for a more gracious host. I hope I can repay your hospitality someday."

He brushed the notion aside with a wave of his pudgy hand. "I have good news. Let us eat together and I will share it."

The servants brought out platters of lamb with honeyed yoghurt, artichokes stuffed with fruit and nuts, and a host of other rich foods. It was my first time eating anything besides soup and I struggled to cut my meat until Kayan Zaaykar quietly did it for me.

"The *Amestris* is due to arrive tomorrow," he said. "The journey to the Hellespont normally takes five or six days, but I've no doubt you can make her fly more swiftly." This last was directed at Victor and Darius. "You will need to avoid the King's fleet, but my captain has experience in these matters."

So he's a smuggler, I thought. And a good one, if it bought him this house.

Kayan Zaaykar took a delicate sip of wine. "I have also received word that the King is sending a force to Bactria to take back the holy urn. I think he is far more worried about Neblis than about you three."

"Has the *Amestris* made the run before?" I asked.

"I have had the privilege of helping daēvas and their bonded reach freedom several times," Kayan Zaaykar said.

"And Eskander truly welcomes them?" Darius asked.

"With open arms."

"What else do you know of him?" I asked. "What's he like as a man?"

Kayan Zaaykar thought on this for a moment. "He is only twenty-two, but already myth and legend swirl around him. He claims to be descended from gods—barbarian gods, of course—and the Greek hero Achilles."

I shrugged. The name meant nothing to me. But Xeros's

line also claimed divine authority. I supposed they all did. And who could prove differently?

"His father was murdered by the captain of his own bodyguard, and Eskander now wears the crown of Macydon. He immediately put down several rebellions. When Thebes persisted, he razed it to the ground."

"Sounds ruthless," Darius said.

"Yes, and no. He has a passion for glory, that is certain, and prefers warfare to diplomacy. But he usually treats those he conquers with respect. It is said he will not tolerate the rape or abuse of women. And he always leads his troops from the front."

"He doesn't force the daēvas to fight for him?"

"He forces no one to fight for him. By all accounts, his men adore him. But he does have a small unit of daēvas, including some who fled the empire during the war."

Victor looked away, uncomfortable, and I remembered that he had been made to hunt down and leash his own kind. Those who got away would have little love for Victor.

"I too was leery of Eskander at first," Kayan Zaaykar said. "When he reached the Hellespont, he drove a spear into the soil and declared that he accepted the empire as a gift from his barbarian gods. But he has vowed to free the daēvas, and the Prophet as well. That is the greatest wish of the Followers."

"Free the Prophet?" I said. "I don't understand."

"We believe he's been imprisoned in Karnopolis since the war," Victor said. "Held by the magi."

"How could he still be alive after all this time?" I asked.

Victor raised an eyebrow. There was only one possibility.

"You think they bonded him?"

"Why not?" Victor said. "No one else understands all the secrets of the cuffs. He's of more use alive than dead."

"I was raised in Karnopolis and I never heard a whisper of this," Darius said.

"Yes, you're every inch one of theirs," Victor muttered.

Darius turned icy blue eyes on his father. "What did you say?"

"You still wear their symbol." Victor nodded at the faravahar around Darius's neck.

"I follow the way of the flame. The righteous path."

Victor barked out a laugh. "Indeed. You pretend to be human, boy, but you're not. What you think is daēva is a pale imitation. A shadow on the wall."

"You tried to kill us," Darius spat. "In the mountains. So spare me your lectures."

Victor scowled. "I don't know what you're talking about."

"You brought an avalanche down on our heads! Nazafareen almost died!"

"That wasn't me," Victor snapped.

Kayan Zaaykar fluttered his hands anxiously. "Perhaps we should call for dessert?"

"Then who was it?" Darius demanded, gripping the edge of the table.

"The Antimagi, perhaps."

"And the slaughter at Gorgon-e Gaz? I suppose that wasn't you either."

"It was unavoidable," Victor said through clenched teeth.

"You may have healed her, but she wouldn't have lost her hand in the first place if it weren't for you," Darius shouted. "All of this is your fault!"

Victor stared at him. When he spoke, his voice was like a knife. "I don't blame you for what they made you into. That can't be helped. I blame you for refusing to see the truth when it's right in front of your eyes."

"And what's the truth?" Darius sneered.

"That you don't belong to them. You belong to us."

"I belong to *no one*!" Darius yelled.

A sudden breeze lifted the hair from my neck. I felt him reach for the power.

"No!" I cried, as Victor's plate flew across the room and smashed into a priceless tapestry.

"You fool," Victor growled.

The table began to quiver, rattling the cutlery and spilling Kayan Zaaykar's cup of wine. I stared at the spreading red pool. I could feel Darius's rage building out of control. If I didn't do something, this would end badly. So I clamped down on the power. Darius's head whipped around.

"Let go of me!" he said.

"No. I won't let you do this."

"It's not your decision!"

Victor bared his teeth in a grin. "Not yours either," he said to Darius.

"I'll let go if you let go," I said.

He battered futilely at the bond. Then he seized a platter and threw it at Victor's head. It missed.

Victor laughed. "I see you have my temper, at least." He glanced at me. "Is he always like this?"

I shook my head.

Victor turned to Kayan Zaaykar, who was discreetly collecting the knives and stowing them in his robes. "I apologize for my Water Dog son. It seems the magi in Karnopolis failed to teach him proper table manners."

"You're not my father." Darius jumped to his feet. "You're a killer and a thief. Just stay well away from me."

Victor mockingly made the sign of the flame. "No dessert, then?" he inquired of Darius's back as he stalked upstairs.

I sighed. "Do you have to provoke him?"

"He makes it too easy."

"They did things to him in the dungeons. You should be kinder!"

"And I spent the last two hundred years in Gorgon-e Gaz. Do you think it was better?"

I stared at Victor. His arrogance staggered me. "You expect him to accept you right away? Darius isn't the only one whose pride makes him blind."

"I'm sorry if being hunted by my own son doesn't make me feel *kind* toward him."

"That's not his fault! He didn't know who you were. And the way you told him...It was only to break his control, make him lose the power. It was a selfish act."

"Yes. And I'd do it again." He stuffed a candied turnip into his mouth. "The boy had to find out sometime. Why not then?"

I shook my head. "Well, you'd better talk to him. I won't keep him on a leash forever. And I don't relish the thought of spending days on a ship, in the middle of sea, with two bickering children who are capable of drowning everyone aboard!"

Victor laughed in delight. "At least they gave my son a Water Dog with some spirit. Those worms at the prison used to quake at the sight of me. They drew straws to see who had to bond me for the day. More than once the loser actually wept."

"Well, you don't scare me," I lied. Then, to Kayan Zaaykar, "Thank you for the lovely meal. If you'll excuse me?"

"Of course, my dear," he said faintly. "By all means. Go after him."

DARIUS'S ROOM WAS AT THE END OF THE HALL,

overlooking the courtyard and the stables. He'd slammed the door behind him. I kicked it back open.

"You need to calm down," I snapped.

"Get out."

I sat down on the edge of his bed. "No."

Darius whirled around. Suddenly, he was on top of me, pinning both my arms with his right hand. I struggled to break free but he was far too strong.

"Don't tell me what do to," he grated. "You're not my master anymore."

I felt something savage in him surge forth. It scared me.

"Stop it!"

"I'm not your pet, Nazafareen," he seethed. "I won't do tricks for you. And you can't take away what's rightfully mine."

Darius's face was only inches away from mine, his blue eyes dark as the sea on a moonless night. A pulse hammered in his throat. I let the power go and he ripped it from my grasp, but didn't use it. How he managed to touch the nexus in this condition, I had no idea. Only that he was capable of tearing the manor house to shreds if he chose to.

"I can when you put us all in danger," I countered, trying vainly to free myself from his crushing weight.

"You're just like *her*." Darius stared right through me, as if he saw someone else lying there. "Kind words and kisses when I please you, but one misstep...Do you know what it feels like to be burned alive?"

"Darius, please..."

"To feel your skin peel off, your bones crack? To be told each and every day of your life how evil you are? That the bond is the only thing keeping your monstrous nature in check? But you wouldn't know those things, would you?" His fury seemed bottomless. "I was so afraid of you when we first met. Wondering what new hell awaited."

"I was afraid too," I whispered. He didn't seem to hear me.

His voice broke, then grew even harder. "Why did you never compel me, Nazafareen? Why?"

"I—"

"You must have wanted to. That's what bonded *do*. No matter how much I prayed for forgiveness, it was never enough. Did you want to hurt me?" He gave me a shake. "Did you? Then go ahead and do it. Get it over with. Make me stop. Make me!"

He hated himself for losing control but he couldn't turn back. He was too far gone now, I could see that. I wouldn't use the bond though. Never that. So I smashed my forehead into his face instead. He rolled away, stunned.

"I'm sorry," I said. "I'm sorry."

Blood ran in a thin trickle from his nose. He stared at the ceiling, the hand wearing the cuff thrown over his head, and I felt the fight drain out of him.

"I deserved that," was all he said.

I crawled over to him. We were both breathing hard.

"I promise, I will never hurt you," I said. Amending it to: "Not with the bond."

He looked up at me. His eyes were so lost. A tear rolled down my face and landed on his mouth. I felt something snap in him. Not the way he had before. Not anger. This was a different tether, one that had been yanked taut for a very long time.

"Father forgive me," he whispered.

Then he slid his fingers into my hair and pulled me down. I tasted the salt of his blood, still warm. Tasted his breath, his tongue. And as I did, I felt him taste me. Felt our desire crash together.

He gently rolled me onto my back, careful to avoid the cuff. Tried to gather himself together.

"We should stop now," Darius said hoarsely.

"No," I said. "We shouldn't."

I took his hand and pressed it to my cheek. I kissed the tattoo on his palm, the triangle with a slash marking him as a wicked daēva. His heart thudded as I stroked his chest, the grooves of his stomach. And then my arms were over my head as he pulled off my tunic. He leaned over me, his faravahar brushing my breasts. Heat flushed my skin as my own heart took up his rhythm as he began to kiss me again.

When I touched his withered arm, Darius stiffened. I held my hand still, but didn't move it away.

"Does it hurt?" I asked.

"No. It's numb. Like it's not even there."

"Then I'll have to touch you places you will feel," I said.

"Nazafareen..."

I arched my back, touching his mouth lightly with my own. He made me greedy, desperate. I had never been with anyone but him. Had never *wanted* anyone but him. Darius kissed me back, pressing me into the pillows, and I felt his walls crumble to dust. His knee moved between my legs. I threw my arms around him, tangling my fingers in his hair. In a heartbeat, we were so far lost in ourselves we wouldn't have noticed if the world was burning down around us.

Agony.

I felt it jolt through his body in a shuddering wave. He gasped, rolling to his back, and I realized too late that I had touched him with the cuff. I tore it off and hurled it across the room. Darius threw an arm across his face.

"I'm so sorry," I said, feeling like a monster. "I forgot..."

"So did I. It's all right."

But it wasn't. I knew now that for him, pain and love and intimacy were all snarled together, and had been for a very long time.

We lay there in a shaft of sunlight, listening to the gulls.

The feel of him next to me was maddening. I was nineteen, not a girl anymore, but a woman. Almost. But I would wait for him as long as I had to. A hundred years, a thousand. It didn't matter.

Only that we were together, and no one would ever take him from me again.

25

He fell asleep as the sun sank below the horizon. I listened to his breath, soft and even. I wondered who the *she* was that he had talked about. Not a magus. Someone else. Someone who had tormented him, probably as a child. I pulled my tunic back on and he stirred.

"Don't go," Darius mumbled into the pillow.

"I'm not. Just a little cold."

"About before..."

"I'm so sorry. I should have taken it off. You know I'd destroy it if I could."

"I told you, I don't want that."

I wanted to ask, what *do* you want, Darius? But the words stuck in my throat.

He studied me in that raw, unblinking way he had, like an animal, or a young child. "I want you to promise me something, Nazafareen."

I nodded. "All right."

"Don't ever hold me against my will again. That's done now. You wear the cuff, but you don't try to control me."

I sighed. "I promise."

Darius held my eyes a moment more, then looked away. How long his lashes were…

"Victor's an ass," I said. "You were right to throw a platter at him."

"Let's not talk about him." He paused. "Tell me about your sister. What was her name?"

"Ashraf." It had been years since I'd spoken it aloud to another person. I thought he would ask me how she died, but Darius instinctively avoided prodding old wounds. He had enough of his own.

"What was she like?"

"Silly. Stubborn. She hated every kind of food except cheese. She pretty much existed on it."

"Did she look like you?"

"People said so. She had a big gap in her front teeth that she could spit water through, quite an impressive distance. She used to chase me around."

"How old would she be now?"

"Twelve."

I tried to picture her face, imagine her as she might be today, but I kept seeing those black almond eyes. The way the wind streamed her hair like seaweed.

"And you joined the Water Dogs because of her."

"Yes. I thought it would make her stop haunting me."

"Did it?"

"No." I turned so I could look at him. "You did."

"Me?"

"I was too busy worrying about what a thorn in my side you were to obsess about it anymore. One nightmare at a time please."

"Thorn in your side?" Darius laughed.

"Among other places."

His fingers trailed along my forearm and lightly traced the skin on my stump. Now I was the one to freeze.

"You're so beautiful," he whispered.

"I'm maimed."

"So am I. I told you, we're a matched pair. Before, you were too perfect. Intimidating."

I snorted, but watching his mouth as he talked was lighting a fire in me again. He was the beautiful one. I was trying to get a handle on myself when the door banged open.

"Daēvas!" Victor shouted. "Many. Moving toward the manor house."

Desire vanished in an instant, leaving cold fear behind. They had found us. *Holy Father, they had found us.* Darius flew out of bed and started pulling his boots on.

"Immortals?" he asked calmly.

"They can be none other," Victor said. He tossed a sword through the air. Darius caught it one-handed and buckled it on.

"What about me?" I demanded.

Victor gave me an appraising look. "Can you use it?" he asked.

"I fight with my left," I said.

"Take mine then." He strode over and buckled his sword around my waist. The weight of a weapon felt reassuring, but I still struggled to contain my panic. I had fought Druj, necromancers, things out of black nightmare, but they didn't scare me half as much as the thought of returning to those dungeons.

"The cuff," Darius reminded me quietly as I started to follow Victor out the door.

It lay on the floor in a shaft of moonlight. How a single object could inspire such simultaneous loathing and yearning in me, I don't know. But I picked it up and slid it back around my stump. A part of him lived in that thing and I had to keep it safe until it could be returned to him, whatever he said.

We ran into the hall, where Kayan Zaaykar was waiting with a lantern, its shade closed to a slit.

"Come," he said urgently. "There's a back way out."

"Not the sewers," I muttered.

"No, a tunnel that comes out six streets away. All the safe houses of the Followers have them."

We hurried down the stairs. As we passed a narrow window, I heard the horses whickering uneasily in the stables. I thought I saw shadows moving in the courtyard but couldn't be sure. I silently cursed our luck. Just a few more hours and we might have been boarding the *Amestris*.

"Where are they?" I asked, my mouth dry as dust. "In the town? Do they know this house?"

"Close, but...I can't tell exactly." Victor frowned. "It's strange. I'm sure I wasn't mistaken."

"I feel it too," Darius admitted. "A presence, but hazy."

When we reached the ground floor, Victor halted.

"I'll slip out through the kitchens and meet you at the docks," he said.

"Why?" Darius asked suspiciously.

"To give them a false scent." He looked at his son. "Don't use the power again, if you can help it. I'll see you soon."

Victor moved down the hallway like a stalking snow cat, and then he was gone.

"He's abandoned us," Darius muttered. "I shouldn't be surprised."

"Don't be so quick to judge," Kayan Zaaykar admonished. "Victor is an honorable man. He'll lead them away. Come!"

He brought us down another flight of steps, winding and made of stone, to the underground level of the manor. It was used as a storage area. I saw crates of wine and fruit. Bushels of onions hung from the low, vaulted ceiling. In the dim recesses was a door, so old the wood looked like pitch.

"The *Amestris* should be here by first light," he said. "She needn't make port. My men will row you out in a longboat. Just hide yourselves until she arrives. I have a warehouse at the docks. Its door bears my sigil, a dragonfly."

"What about you?" I asked.

Kayan Zaaykar shrugged. "I am an old man. My children are all grown. My beloved wife has been with the Holy Father these last five years now." He grinned. "And I am a very good liar. I will say you held me hostage. They cannot prove otherwise."

I took his hands in mine. "Thank you, Kayan Zaaykar, for everything."

He made the sign of the flame, and I returned it.

"The Prophet protect you," he whispered, unlocking the door.

Darius's eyes suddenly went wide. He threw himself against it, but it was too late. Immortals poured through, filling the space even as I reached for the hilt of my sword. Too many. Power surged for an instant through the bond before it was cut off, as easily as snapping a thread. I slashed at a soldier in red. He jumped away. Something struck me on the back of the head, a stunning blow. I fell to my knees. The next one knocked me flat.

I gasped for breath as a boot pressed down on the side of my neck. Spots danced in front of my eyes. I wrapped my hand around the soldier's leg, tried to push it off, but it was like being buried under the mountain of snow. A paralyzing weight that wouldn't budge.

My vision turned red, then black.

BLINDING PAIN. I OPENED ONE EYE. MY ROOM. I WAS BACK in my room, the bed soft beneath me.

A nightmare...Only a nightmare.

So why does my head hurt so much?

Some tiny sound signaled another presence. Not Darius. He was downstairs. My eyes flew open.

"Where's Victor?"

I tried to rise and was backhanded. I turned and retched over the side of the bed.

"Take a moment."

I lay very still until my vision cleared again. Ilyas was sitting in the chair, the one Darius had told me stories from. His long legs were crossed at the ankles.

"What have you done to Darius?" I whispered.

"Give me Victor and I'll let you both go."

So they hadn't caught him yet. I felt a tiny flutter of hope.

"Or what? You'll take my other hand?"

"I could do that." The way he said it sent chills along my skin. There was no malice. No heat to his words. Just pragmatism. "But it would be simpler if you told me."

"I don't know. He left."

"When?"

"Just before you arrived."

"I see. And did he say where he was going?"

"Only that he would try to lead you away."

Ilyas absently stroked the cuff. "The King wants Victor badly. His own daēva betrayed him. He's quite irate."

I was afraid to ask, but I had to. "What has he done to her?"

"Locked her up, for now. The Numerators think she should be given to the fire in Darius's stead. They've been cheated of their prize and they're none too happy about it." He sighed. "The King trusts them above the magi, and even the Immortals, because they haven't harbored traitors. There's a purge coming, Nazafareen. We will discover how deep this corruption goes."

He was talking to me like the old days. Like his second in command.

"War is imminent," Ilyas mused. "On two fronts. We can't have loose daēvas running around. Especially not when they're planning on running to Eskander."

Did he know about the ship then? I resolved to keep him talking as long as I could.

"How did you find us?" I asked.

"Someone used the power in this manor yesterday. Very foolish of you. Immortals had already searched the town, but I thought it prudent to leave a few behind to watch for such things."

I closed my eyes. Darius had let his anger get the better of him, and Victor had pushed him into it. *Idiots*. I could no longer sense the power through the cuff. They were blocking it somehow.

"How did you cloak yourselves? Darius had no idea your men were there until the last instant."

Ilyas assumed the patient, slightly bored lecturing tone he used in training.

"Daēvas cannot sense Druj. Why?"

"They're dead."

"Precisely. They exist behind the veil. The Immortals have refined a similar technique."

"Sounds like necromancy."

"*You* did it," Ilyas said. "In the woods. It's the only way you could have eluded us."

"That was different. I sought the light, not the darkness."

He shook his head sadly. "I'm afraid you can no longer tell the difference, Nazafareen. Now, let's go back to Victor."

"I know you won't let us go," I said. "No matter what I say."

He studied me. "I haven't taken the cuff from you," he said. "Do you know why that is?"

I didn't answer.

"It's because I think you need to learn a lesson. And the only way to teach it to you is to let you experience everything he does."

My chest tightened. "Please, Ilyas. Whatever you're thinking—"

"Tommas agrees," he said. "He told me so."

"Tommas is dead!"

"Because of Darius," he agreed. "But he lives in me still." Ilyas leaned closer. "I think you know where Victor went. And you will tell me, one way or another. I'm not returning to the King empty-handed a second time."

I held my left arm out, trying to control the trembling.

"Take it," I said. "Take my other hand, if you don't believe me. I swear to you, Ilyas, we don't know where he is. Just don't...don't hurt Darius again."

"Your loyalty is admirable. I would have done the same for Tommas. But we're past that now." His tone was almost kindly when he added, "Perhaps the old man will break before you do."

✲ 26 ✲

Two Immortals were waiting outside the door. They dragged me downstairs, where Darius had been tied to a chair. A blue *qarha* was wound around his mouth. At least two dozen more soldiers filled the room. Up close, the daēvas' infirmities were more obvious. Missing ears and eyes, contorted limbs. Still, they were formidable, battle-hardened men. Then I saw Tijah.

She glanced at me, and looked quickly away. What had Ilyas told her? I couldn't believe Tijah would turn on me, but she'd let them bind Darius and was making no effort to stop this. As usual, Myrri just stared off into space.

Ilyas walked over to Darius. He seized a fistful of hair and lifted his face up.

"I'm aware that you have a high threshold for pain," he said. "But know this. What you feel, *she* feels. If you continue to be obstinate, we'll try it the other way around. So I'll ask you one last time: where's Victor?"

Darius glared at him. Then he shut his eyes. As in the audience chamber at his trial, he seemed almost serene. I realized with terrible sadness that he'd learned a long time ago to accept this as his fate. Torture was a known quantity and he didn't fear it.

I did though. My stomach clenched when Ilyas rolled up the left sleeve of Darius's tunic. He unsheathed his knife—the same knife that I longed to bury in his throat—and proceeded to cut into Darius's withered arm. A muffled groan escaped the *qarha* but I felt nothing. Even as blood ran down his arm and dripped to the floor.

What had he said?

It's numb. Like it's not even there.

I released a breath and twisted my face in feigned distress, inwardly shaking with relief that Ilyas had chosen that particular spot. He probably thought the infirmity would make the pain worse. Darius made a show of straining against the ropes that held him. Tijah's eyes were rooted to the floor, her face tight, but still she didn't intervene.

Finally, Ilyas ripped the *qarha* off. I could see he was frustrated. That his cool façade was starting to fracture.

"Where is Victor?" he hissed.

Darius glanced down at the mess of his arm. "All right. If you must know, he said he was off to have some sport with your barbarian mother. I hear she—"

Darius's teeth rattled in his head as Ilyas cracked him across the face. He raised the knife and I suddenly knew that Darius wanted Ilyas to kill him before Ilyas decided to put *me* in that chair.

"Please," I begged. "Please don't, Ilyas. Please. He didn't mean it."

Ilyas turned, hatred burning in his grey eyes. "Is she right, Darius?" he asked softly, not looking at him but at me. "Did you not mean it?"

I searched Ilyas's face for some sign of humanity, although I should have known better by that point. He didn't flinch from my gaze. He harbored no guilt, no mercy. He was *enjoying* himself. And I knew then that he planned to watch me as Darius died.

I kicked the soldier who was holding me in the shin and began to struggle wildly. He swore and lifted me off my feet in a bear hug. I saw Tijah take a small step forward, hand on the hilt of her scimitar, as the candles guttered. A breeze swept the room. It smelled strongly of the sea, and the night-blooming flowers in Kayan Zaaykar's garden. The Immortals stiffened, half drawing their swords.

Victor appeared in the doorway, incandescent with rage. An avenging angel—or devil, I no longer cared which. Only that he slayed them all where they stood. But he didn't move. And then I noticed the glint of metal at his wrist. The three missing fingers.

Someone gave Victor a hard shove and he stumbled into the room.

"We caught him trying to climb into an upstairs window, captain." It was Lieutenant Kamdin, the one who had taken me to visit Darius in the dungeons. I cast him an imploring look. He seemed troubled at the scene in the room, but then his face hardened again.

"Victor's cuffed?" Ilyas blinked in surprise.

"We set a trap. He walked right into it." Kamdin sounded as astonished at his luck as Ilyas.

"Give it to me," Ilyas said.

Kamdin flicked a catch and the cuff on his own arm opened. It was one of those designed for battle, to be removed at will. Ilyas snapped it on his wrist, just above Tommas's, and Victor gritted his teeth. At least he was smart enough not to attack. They would have just beaten him senseless.

I watched a mix of emotions wash across Ilyas's face as he registered the bond. Distaste, but also triumph and a strange sort of contentment.

"Make ready to return to Persepolae," Kamdin told his men.

"No," Ilyas said.

"But—"

"The King asked for Victor's head."

Silence greeted this statement.

"He's too dangerous to live," Ilyas said softly.

"We didn't expect to take him," Kamdin said. "Perhaps he should be returned for questioning."

"Did the King not give me command of this hunt?"

Kamdin's lips thinned. "Yes, captain."

"I think his son should be the one to do it. He claimed loyalty to the empire. What better way to prove it?" Ilyas wiped his blade clean on Darius's tunic and sheathed it. "Bring them both outside."

The sky to the east was blushing pink as we assembled in the courtyard. Kayan Zaaykar was also dragged out from a back room. He looked a bit roughed up, but not badly injured. He held his head high, as if the Immortals trampling his garden were invited guests. A man determined to die on his own terms.

"Single combat," Ilyas announced. "Cold iron only." He looked at Darius. "If you think to use your weapon on anyone besides Victor, I'll take the rest of her arm." He moved to stand just behind me. I felt his knifepoint at my back.

"Leave the girl alone!" Kayan Zaaykar cried.

"Shut up, old man," the soldier holding him grumbled.

"You don't have to do this," I said. "We all know he's going to kill me anyway."

I could tell from their faces that the Immortals were uneasy with the situation. But they were the empire's most elite soldiers, trained to obey without hesitation. This was not the first brutality they had witnessed and it wouldn't be the last. Two of them stepped forward and laid their swords on the ground. Not as an act of protest. So Darius and Victor could pick them up.

As the first molten sliver of sun broke the horizon, I saw a white speck in that expanse of dark ocean. The *Amestris*.

Turn back, I thought, my heart a stone in my chest. Turn back or they'll kill you too. But the captain had no way of knowing. He would make port and Immortals would be waiting for him. I knew Ilyas. Once we were disposed of, he'd tear this town apart. A large ship belonging to the traitor Kayan Zaaykar would hardly escape his notice.

"Arm yourselves," Ilyas ordered.

"If you do this, he wins no matter what happens," I said.

Ilyas's knife dug deeper. Not breaking the skin, but a hairsbreadth away.

Darius went for the swords first, his face expressionless. From the moment they had seized us, he hadn't stopped probing, trying to touch the nexus. A dozen of the Immortals in blue—the daēvas—kept their eyes on him at all times, I noticed. They were doing something to contain him. If only I could figure out what...

Victor and Darius now stood in the center of a loose ring of Immortals. Their gazes were locked but neither had raised his weapon.

"What is in it for me?" Victor asked casually. "If I win?"

"You keep your head long enough for the King to pass judgment on you. You're one of his most prized breeding stallions. He might even spare your life." Ilyas's knife moved from my back to my throat. "*Fight*," he said.

Metal rang on metal as Victor suddenly stepped forward and swept his blade in a lightning arc at Darius's head. Darius got his own blade up just in time to parry the blow. They circled warily, testing each other's skill. Despite his two-century-long confinement, Victor hadn't forgotten the finer points of swordplay, I saw with a sinking heart. His missing fingers didn't seem to hinder him the way Darius's arm did. This was the man who had killed more Druj in the war than any other daēva, and it wasn't just by using the power. He was an expert opponent. And Darius had lost a fair amount of blood.

The Immortals moved back to give them more room, and then the duel began in earnest. So fast I could hardly follow it. Only the clash of iron and grunts as they went at each other in a frenzy. I wanted to scream at them to stop it, but the tip of Ilyas's knife was pressed to the tender spot just below my ear and I feared to make even the smallest movement.

The sun rose higher and still they fought. Darius staggered with exhaustion. Victor was slowing too, but he had six inches of height on his son and a longer reach. Finally, Darius lost his footing on the dew-slick stones. He fell to one knee, bringing his sword up to vertical. In an instant, Victor had hooked his own blade around it. He twisted the hilt, sliding down the outside of Darius's blade, then jerking it in towards himself. Darius's sword flew through the air, landing a few feet away. The tip of Victor's own blade now rested against Darius's heart.

"An entertaining match," Ilyas said. "Finish it then."

Victor turned. "Go to hell," he said, throwing his sword to the ground.

Darius looked up in surprise. Then Victor was doubled up on the ground, writhing in pain, as Ilyas punished him with the cuff.

"Pick up your sword!" Ilyas grated at Darius. "Finish it or I'll do it myself!"

I scanned the faces of the Immortals. Lieutenant Kamdin was scowling, but to defy Ilyas would be tantamount to mutiny. He'd be executed himself.

Darius crawled over to his father, trying to keep him from

injuring himself as he flailed on the stones, jaw clenched tight. Victor didn't want to give Ilyas the satisfaction of screaming, but every nerve in his body was alight with agony. Tears of impotent rage sprung to my eyes. There was no limit to Ilyas's insanity. He was a rabid dog loosed among us, and no one had the courage to put him down.

And then a thin, girlish figure slipped quietly through the ranks of the Immortals. Her brown eyes were not so dreamy now. Not at all. She made a hand sign at someone behind me. Forefinger and thumb touching in a circle, followed by a quick flick of the wrist. I knew it meant *now*.

The knife at my neck drew a pinprick of blood, then fell away as a sword erupted through Ilyas's chest. Not a regular sword. This one had a wicked curved tip. A scimitar.

Kamdin reacted instantly. "The cuff!" he bellowed. "Get it back before he dies!"

One of the Immortals, a giant of a man wearing the red, dove for Ilyas's falling body. An invisible wall slammed him back. Myrri. My mind raced, even as my heart filled with a savage glee at Ilyas's agonized cries. The cuff...

I threw myself on top of Ilyas, fingers fumbling for the catch.

"Hurry!" Tijah shouted. She stood over me, scimitar raised in a fighting stance. The daēva Immortals still trained their focus on Darius, holding him back. They couldn't work the power to attack me. But the rest now stormed toward us, weapons out and teeth bared in snarls.

I felt around the rim of the cuff. It seemed smooth. Unbroken. But I had seen Kamdin open it. Ilyas twitched weakly, his grey eyes finding mine. He opened his lips and a bubble of blood escaped. He was trying to speak, but I didn't care what he had to say.

I ran them underneath a second time. My fingers touched a slight indentation. I pressed it and the cuff popped open.

What would happen when one person bonded two daēvas? I had no idea, but I was about to find out. I snapped the cuff around my own wrist just as the first wave of Immortals hit us.

Victor. He surged into me, all fury and vengeance, like a thunderstorm breaking after months of drought. The rush of power through the bond swept away whatever had been blocking Darius. He too filled with it, to bursting, and I stood trapped between them, opposing forces both sucking power through the cuffs at the same time. It was like standing amidst two oceans crashing together in a narrow strait.

I literally went blind for a moment, my senses withdrawing from the onslaught like a rabbit hiding in its burrow. Power swirled around me as Victor and Darius lashed out at the Immortals, and their daēvas retaliated in kind. My whole right arm felt frozen solid. I had the disorienting sense of being in *three places at the same time*.

I forced my eyes open just as the huge Immortal who had first tried to take the cuff loomed in front of me. He reached for my arm. I couldn't let him take it. *I couldn't*...If they got Victor back, we were lost. It was only his fearsome strength that was keeping their superior numbers at bay.

Without knowing exactly what I was doing, I reached though the twin bonds, through Victor and Darius both, and let go of myself just as I had in the woods when we hid from the Immortals. I reached not for the power, but for the nexus itself. The place where all things were one. The sounds of fighting faded away. I felt the cool morning air on my skin. Smelled the tang of the sea. A place of perfect calm and emptiness.

That shining pool ran into me and I understood that you could only touch it by surrendering. Victor had tried to tell me that, in his own way.

I sensed invisible lines girding the earth, a web leading

north and south, and watched as a flock of geese passed overhead, following those lines as if they could see them too. I felt the movement of the sea and everything that swam within it, the quiet contentment of Kayan Zaaykar's flowers as the sun kissed their petals. Things were solid, but not solid. The stones beneath my feet also had air, and the air contained water, and the water in turn had particles of earth. The strands of these three elements coiled and undulated, separate but weaving together in an intricate tapestry of matter as far as the eye could see.

And underneath all of that was a humming, crackling thing, like a deep ocean current. Not an element, but a *force*.

This awareness coalesced in an instant, although it seemed much longer. The Immortal's hand still reached for the cuff. He had fine brown hairs on the backs of his fingers, and a small moon-shaped scar on his wrist. I felt his heart pumping. The ebb and flow of his blood through his veins. And with a thought, I reversed the direction of it. He made a terrible croaking sound and fell to the ground, muscles jerking. That force, whatever it was, flared like the lake at the Barbican when the High Magus tossed a torch into its volatile depths.

I heard distant screams, followed by sudden silence. Shock echoed through both bonds. The nexus vanished, popping like a soap bubble, and I was back in the courtyard again, a dead man lying at my feet.

"Gods, what did you do?" Victor said softly.

"I..." My left temple began to throb. "I don't know." He and Darius were both staring at me like they'd never seen me before. Tijah frowned in confusion, but Myrri studied me with a wary, considering sort of look. Like I was a dog that had seemed tame but turned out to be three-quarters wolf.

Then, in three long strides, Darius was at my side. He gently touched my chin and his fingers came away red.

"Your nose is bleeding," he said. "You worked water. I felt it. Are you all right?"

"I think so, yes." I swiped a sleeve across my face. I hadn't even noticed.

"You linked the three of us together. Holy Father, the surge...we should all be dead."

Darius glanced around the courtyard. The Immortals were down, their swords scattered where they had fallen in that instant of pure destruction. A few still stirred weakly, including Lieutenant Kamdin, but I found I didn't want to finish them. I couldn't stomach any more violence today.

"Leave them," I told Victor when he raised his sword.

He arched an eyebrow. "You command me, girl?"

I felt his irritation. Holy Father, two of them in my head now...

"Only in this," I said firmly. "Ilyas is dead. The others were acting on his orders. And you'll need them later. Let these men carry the tale of your mercy back to Persepolae. It will help to win their hearts."

Victor frowned, but he saw the logic in my words and lowered his blade. "What you did just now...There is only one other human I have ever known who could touch the power."

"Did he wear the cuff?" I asked, intrigued.

Victor slowly shook his head. "No. He's the one who made them."

"The *Amestris*!" Kayan Zaaykar pointed to the harbor. Her square sails were clearly visible now, driven before a stiff wind that brought her swiftly toward shore.

"We will speak more about this later," Victor said, pinning me with his predatory black eyes and stalking over to the smuggler. I stood there, wondering if I had really just heard him say the Prophet Zarathustra could wield the power, as Darius swept Myrri off her feet in a one-armed bear hug. She grinned ear to ear.

Then Tijah was at my side, a pained expression on her face. "I'm sorry I didn't kill Ilyas more quickly," she said. "He watched me like a hawk. He never trusted me."

"Better late than never." I squeezed her hand. "It's not your fault. I never blamed you for anything."

"I'm so sorry," she began, her gaze straying to my pinned sleeve.

"No need." I kissed her cheek and walked over to Darius. There was one last thing I had to do.

"Give me your sword," I told him.

He studied my face for a long moment, then wordlessly handed it over. I went to Ilyas's body. He lay on his back, eyes open and staring into the sun. I tested the edge of the blade against his copper hair. Razor-sharp. The Immortals kept their weapons in good order. I positioned the tip where I wanted it to land. Then I raised it high and brought it down with all my strength, cleaving Ilyas's hand from his wrist in three strokes. I removed the cuff, feeling its cool weight in my palm.

There was nothing there. No presence. No ghost. But I would still make certain that Tommas rested in peace.

We found the Immortals' mounts tethered a short distance away and galloped through deserted streets down to the harbor. The residents of the town had shuttered them-selves in their beehive-shaped homes. They must have seen the battle raging at the manor house on the hill. I felt hidden eyes on us as we passed, but no one seemed to feel the desire to inquire into our business.

As promised, Kayan Zaaykar had a longboat waiting to row us out. My spirits lifted as we pushed away from shore, although my stomach was less certain. I had never been on the sea before. My only experience with boats was the rafts supported by inflatable bladders that the Four-Legs Clan used to cross rivers during their trek, and those had a tendency to tip if someone scratched their nose.

"Gods, don't tell me you suffer from seasickness," Victor growled. "That's all I need."

I kept my eyes fixed on the horizon. Wide and blue and undulating like a serpent. I'd heard there were monsters in the Midnight Sea. Things that could swallow a warship in one bite. But the lands of the empire lay behind us, and I wouldn't look back.

I gave Victor my brightest smile, despite the queasiness in my guts.

"How do you feel about figs?" I asked.

❧ 27 ❧

The captain of the *Amestris* was surprised to find his employer presiding over the longboat with torn robes and a goose egg on his eye, but he immediately grasped the need for haste and a minute after we were hoisted aboard, he was shouting at his men to steer the ship out to sea again.

She had two masts, with one large sail and one smaller sail, as well as banks of oars.

"My cabin is yours," he told Kayan Zaaykar with a bow.

"You are most kind," Kayan Zaaykar replied solemnly. "I hope you still keep a cask of that strong Attican wine handy? I could use a cup or two."

The captain grinned. He wore his dark hair at shoulder length, and his skin looked like old leather, with deep creases around the eyes that signaled an amiable disposition. "Always, my lord," he said.

They went off together, and two sailors showed the rest of us to cramped quarters below decks. I curled up in a bunk and stayed there for the next three days, reluctant to move even my head. Tijah visited each morning and evening to bring me water and change my revolting bucket. She reported that Darius and Victor were in the same condition, and blamed me for it.

When I dreamed, it was always of fire. Sometimes a blazing inferno, other times a single flame wavering in the dark. I felt an irresistible urge to reach for it, to seize that wild energy and let it flow through me. I knew I couldn't, that it would burn me alive. But the urge would grow until I could no longer stop myself. And then the fire would fill me, and I would hear screaming. I would look at my hands—for in the dream, I still had both—and I would expect to see them charred, but they would appear fine. The screaming came from Victor and Darius, their bodies blackened, smoking ruins...

It made me terrified of fire. Fortunately, there wasn't much to be found on a wooden ship. But the superstitious part of me wondered if the dream was not a foretelling of events to come. I knew I had to learn to control what I had done, lest I accidentally repeat it. But I had no guide. No one who understood how it worked for a human.

Eventually, I grew accustomed to the constant rocking of the ship and ventured up on deck for some fresh air. The sun polished the water like a silver coin. I made my way to the rail, through a baffling web of ropes, and watched our wake trailing in the distance. The shore was a dark line to the left.

"Feeling better?" Tijah stood at my elbow, looking fresh as a lotus blossom.

"A bit." I smiled ruefully. "I no longer wish to die at least."

She laughed. "I never thought there could be so much water in one place." Her eyes grew pensive. "The world is wide, Nazafareen. Wider than I ever imagined."

I rested my head on her shoulder. "And I hope you get to see all of it someday."

Tijah made a small noise of agreement. Her voice lowered as she said, "What did you do back there? Did you really use the power?"

"I think I must have."

"That's not supposed to be possible."

"I know."

"Myrri says she's never seen anything like it. Do you think it's because you bonded two daēvas? Or maybe because they are father and son?"

I shrugged. "Tijah, I honestly don't know. It just kind of happened." Which was partly true.

She sighed. "So Victor...what's he like?"

"Pigheaded. Prideful. Very strong. A little scary."

"A mirror image of his son, in other words?"

I laughed. "In many ways, yes. Not in others."

She was silent for a moment. "About Ilyas..."

"You killed him in the end. That's what matters."

She chewed her bottom lip. "After you were arrested, he had me locked in my chambers. He knew how close we were."

"I thought that maybe he had discovered your secret," I said, glancing at the sailors bustling around on deck. None were close enough to hear us.

She shook her head. "If he had, Ilyas would have handed me over to my father without hesitation."

I knew she was right. He always did what he thought was correct, no matter the consequences. There were no shades of grey in Ilyas's moral universe. Only sin and virtue.

"I was out of my mind with worry, but Myrri urged me to bide my time. To convince him of my loyalty. She said it was the only way I could help you."

"It makes sense," I conceded.

"I had to beg him to come along on the mission to bring you back. He finally relented, but I saw in his eyes that he was still suspicious. I knew I would have only one chance. So

I waited until he was distracted. I'm sorry for what he put you through." Her face hardened. "He will be punished in the afterlife for it."

I thought of the cuff I had taken, wrapped in a scrap of cloth and stowed beneath my pillow.

"Ilyas was punished in this one too," I said.

WITH MY OWN SEASICKNESS PASSED, DARIUS AND VICTOR also emerged into the light, blinking like deep-sea fish dragged up from the depths. Each occupied a distinct part of my mind. I was starting to feel like conquered territory, like I was being carved into satrapies, each with its own little despot in charge. At least the two of them seemed to have reached a truce. As strange as it was, forcing them to fight each other might have done more to leech the poison from their relationship than anything else would have.

Victor accepted the bond with surprising good grace. He knew I'd had no other choice. He was trapped in the cuff until it was broken, regardless of who wore it. And I was infinitely preferable to Ilyas, or a Numerator, or the guards at Gorgon-e Gaz. I didn't hold his power in check. It was his for the taking.

Darius was far unhappier about the situation than Victor. He had no wish to share me with anyone, let alone his father. Darius took his revenge in petty ways, like performing the water blessing on deck each morning in full view of the entire crew. He would conclude the ritual by ostentatiously kissing his faravahar, as Victor shook his head in disgust. But Victor never said a word about it again. We were stuck with each other for the present. There was nothing anyone could do about it short of offering to bond Victor themselves, and I wasn't getting any volunteers.

I'd been waiting for Victor to make good on his promise, so when the two of them corralled me after breakfast the next day, I girded myself for a lengthy interrogation.

"You used the power," Victor said without preamble. "How?"

"I don't know. It's a bit of a blur." And it was. That whole awful day was a blur.

"Try it again. Now."

"I haven't—"

"Just try."

I sighed and closed my eyes. Tried to seek the nexus, to surrender to it. I could sense twin pools of power shimmering at the edges of my vision, as always, but when I moved toward them, they receded, like the vanishing point of the horizon. Eternally just out of reach.

"I can't do it with you staring at me like that," I said, feeling defensive.

"Leave her be," Darius said quietly.

I cast him a grateful look.

Victor scrubbed a hand against his jaw. "It was Zarathustra's intention that the cuffs work in this way. I felt the surge. It should have broken all of us. And yet you walked away with a nosebleed, while Darius and I were untouched."

"Is it true what you said? That the Prophet had this ability too?" I asked, as Darius looked at me in surprise.

"He concealed it from the other magi, but yes. That's how he made the cuffs in the first place."

"Those lying, hypocritical —"

"I don't disagree," Victor cut in calmly. "The question is what else you can do." He paused. "Such as break the link."

"If I understood how to do that, you know I would," I said wearily. "In a heartbeat."

Victor stared at the distant shore. "She was supposed to be on this ship with me." I knew he meant Delilah. The day before, he'd finally taken Darius aside and told him the truth about his mother. "But as long as she wears the cuff, the King owns her, body and soul. Gods, I'm helpless! You can't know what that feels like."

Of course, I did. His pain was my own.

"We will return for her," Darius said grimly. "And when we do, there will be an army at our backs."

Victor nodded. Then his gaze narrowed. "Sails," he said, pointing far out to sea. "The triremes of the King's fleet."

They ran to alert the captain. Short and wiry, he exuded an air of calm authority.

"Yes, we just spotted them," he said. He squinted at Victor and Darius. "The *Amestris* has the wide hips of a matron, Father love her, and those triremes are built for speed. She can't outrun them on her own."

"Don't worry," Darius said. "I'll get Myrri. We'll be gone before they even notice us."

The captain bellowed orders and the crew leapt to work, trimming the sails and doing all sorts of mysterious things with knots and ropes. The three daēvas gathered at the stern and began to breathe deeply. A wind sprung up, whipping spindrift along the surface of the water. The Amestris lurched forward as it filled her sails. I laughed in delight, grabbing the rail as the ship tilted to one side and plowed through the waves, gaining speed with each minute.

Soon the King's fleet had disappeared from view. I went down to my cabin and retrieved the bundle from under my pillow. When I returned, the daēvas were still there, flushed with power as they carried us away from danger. I stood silently, watching them.

And for one bittersweet moment, I saw a golden-haired boy, legs spread wide on the rolling deck, laughing as he called the wind. Another, slightly older boy stood at his side, copper curls blowing back from his forehead, his grey eyes alight with mischief.

I leaned over the rail and opened my hand. The cuff gleamed as it fell, snarling lions somersaulting end over end. It hit the waves with the tiniest splash. And then it sank, all the way to the bottom of the sea.

❧ 28 ❧

We passed through the Bosporus strait, and into the body of water the Greeks called the Propontis. I knew from my lessons with the magus that Xeros the First had come this way with his warships, bent on conquering the Free Cities and bringing them into the fold of the empire. He'd made it all the way to Athens before they drove him back with fire, the single defeat in our two hundred-year history. Now Eskander intended to take the same route, straight to Persepolae.

Where the Immortals would be waiting for him.

I knew how lucky we were to have escaped. They were unprepared for the sudden burst of power through the bond. But five thousand of them together? No human army could face that.

Well, it wasn't my problem any longer, I reminded myself. I'd managed to crawl out of the belly of the aurochs, and if Eskander wanted its hide for his wall, he could hunt it himself.

The *Amestris* made steady progress through the inland sea. My nausea was less on deck, so I found a corner out of the way of the crew and watched the forested shore slide past. One morning at dawn, I saw a great flock of birds. They must have numbered in the tens of thousands. I stood at the bow, open-mouthed with wonder, as the flock split in half, then rolled together like waves breaking. They whirled in tight spirals, dancing apart, then together again, each bird banking at precisely the same instant as if they shared a single mind.

"Starlings," one of the sailors said. He had paused in his work to watch. "A good omen."

I sensed Darius standing behind me.

"The magi call it a murmurration," he said.

"It's like they share the bond," I whispered, riveted by the gorgeous spectacle.

"The starlings overwinter in Karnopolis. I've seen it there, many times."

He had been distant since we boarded the ship and I knew why.

Victor.

Until the bond was broken, his father would be privy to my every emotion and sensation. It was awkward, to say the least.

"I've been thinking," he said. "About the Prophet. Do you believe he lives?"

"I don't know. Anything is possible."

"The histories say he died in the Battle of Karnopolis. Our first victory, when the daēvas drove back the tide of Druj. I've been to his tomb. It draws pilgrims from around the empire."

"The Numerators wouldn't have existed yet," I said. "So it would have to be the magi. But would they keep such a secret? He was one of their own."

"The city was besieged. An army of Revenants battered at the gates. I think they would have done anything to keep them out." Darius stared at the water. "If Eskander marches on Persepolae without the fire, it will be a slaughter. Of both sides, most likely." He paused. "And the King has my mother."

I took his hand. I had thought the same thing. It was a perfect disaster that the necromancer had gotten away.

"How did they come to be bonded?" I asked. "She must have been at Gorgon-e Gaz with Victor, if you were born there."

"Shortly after they sent me away, Artaxeros came to inspect the prison. He saw Delilah and wanted her for his own. So he took her."

I hadn't realized that such things went on, but then I hadn't *wanted* to know either. How easy it is to commit savagery when good people turn their eyes away.

"She told me who she was," I confessed. "I kept it from you. I'm sorry, but it's what she wanted."

He didn't say anything.

"They would have killed you. Or used you against her."

He sighed. "I know. It doesn't change the fact that I abandoned her."

The starlings took a final sweeping bow, then flew into the rising sun. I watched the dark cloud dwindle to a speck on the horizon.

"Where do you think the holy fire came from?" I asked. "Was it truly a divine gift?"

He slowly shook his head. "I think Victor is right. That the Prophet made it somehow."

"I've been dreaming of fire, Darius," I admitted. "Terrible nightmares."

"Are you asking if they're mine?"

"I did wonder," I said.

"No." He frowned. "Do you think it means something?"

"I have no idea." I struggled to keep the frustration from my voice. "I thought I understood the cuffs, how they worked. But the only one who truly does hasn't been seen in two hundred years. And I'm so afraid I'll make a mistake."

"Maybe I can help you," Darius said.

"How?"

"There are simple exercises they taught us as children. You can practice them if you like."

We decided to start with water, since I had worked it before. Darius lowered a bucket on a rope and dipped it in the sea. Then he found a cup and said he wanted me to fill it without touching the bucket.

"Close your eyes and listen to all the sounds around you," he said. "Focus only on that."

At first, I heard only the wind sighing in the rigging, the creak of ropes and splash of the waves against the hull. But the longer I sat there, the more I began to detect subtle sounds. Bare feet moving on the wood. The murmur of voices below deck. The scrape and snap of the sails changing direction. A muffled, steady thumping that I knew was his heartbeat.

The sounds ebbed and flowed, until they no longer seemed separate. It was like listening to music without trying to pick out individual instruments.

"Can you sense the bucket of water?"

I felt very relaxed, almost drowsy but alert too. "I think so. Yes."

"Try to lift a spoonful."

Easy. I exerted my will on it, imagining the water rising into the air. Nothing happened. It slid through invisible fingers. I tried again. And again.

"Try to clear your mind," Darius suggested.

"I *am*," I hissed.

Gulls. Splashing. Wind. Grinding, of my teeth. One little spoonful. That's all I wanted.

I could see the water in my mind, luminous with power, but still it resisted me.

"You're trying too hard."

I opened my eyes and gave him an angelic smile. "You wish me to fill the cup?"

"Nazafareen..." Darius started to scoot back but it was too late. I seized the bucket and upended it on his lap.

"There. I did it! Are you pleased?"

He looked down at his pants. Then he raised the cup in a toast. "To my bonded, who could teach patience to an oak tree, stoicism to a martyr, and temperance to a saint. Her gentle nature rivals the trembling doe of the forest..."

I started to laugh. "Don't forget that I sing like a nightingale."

"And spout like a whale." He stood up, dripping, and refilled the bucket. When he sat back down, the grin on his face was nothing less than evil. "We're going to try this again. Picture a flower this time. Any one, it doesn't matter. Hold it in your mind. And Nazafareen..." He leaned toward me. "If you do that again, I'll drop half the sea on your head."

"You're a tyrant and a bully," I sulked.

"Flower," he barked. "Now."

Two hours later, I had managed to fill and empty the cup three times. On the last occasion, I threatened to pour it down the back of his tunic if he didn't let me stop, and Darius relented.

"Tomorrow, we do it again," he said.

"You just like bossing me around for a change," I said, feeling mean and petty and exhausted.

"It is rather fun," he said. "When you're concentrating, you bite your lower lip in the most adorable—"

I threw the cup at him and stalked down to my cabin.

"Sick again?" Tijah asked when she saw my face. She and Myrri were playing a game of dice on her bunk.

"Of Darius, you mean? Then the answer is yes," I grumbled, stuffing a pillow over my head.

Tijah laughed long and hard. "So he won't put up with your crap anymore? My heart's breaking for you, nomad girl."

I made a rude noise. But as usual when I let my temper get the best of me, I was starting to regret it. I would apologize to him later. Thanks to Darius's help, I had taken a small step towards controlling my gift. I would never get my hand back, but if I truly mastered using the power, I would be strong again. For it was my own weakness that frightened me the most.

❧

As it turned out, I was spared any further lessons because the next day, the *Amestris* finally reached the Hellespont, which looked like a narrow, winding river. The captain explained that it was a tricky place to navigate because the currents flowed in two directions simultaneously—northeast and southwest—between the Middle Sea and the Propontis. He required the daēvas' help, so I was alone at the rail when I first saw the town of Sestos on the opposite bank, and the force that occupied it.

I counted more than a hundred and fifty galleys anchored in the harbor, each with three banks of oars. Eskander's army camped on the shore, their tents and picket lines stretching as far as the eye could see. It was all very clean and orderly. Cavalry drilled in an open area, wheeling and maneuvering their horses as tightly as the starlings.

The *Amestris* was known to the Macydonians, and we were greeted by soldiers wearing armored breastplates, with strips of thin leather protecting the upper arms and hips, leaving the legs bare. Most wore a simple conical helmet, but the officer who addressed us sported a horsehair crest with a gold laurel wreath worked on the side. I didn't understand the tongue he spoke, but Kayan Zaaykar seemed fluent in it.

"The King awaits us," he said. "We are to follow this officer."

It was the second time I was about to deliver bad news to a god-like figure, and I'd be lying if I said I wasn't afraid. But we were already in the jaws of the wolf and there was no turning back now.

As we walked through the camp, drawing curious stares from the soldiers, I noticed a row of strange-looking wagons. Each had vertical braces that supported a long wooden beam with a cupped end, almost like giant spoons, tilted at an angle. I'd never seen their like and wondered what they were used for.

I was about to ask Kayan Zaaykar when we arrived at a tent that was larger than the rest, with a spear thrust into the ground a few feet from the entrance. When the officer drew the flap aside, I expected to see the luxurious amenities that Artaxeros reportedly enjoyed on campaign. But the tent was austerely furnished. Three men stood around a table, studying a map. All were young, but one stood out from the rest.

He was shorter than his companions and clean-shaven, with curly, dark blonde hair. There was a sternness in his face, and also a kind of restless energy. When he turned to us, I noticed that one eye was brown, the other blue. He wore no crown or other regal insignia, but our escort addressed him with reverence. Their language was strange, both fluid and harsh-sounding to my ears.

Eskander's penetrating gaze swept over us. He switched to our tongue, although it was halting and heavily accented.

"Where are the other daēvas?" he asked.

"We were beset by Antimagi," Victor said. "I am the only survivor."

"Antimagi? Where?"

"On the Salt Plain, near to Persepolae."

"That is ill news." Eskander laid a fist against his heart. "I mourn your loss. Their sacrifice shall not be forgotten."

I suddenly realized that I never asked Victor anything about them, let alone told him I was sorry, and felt ashamed.

"There is worse," Victor said quietly. "The urn is in the hands of Neblis."

Eskander stared at him for a moment. His eyes flashed dangerously, and I waited for him to erupt in a fury. Without the fire, he would be forced to face the Immortals. His army was large, but unless half of it was daēva, he'd be at a fatal disadvantage.

Of course, he had no guarantees if they were freed either. I supposed Eskander believed they would be grateful enough to him as a liberator that they would choose to fight with his army or simply flee the city, but not turn on *him* too. At least two of the Immortals had helped Delilah, so she must have some influence over them.

But I also knew that people could be unpredictable, and as much as I agreed that the daēvas deserved their freedom, the thought of those cuffs all shattering at once made me want to be far away when it happened.

"Gods curse her," Eskander said at last. "This changes matters. But we are not unprepared for such a turn of events." Eskander shared a look with the man next to him. He had tanned skin and eyes the color of an eggplant, black with hints of violet. He was also daēva, I was certain of it, although he wore no cuff.

"I intended to track the necromancers who took it all the way to Bactria, but I needed to see my wife first," Victor said. "When I returned to Persepolae, the gates were barred with fire. I learned in the town that a Water Dog daēva had been arrested for treason, and that he and another had somehow escaped the dungeons. I guessed who it was. I did not wish to abandon these two," Victor admitted, glancing at me at Darius. "They were being hunted by the King."

So he hadn't just been *passing by* after all. He did care about Darius, even if he was too proud to admit it.

"Who do you bring me then?" Eskander asked.

"My son and his bonded, along with two other former Water Dogs who renounce the empire." Victor paused. "And this is Kayan Zaaykar, owner of the *Amestris*."

Eskander nodded politely at the four us, and clapped the smuggler warmly on the back. "I'm glad to finally meet you. The Followers have been a true ally."

Kayan Zaaykar bowed low and kissed Eskander's hand. "An honor, my King," he murmured.

"This is Hephaestion," Eskander said, gesturing to a tall, handsome man with the same fair Macydonian looks. "He commands the cavalry of the Companions. And Lysandros. He leads my small force of free daēvas."

"We already know each other," Lysandros said. "Do we not, Victor?"

Victor met his gaze with defiance.

"A pity they sent you to Gorgon-e Gaz after such faithful service. I warned you that Xeros couldn't be trusted."

"I never *trusted* him," Victor muttered. "I had no choice."

"None at all? I think we always have a choice. But what a relief to know the infamous Victor has returned to the fold. I'm sure you're perfectly trustworthy now. Even if you claim to have lost the urn, which was the sole purpose of helping you escape your prison."

"Lysandros," Eskander said warningly.

The daēva flashed white teeth at Victor. "Apologies. We're all on the same side now. I suppose it's petty of me to hold a grudge for two hundred years. Doubtless you've paid the price for your folly."

"Enough," Eskander said mildly. "I am left with no choice

but to take Persepolae by force. I had hoped to avoid it, but the gods have seen fit to arm me with the means to do so, and I will not turn back."

"What do you mean?" Victor asked.

"I will use fire."

"If you mean arrows, the Immortals will just use air to extinguish them—"

"Not arrows. A new device called a catapult. It can throw Greek fire over the walls."

"But...the whole city will burn!"

"Defiance carries a price," Eskander said calmly. "I sorely regret the loss of the daēvas. Their bondage is immoral. But if I am unable to free them, I will have to kill them."

"Artaxeros has my wife!" Victor rasped.

"What would you have me do? If he opened the gates, I would gladly spare all within." Eskander's lips quirked. "But that is as likely as Hephaestion here kissing my boot."

"Give me a ship," Victor said. "I will take the fire back for you."

Eskander frowned. "From Neblis? Such a mission would be certain death. Besides which, no one knows where the witch's stronghold is."

"I do. I escaped from it once before. A long time ago. And a single daēva might sneak in where an army cannot."

"Two daēvas," Lysandros said. "I would go with him."

Victor's eyes narrowed. "I didn't ask for company," he said.

"And I don't particularly relish yours," Lysandros retorted. "But if you fail, every one of those daēvas will die. And frankly, I'd rather bet on myself." Lysandros said to Eskander. " You'll have to face Neblis eventually. The only question is whether it will be on her terms, or yours."

Eskander shook his head. To Victor, he said, "You actually believe you can take it from her?"

Victor grinned. "She fancies me. And her stronghold is not as untouchable as she thinks. Neblis is an arrogant woman. She'll expect a full-scale invasion, not a sneak thief."

Eskander turned to Lysandros, and another of those unreadable looks passed between them. "What if I don't wish to give you up?"

"Then you may command me to stay. But you know my heart's wish has always been to see my brothers and sisters freed from their fetters. It's why I came to you in the first place. If you massacre the Immortals, it will be a stain on your victory. And there are still the other old ones in Gorgon-e Gaz to consider. They would gladly fight at your side if you free them. And you will need them when you march on Bactria. There are still the Druj to consider."

Eskander's expression darkened, but he was not an irrational man. He knew Lysandros had a good point.

"If I may?" Kayan Zaaykar ventured.

"Go ahead," the King said.

"If you had the Prophet, you might not need the fire. He is revered by all, including the Immortals. We know that Xeros twisted his teachings, even if we are not believed. But to hear the truth from the mouth of the man himself..."

"So you believe he lives?" Eskander asked.

"I do. His tomb lies empty."

"That proves nothing," the young King said gently.

"If I may explain. When Zarathustra was deposed as High Magus of Karnopolis, his closest friends in the magi fled the city. They formed what would become the Followers. There was already a longstanding schism in the magi over whether the daēvas were angels or devils. Over time, they recruited a few others who were sympathetic to the cause."

"Which was...what exactly?"

"That a great wrong had been committed against the daēvas. They knew the truth, but no one cared to listen. Most people had never even seen a daēva. Half thought them witches already. It was no great stretch to convince the populace they were Druj, and that Zarathustra had sanctioned it."

"They say he was killed by a lich," Eskander said. "That it drifted over the walls during the siege."

"That's a lie," Victor put in quietly. "I saw him alive after they'd announced his death and appointed a new High Magus. It was only for an instant, on the night after our first victory against the Druj. The hour was late. I was passing the stables behind the Temple and saw a man surrounded by magi. I ducked into the shadows and watched. They were escorting him somewhere. He wore a hood and his hands were bound, but I caught a glimpse of his face. There is no doubt it was Zarathustra."

"With all due respect, that was two centuries ago," Eskander pointed out. "Has he been seen since?"

Kayan Zaaykar shook his head. "No. The years passed, and most of his Followers gave up hope. Only a few kept the faith. My great-grandfather was one of them. Eventually, he gave up the robes and married, but he told his son what he knew, and my father told me. We kept in touch with the others, but there was little news to share. Then, about six years ago, one of the Followers in Karnopolis was called to give the final rites to a brother magus."

"You count magi among your numbers?" Lysandros asked. "Besides the two Purified?"

"Not many, but some. Just before he took the blessing, the dying man admitted that he had tended to a secret prisoner since he was first raised to the robes, although he would not speak his name. But he said it was a holy man. *The holiest of all.* The Follower covered his shock and pressed for more details, but the magus refused. If he had not been dosed with poppy and mandrake to dull the pain of his illness, I'm sure he would never have spoken of it.

Afterwards, he seemed very frightened. The magus was dead by morning. None but our member knew of his confession."

Kayan Zaaykar noted Eskander's skeptical expression and finished his tale in a rush. "We do not know where in Karnopolis they are holding him. When you gathered your army, my King, we decided the time had come to act. So we devised our plan to free the prisoners at Gorgon-e Gaz and take the holy fire. It would have worked if not for the necromancers. But I do believe the Prophet lives. And that he is somewhere inside the city walls."

"Hephaestion," Eskander said. The taller man looked up. "What is your counsel?"

"I think you have a better chance of finding the Prophet than taking the fire back from Neblis, although both are poor odds."

Darius stepped forward. "I know the city well and have some skill as a tracker. I am willing to lead the search."

I stared at him. Karnopolis. The seat of the magi. His childhood home, where they had done unspeakable things to him. Stronghold of the Numerators. They would probably catch us and flay us alive within five minutes, if we even got that far.

"I'll go with him," I said.

"I wouldn't ask that—" Darius began.

"You're not. I'm telling you."

In my heart, I was far from certain that this wasn't a fool's errand. But I would not allow Darius to face them alone. And I wanted more than anything to understand my gift. This might be the only way.

"We will go as well," Tijah said without hesitation. Myrri nodded.

"There is something else. Something we can make use of if we have to fight our way out." Darius looked at me. "She can touch the power. Not only that, she magnifies it, like oil poured on fire."

I tried not to wince at the analogy.

"Impossible," Lysandros said flatly.

"I felt it also," Victor said. He held up the cuff. "She is my bonded too."

They all stared at me. I wished Darius had given me some warning. I felt like a mouse that had just been dropped into a nest of starving hawks.

"What is your name?" Eskander asked.

"Nazafareen."

He tilted his head. "It is one of the virtues of the empire that they allow women to fight for them. You were a Water Dog?"

"Yes."

"And you swear allegiance to me now?"

I dropped to the ground to perform the prostration, as I knew he must expect. "Yes, Eskander...I mean, my King. My sword is yours, until victory or death, whichever comes first."

I was shocked when I felt his hand on my elbow, lifting me to my feet.

"Is what Victor tells me true? You can use the power?"

"I...yes. To a degree."

"And you wish to go to Karnopolis with your daēva?"

I nodded.

He thought for a moment. "I have no wish to kill slaves. So I will give you each a ship and whatever else you require. You have until the feast day of Zeus, four weeks from now, to bring me the Prophet or the holy fire." His tone hardened. "Then I will cross the Hellespont and no man shall stop me."

I shared a look with Darius. One month before the city burned, and his mother with it. If the Prophet did live, they had kept him hidden away for more than two centuries. What hope did we have of finding him? Perhaps as much as

Victor did of slipping unnoticed into Bactria and seizing the urn from under Neblis's very nose.

But I had no doubt that Eskander would keep his word. *Ruthless*, Darius had called him. Yes, he was that. Not cruel or bloodthirsty, just inexorable, like the tides or the movement of the sun. I could feel it standing in his presence. He was a man bent on leaving his mark and anyone who got in the way would find themselves flattened.

"I plan to march to the ends of the world and the Great Outer Sea," the young King said, his mismatched eyes shining with certainty. "And it's Al-ex-an-der." He smiled. "You Persians always butcher my name."

EPILOGUE

The nine Antimagi rode across the Great Salt Plain. They didn't stop until they reached the sharp teeth of the Char Khala, and then only to exchange half their captives for fresh ones at a village in the foothills.

The one who carried the urn went by the name of Balthazar. He was old, although not nearly as old as his mistress. He knew she would be displeased that they had failed to take the daēva called Victor, but he hoped that the prize he brought would blunt her anger. Balthazar feared very few things in this world, and even the world beyond the veil. Neblis was one of them.

They crossed the mountains and rode on into Bactria. Occasionally, they passed the ruins of a village. Vines and creepers wound through empty doorways. Birds nested in the thatching of collapsed roofs. Another few decades, he thought, and the endless forest would erase even those few traces of the people who had once lived here.

Balthazar knew these woods were full of game, creatures that had never heard a human footstep. But they instinctively stayed away from the party that passed through the woods, and the Antimagi saw no sign of life until they reached the shores of the lake.

It shone like a mirror in the light of the setting sun. A breeze lifted Balthazar's dark hair from his brow, but it didn't disturb the surface. Not a single ripple marred that smooth expanse of silver. It was another peculiarity of the lake that while it was girded by tall pines, they cast no reflection.

"One of you, pay the price," Balthazar told his companions. "And do it quickly, before night falls."

He had no wish to make the passage in darkness. The veil was a strange place, and stranger yet when the forces of night held sway. The things in the lake feared him, but they grew bolder after the light of the sun faded, and Balthazar was tired. He had nearly died in the dome, and wanted only to see his queen.

One of the Antimagi dismounted, yanking his captives down after him. He chose one at random and shoved her to her knees at the edge of the lake. She looked at him with terrified eyes. They always seemed to know, at the end. To come back to themselves enough to scream, or even beg. This one did neither. Only made the sign of the flame with one manacled hand, and cursed them in the eyes of the Holy Father.

How can she still believe? Balthazar wondered wearily. How can she cling to a God that would allow he and his brethren to do as they wished with His children? And yet they always did, the fools. In such moments, he never forgot that he had been one of them, a very long time ago.

The Antimagus spilled her blood into the lake. It pooled on the surface for a long moment, then sank slowly into the depths. Balthazar spurred his mount forward. He heard the Revenants tearing through the earth behind him, but didn't look back. His companions would dispose of them, or command them to wait. Their mistress did not permit Druj within her walls.

Balthazar gripped the urn in his gloved hands, ignoring a stab of worry. He had studied its contents with great interest during the journey. The flames that leapt within were blue and cold. In typical grandiose fashion, Old Zarathustra had called it holy fire, but it was merely alchemy, although of what sort the Antimagus was uncertain. No one had ever replicated it. The fire seemed to burn without fuel. Would passing through the veil extinguish it?

The water rose to the animal's withers. It rolled its eyes, but it had made the passage before and understood that there was no choice. Balthazar's captives were another matter. He felt their dread, bordering on panic, and sent a pacifying jolt through the chains that left them slack-jawed. *Too much.* Balthazar's lips tightened. She would want to question at least one of them. He was tired indeed to be so careless.

Deeper they went, until the lake reached Balthazar's chest. It had no real weight or substance, this liquid. For it was not water at all.

He took a deep breath. He couldn't help himself. It was unnecessary, but there are certain things the body insists on doing, and he allowed himself this weakness because it reassured him.

A moment later, he was fully immersed in the twilight world beneath the lake. Tall grey weeds swayed as though brushed by an invisible current. It surprised him that anything grew there, considering the nature of the place. He had come to the conclusion that they were part of the lake's defenses. That they served as camouflage for the denizens of this limbo, whose cold gaze he could sense as he rode deeper, toward the middle.

Look, but do not touch, he thought grimly. I am her

favorite consort, and she will punish any who interfere with me.

Shadows moved among the reeds. Balthazar kept his eyes straight ahead. At last he saw the marble of the palace, gleaming palely like the skin of a fresh corpse.

He rode through the gates and the fey atmosphere vanished. Lush gardens bloomed in the half-light, bursting with dark color. Balthazar's gaze did not linger on the structure itself. The strange angles and twisted towers. Doing so was an excellent way to acquire a blinding headache, and he was on his way to one already. But a quick inspection of the urn revealed the fire burned still. He let out a slow breath.

Mute servants ran out to take his horse. No one ever spoke in The House-Behind-the-Veil, not unless Queen Neblis had asked them a direct question. These were dressed in long white tunics that flowed gracefully. Their mistress liked pretty things. Only the most attractive of the unlucky souls caught by the Antimagi were permitted to attend her, though their looks tended to fade quickly.

Balthazar barely saw them. He passed tinkling fountains and ancient olive groves, his captives pattering obediently behind. The closer he drew to his queen, the more he had to fight the urge to run to her. To prostrate himself on the ground and beg forgiveness. The weight of his failure felt overwhelming. He fought it, knowing it was unnatural. He wasn't even certain she did this to him on purpose. It was simply her nature, to shape others around her will. She was the hammer and forge, Balthazar the base metal.

But he was the strongest of the Antimagi, the one she trusted above all others, and he would not lower himself in her eyes by crawling to her on his belly like a dog.

"My Queen," he said, dropping to one knee, for she did expect a certain degree of deference.

Neblis sat on the rim of a circular pool. Unlike the lake,

which had the opaque yet lustrous aspect of quicksilver, this was pure blackness. She wore a gown of blue silk, with matching slippers. Her appearance changed with her mood, but today she had white hair and golden eyes. The latter had the same intensely curious, birdlike look they always did, and that he would have recognized no matter the color or shape.

"You come alone, Balthazar," she said. "Why?"

He didn't bother with excuses. "The others are dead. Victor escaped. But I brought you this in his stead." He held out the urn. "From the Barbican itself."

Her golden eyes widened a fraction. "The fire?"

"Yes, my Queen."

Neblis took the urn in slim fingers, turning it this way and that.

"He was taking it to..." The Antimagus stopped himself from speaking Delilah's name just in time. "The King's whore."

"To free her?"

Balthazar didn't dare answer.

"Even after all this time..." Neblis's tone was light, but there was an edge to it. "Poor thing. I wonder if he will come after it?"

"Someone will," Balthazar said. "If not Victor, the Macydonian invader."

She looked at him, her gaze impenetrable. "So you would bring them down on me?"

"I...Of course, that was not my intention." Balthazar tried to control the quaking in his bowels. "If you wish it, I will take it back over the mountains immediately."

Neblis smiled and Balthazar felt the world right itself again. "No. You did well." She tapped a nail against one pearly tooth. "I have no unholy bonds to break, but perhaps new ones could be forged. Do you know how to use it?"

"No, but this one does." Balthazar gave the chains a heave

and his captives stumbled forward. Two teenaged boys and a Purified. "He is one of the magi that guarded the fire. See his hands?"

Neblis wrinkled her nose in distaste. "Savages. Make him speak."

The Purified stared straight through her. His lips were flecked with drool. Balthazar sent a tentative probe of power through the chains. The mind there was fragile as an old eggshell. His palms began to sweat. *Thoughtless!*

"You always were too heavy-handed," Neblis sighed. "Using a cudgel when a gentle slap would suffice. Give him to me. And remove the collar first."

Balthazar obeyed, letting the Purified sink to the ground at the very rim of the pool. He himself took a step back. The thing that lived in that black hole made the fauna of the lake seem tame and benevolent.

Neblis laid her palms on each side of the Purified's head. He jerked once, then subsided. But his brown eyes now looked more dreamy than vacant.

"What is your name?" the queen asked, her voice low and musical.

"Mahvar," he said instantly.

"How are the cuffs forged? What are they made of?"

"Are you the Prophet?"

Neblis shot Balthazar an amused look. "Yes, my son. You can speak to me freely."

"Praise the Holy Father. How did you break free?"

"What do you mean?" Her hands tightened on his face and he grimaced, but Neblis seemed not to notice.

"I dreamt of your prison. Cold and deep. All I have done was for you, the highest of all mages..."

"Prison?"

"Oh, the wickedness that has been committed in the name of the Holy Father. It shames us all!"

"Where?" Neblis nearly screeched.

Balthazar watched his queen with apprehension. Pinpricks of blood welled in the Purified's eyes. Balthazar weighed the wrath he would incur by intervening against the loss of their only source of information. He knew she harbored a deep-seated hatred for the so-called Prophet, even greater than Balthazar's own. But they had both assumed him dead these many years.

"Where is this prison?" Neblis demanded.

"Karnopolis," the Purified choked out. "Do you not remem—"

His words cut off as she savagely twisted his head to one side.

Balthazar's queen breathed heavily for a moment, her face flickering among the dozens she could call on at will. It dizzied him to watch it, so he stared at the substance of the pool instead. That too was mesmerizing, in its own way. Layers of darkness, like peering into a tunnel that went down and down and down...

"Balthazar!"

His head snapped up.

"I have a new task for you." She looked like a pretty dark-eyed girl of Babylon now, a city Neblis had known when it was still a scattering of mud huts on a fertile plain.

"How can I serve, my Queen?" he asked, although he already knew.

"You will bring me Zarathustra. Alive. If he is to be a prisoner, he may as well be mine." She rose, stepping one delicate slipper over the body of the Purified. "And get rid of that."

"What of Victor?" Balthazar asked.

"I think he will come to me." She smiled cheekily, and Balthazar felt a pang of jealousy. "He won't be able to resist my charms."

"No man could," Balthazar muttered.

She peered at him, birdlike again. "Do you love me?"

"You know I do." His heart ached in his chest as she held his eyes. Her beauty was dizzying, exquisitely painful, like a parchment-thin blade between the ribs. Even when he slept, she filled his dreams. The scent of her, a delicate, honeyed poison.

"Then don't fail me a second time."

Neblis paused to pluck a crimson flower, then wandered into the grove. Balthazar watched her until she was lost to his sight. He felt outpaced by events. As though he fought a war on too many fronts to keep track of. Alexander would move soon, but in what direction? The empire tipped on a knife's edge, and it was Balthazar's duty to ensure that when it did fall, it went straight into his queen's lap. If only she hadn't killed the Purified...But Zarathustra would be an even better substitute. He'd *made* the cursed fire. And Balthazar had his own bone to pick with the old man.

Karnopolis. The last time he had been to the city, he wore the robes of a magi. That had been before the war. Before they cast him out as a heretic. Did any still live who would remember his face? Balthazar very much doubted it. And if he wore the robes again, he would blend in easily with the hundreds of other magi in the city. A jackal among rabbits.

Balthazar lifted the Purified in his arms and contemplated just heaving him over the rim of the pool. In the end, he decided to dispose of the body elsewhere. The lake, perhaps.

Some things were best left undisturbed.

NOTE TO THE READER

First I want to say thank you for reading to the end! Since this book is set in a real time and place, but with many—okay, mostly—fantasy elements thrown in, I thought I'd take two more minutes to clarify.

This story began with the daēvas. In the Zoroastrian religion, they're evil spirits that embody every imaginable sin. But it wasn't always so. They started out as gods that were later considered false. They were demonized, in other words, which I found fascinating. And I loved the word daēva. It seemed beautiful and mysterious. And I began to imagine how such a downfall might come about.

The Midnight Sea is not at all an alternate history, although it is set in a specific time period: the collapse of the Achaemenid Empire, around 330 B.C. Alexander the Great defeated the Persian King, Darius III, in two decisive battles and went on to take the capitals of Persepolis and Susa. I couldn't resist weaving a (very twisted) version of those events into my story.

But the wicked king in The Midnight Sea bears little resemblance to Darius III, who may have been a mediocre general but didn't seem like a bad guy. In fact, the empire he ruled was pretty benevolent as empires go. Although Zoroastrianism was the official religion, other practices and customs were respected, gay people weren't persecuted, and women had property rights and could be economically independent. The Persians had the world's first charter of human rights (and the first postal system), among many other achievements.

They invented polo, which they called chaugan, and the letter from the king to Alexander taunting him with a mallet and ball was real. Other real things: The Hall of a Hundred Columns (where my Darius was sentenced), the general description of the palace complex at Persepolae, and the ass-kicking Pantea, who had command of the Immortals during the reign of Cyrus the Great and was sort of the sheriff of Babylon.

Alexander did hurl a spear into the ground and claim the Persian Empire for his own, although it was after he crossed the Hellespont. One of the best stories I read about the Hellespont involves the Achaemenid King Xerxes, who got so mad when a storm destroyed the bridge he'd made (in an attempt to invade the Greek mainland) that he ordered his soldiers to administer three hundred lashes to the strait and throw manacles in the water. That'll teach it!

Most of my place names are made up, but correlate roughly to a map of the empire at that time. The Midnight Sea is the Black Sea, the Salenian Sea is the Caspian, and the Middle Sea is, of course, the Mediterranean. The Great Salt Plain is Iran's central plateau, known today as the Dasht-e Kavir, or Great Salt Desert.

I also want to stress that my version of Zoroastrianism is only superficially related to the real religion, which many people still practice around the world. This is obviously a work of fiction, and the real magi did not oppress any supernatural beings, although they did worship fire and preach good thoughts, good words and good deeds, which I think sounds nice.

Dogs had a special place in Zoroastrianism. Weirdly enough, the holiest of them all, Water Dogs, were actually otters and were believed to hold the reincarnated souls of a thousand former actual dogs. Still with me? Well, killing one was just about the worst thing you could do, and was reportedly a capital offense.

What else? Zarathustra is the Greek name for Zoroaster. He died in 551 BC, at the founding of the Achaemenid Empire. He preached the importance of being good and kind and honest in this life, which I agree with wholeheartedly.

The word Druj comes from the ancient Avestan language, and means the embodiment of evil and sin.

The Char Khala range is the Caucasus. As far I know, Bactria was never infested with Undead demons. But I will be returning to my Bactria, the lair of Queen Neblis, and so will Nazafareen and Darius. I hope you'll come with us.

I encourage you to sign up for my newsletter at katrossbooks.com so you don't miss new releases or special offers. And if you have a moment to leave a review, they're a huge boost for authors and help us to keep writing books at affordable prices.

Cheers, Kat

BLOOD OF THE PROPHET

Continue the story of Darius and Nazafareen with a sneak preview of Book #2 of the Fourth Element Series...

CHAPTER ONE

"We are here."

Shuffling feet paused before an iron-bound door. A single torch cast a pool of wavering light on rough stone walls stained black with mildew. The torch had been soaked in an aromatic resin called galbanum which, when first lit, would give off a bitter and peculiar scent. After it burned for a few minutes, however, the resin mellowed to something reminiscent of green apples or evergreens. But even the sweet smoke failed to mask the air in the tunnel, which had a dank, unpleasant quality, as though it had absorbed the darkness pressing in from all sides.

The Numerator holding the torch raised it to examine the door more closely, then gave a satisfied nod. His face was all hard planes and angles, yet none of them seemed to fit quite right, like the walls of a shoddily built house. Thinning brown hair swept back from a high, pale forehead.

"Are you certain?" asked the second man. "This section has been bricked up for decades."

"I am certain." An elegant finger traced the hinges. "See?

There are no signs of rust. Check the map yourself, Hierarch. This is the place."

The honeycomb of tunnels beneath the temple district of Karnopolis had been used for many things over the last thousand years. When invaders came to loot and burn, as they often did in the city's early days, the magi would hide there until it was safe to come out. Later, the tunnels had served as wine cellars, smugglers' dens and, naturally, dungeons.

But peace had now reigned for more than two centuries. Most of the tunnels had fallen into disuse, and few remembered they even existed. Only one prisoner remained. He had been there a very long time. In fact, he should have died decades ago and no one knew for certain why he hadn't, although they had their suspicions. The prisoner was both feared and pitied, a relic from the war left to quietly gather dust in the darkness. When they thought of him at all, it was mainly to wonder when he would die and spare them the indignity of his upkeep.

The two Numerators who stood outside his cell were the first people other than his jailers to come see him in recent memory. Food and water arrived twice a day through a slot in the heavy oak door, and a bucket of waste was removed, but the prisoner had not spoken in a generation except to request certain harmless items, such as pens and vellum, which no one objected to. Until recently, only the King and a handful of magi knew he still lived. He had been one of them once, so they refrained from killing him outright. That might be considered a sin in the eyes of the Holy Father. The prisoner also had certain arcane knowledge he refused to share, so it was only prudent to keep him around in case they needed it someday.

That day had now arrived.

"Is this truly necessary?" the older Numerator demanded.

He was the head of their order and a hard man, but the thought of seeing the prisoner made his voice quaver.

"If we are to take charge of him, it would be wise to assess his condition first," replied the much younger man, whose name was Araxa.

"I know that," snapped the Hierarch. "But do you not find it strange he still lives?" He made the sign of the flame, touching forehead, lips and heart. "There is some dark magic at work here."

"It must be related to the cuff he wears," Araxa said. "They have assured me it keeps him docile. If he could have broken free, he would have done it years ago. I do not deny he is dangerous. That is why we must take him from the magi before their incompetence causes yet another disaster."

The Hierarch nodded his grey head. "It is a blessing that the King has charged us with purging the magi of traitors. They've probably been infested for years."

The Numerators of Karnopolis despised the magi, and vice versa. As the Hierarch's spymaster, Araxa had been given the task of leading this purge. One of his first acts was to demand the transfer of the prisoner to the Numerators' custody. He had been shocked to discover the old man still lived, both because it shouldn't be possible and because Araxa traded in secrets. He had informants in the magi, but none had ever breathed a hint of this. It was only after two of their own Purified had brazenly stolen the holy fire that the King revealed the truth. The Prophet Zarathustra had been—quite literally—under their noses for the last two hundred years.

"By the time I am finished, the magi will be grateful if we allow them to crawl back to their flyspeck villages," Araxa said. "Their power will be broken, and the Numerators will be given full control over the daēvas as well. Then we can dispose of them as we see fit."

The Hierarch frowned a little at this. "But we need the daēvas to fight for us."

"Only to defeat the Druj once and for all. Let them serve their purpose and return to hell, where they belong." He gave a sly, reptilian smile. "They may heal quickly, but they are not immune to a knife in the heart. Or fire."

"Perhaps." The Hierarch waved a blue-veined hand. "Are there no guards?"

"Not in a hundred years. They say he has never attempted to escape. No one even remembers these tunnels exist, Your Excellency. And a man could stumble around in the dark for weeks without finding a way out."

"It is still a foolish risk."

"As you say. In any event, it will soon be a moot point. I agree he cannot be left down here. Not with devil-worshipping heretics running loose, and traitors amongst those who are supposed to be his keepers."

The Hierarch cleared his throat with a wet *harrumph*. "Let's get this over with. Open it."

Araxa produced a crude bronze key and turned it in the lock. He thrust his lantern through the door first, expecting darkness, but the chamber beyond was filled with candlelight. A straw mattress had been pushed against one stone wall. The Hierarch wrinkled his nose at the smell wafting through the doorway, stale and waxy and animal. He clutched his pristine white robes and peered over Araxa's shoulder with morbid curiosity. What state would the prisoner be in after two hundred years in a windowless cell? He had been offered chances to repent, to return to the fold. But Zarathustra was a stubborn man. And apparently a mad one.

Araxa drew in a sharp breath at the scene before him.

"It's a wonder he hasn't burned to death," he said. "The magi truly are fools to have indulged him so."

Stacks of vellum towered from floor to vaulted ceiling,

many of them mere inches away from wavering candles. One wall appeared to be devoted to charts of the heavens, drawn from memory. Another was covered with incomprehensible diagrams, while the stretch nearest the door consisted of sketches of goats, some with disturbingly human eyes. There was no rhyme or reason to it that Araxa could discern. It was the cell of a lunatic.

He knew the old man had been considered a genius in his time, an inventor and alchemist. Ironically enough, he had even designed the gold cuff trapping him in this place.

"I've run out of ink," a tremulous voice said. "You promised me ink two months ago. Have you brought it?"

The Numerators exchanged a look. "I'll see that it's done," Araxa said soothingly, with no intention of doing so.

The Prophet Zarathustra, believed by all the world to be dead, sucked his rotten teeth and turned back to the vellum between his knees. One filthy, ragged fingernail scraped its surface as he traced intricate symbols on it, long grey hair hanging in cobwebs across his face. Within moments, he seemed to have forgotten anyone else was there.

"You see?" Araxa said. "He'll give us no trouble."

"Make the arrangements," the Hierarch said. "And burn these papers once he's gone. They're nonsense, but they could lead to questions we don't wish answered. How many know of his existence?"

"The High Magus of Karnopolis, of course. The King and his closest advisors. A handful of magi who see to his daily needs."

"Put the last ones on your list to be questioned," the Hierarch said. "I wouldn't be surprised if they had ties to the so-called Followers."

"They are already on it," Araxa said. "At the top."

"Good." The Hierarch took a last look at the prisoner, shook his head in disgust, and exited the cell, Araxa at his heels. The iron-bound door was once again locked. Araxa lifted the torch and they retraced their steps through the darkness. Altogether, the spymaster was pleased with the situation. He had worried the Hierarch was too old and weak-minded to do what needed to be done, but that no longer mattered, since he had ceded authority over the entire affair to Araxa.

"Would you join me for a cup of wine in my study?" the Hierarch asked as they reached the final passage leading out of the labyrinth. "It does ease my gout."

Araxa smiled. Thoughts of poison danced in his head, but the time was not yet right.

"I'd be delighted to, Your Excellency," he said.

CHAPTER TWO

I used to think the stars were angels. A great army waiting for the last battle against the Undead Druj. The light shone from their swords, which were made of silver and inlaid with precious stones. When the time came to return to Earth and pass judgment on the wicked, this celestial horde would be led by the Holy Father himself, riding a stallion that breathed cold blue fire.

Really, it made perfect sense.

Then my daēva, Darius, told me the stars were actually suns, only very far away. That they were, in fact, flaming orbs of vast magnitude. This flew in the face of all reason. Next he would claim the Earth was a sphere as well.

But as I lay on my back, listening to waves lap at the ship's hull and staring up at the dome of the night sky, I knew he was right. I could sense their ferocious energy myself now. It made me uneasy. I dreamt of fire often these days. The dreams always ended with my daēva dead, his blood boiled in his veins, and me untouched.

"What's wrong?" Darius asked. He sensed my discomfort thanks to the bond that joined us, although not what caused it. He couldn't read my mind—a fact for which I was eternally grateful.

"Nothing. Tell me more about Karnopolis."

He sighed. "I've already told you everything I know, Nazafareen."

"Tell me again."

I glanced over at Darius's profile, the beaky nose and short-cropped hair. I had only kissed him once but I wanted to again. Desperately. Yet the walls between us had fallen back into place. It wasn't so long ago I was his mistress, and he little more than a slave. It didn't help matters that I was also bonded to his father, Victor, whom he hated, and that we were going back to his childhood home, a place with terrible memories for him. Either way, Darius was in a fragile state of mind. Outwardly he seemed calm. But I knew he felt afraid. I did too.

"It is the greatest city in the empire," Darius said. "Ten times older than Persepolae, at least. Its architects had a love of symmetry, so Karnopolis forms an enormous square, precisely fourteen leagues on each side and boasting two hundred and fifty watchtowers along the walls. I know the temple district best, where they keep the daēvas. It's usually full of pilgrims, so we should be able to blend in."

I snorted. "Yes, a girl with only one hand and a boy with a withered arm. No one will notice we happen to match the description of the most wanted pair in the empire, I'm sure."

"Such things can be disguised," Darius said. "Are you having second thoughts?"

"No," I said. "Those came days ago. More like eleventh or twelfth."

"You did volunteer for this."

"Oh, I'm not complaining. Just stating the obvious. If the Prophet even lives, they will have him in some hole so deep and dark he could not be found in two years, let alone two weeks." I propped myself up on one elbow. The sky in the east was beginning to lighten. I could see a series of rugged islands in the distance, their little white and blue houses clinging like barnacles to the cliffs. "But we have to try. And if I get to kill some Numerators, so much the better."

Darius smiled. "How bloodthirsty you are, Nazafareen."

"Only for the daēva-hunters. And the magi." I thought for a moment. "The King, of course. We may as well throw in all the satraps while we're at it."

"Yes, it's a short list you've got." He paused. "Speaking of killing, have you been practicing?"

I knew he meant with the power. I shouldn't even be able to touch it. Manipulating the three workable elements— water, air and earth—was a daēva talent and I was human.

"Yes," I grumbled. "It's like trying to bail out a boat with a leaky bucket. Plenty of frenzied activity, but you still end up at the bottom of the ocean."

"Give it time."

"That's what you always say. And it's the one thing we haven't got."

"We did fine before," Darius pointed out. "You can still fight with a sword. I'm strong enough in the power for both of us."

He could be tactful and even kind when he chose to, so Darius didn't even glance at my missing hand. Yes, I could still hold a blade with my left—which luckily was my strongest. But it was ridiculous to pretend my skill was the same.

"I can't shake the feeling we're skipping into a pit of quicksand," I said. "Let's just get that cursed old man as fast as we can and be on our way."

"Don't speak ill of the Prophet." Darius frowned. Unlike me, he was still devout. "He didn't mean for any of this to happen."

"How do you know? Because Victor says so?"

Darius's blue eyes glittered dangerously at the mention of his father. "Zarathustra was...*is* a good man. His intentions were distorted."

"That's one way of putting it. It's thanks to him the daēvas were enslaved." I blew out a long breath. "Let's not argue. What he is makes no difference to me. He just needs to live long enough to convince the Immortals in Persepolae to throw down their swords before Alexander burns the city to the ground. After that, I don't give a fig what happens to him."

We watched the sun rise in brittle silence. I didn't understand why Darius still clung to the Way of the Flame after all that had been done to him. His left arm was a withered husk because of the bonding process. The cuff had maimed him—another thing the magi had lied about. They claimed the daēvas' infirmities were their Druj curse. But they weren't Druj. Not even close. Frankly, I had no idea what they were, or where they came from. Darius didn't either, which was part of his problem. He couldn't face giving up all he believed when he had nothing to take its place.

"Quarreling again?" Tijah flopped down beside me, joined moments later by her own daēva, Myrri. They could have been sisters, both tall and slender, with tilted eyes and pretty skin the color of strong tea. Tijah wore her hair in dozens of small braids, while Myrri's hung in springy curls to her shoulders. The bond had taken Myrri's tongue, so they used a system of hand gestures to communicate. Myrri's fingers flashed and Tijah laughed.

"Not in the least," I said. "We were just admiring the view."

"Well, take a look on the port side," Tijah said with a grin. She was from the desert lands of Al Miraj and had never seen a pool of water much larger than she could hop across. She found the ocean fascinating, and had spent much of our journey from the Bosporus cajoling the crew into teaching her their seafaring lingo, which she liked to show off at any opportunity.

I raised my eyebrows at her pleased expression.

"Land ho," she said.

Darius and I jumped to our feet and ran to the opposite rail, where the ancient city of Karnopolis crouched in the morning sun.

"Holy Father," I breathed, forgetting for a moment I was supposed to be a heretic.

Until I was thirteen, I had never set foot inside a house. My people were nomads. We lived in goat-skin tents and drove our herds over the mountains twice a year. When I left my clan to join the King's Water Dogs, I had lived in Tel Khalujah, which seemed a bustling metropolis. And when I first saw the summer capital of Persepolae, I'd realized Tel Khalujah was just a backwater.

But Karnopolis...It was fifty times larger than Persepolae. As we sailed into the harbor, past fishing boats and cargo ships and the sleek triremes of the King's Navy, I gawked at the famous wall surrounding the city. It curved down to the Middle Sea like a sheer cliff, casting sharp-edged shadows on the white stone buildings within. Odd-looking trees with large fronds and no lower branches swayed in the breeze along the waterfront.

"My father—may the gods cause his manhood to wither and fall off—said they race chariots atop the wall," Tijah observed. "I'd like to see that sometime."

"Karnopolis has every amusement, despite the best efforts of the magi to suppress sinfulness," Darius said dryly. "Unless I'm mistaken, the address we're going to is deep in the belly of the pleasure district."

Tijah grinned. "Why does it not surprise me the smuggler

has unsavory friends? Well, we are less likely to be scrutinized there, I suppose."

"Do they have special daēva gates, like in Persepolae?" I asked. It had only just occurred to me, but if they used the fire test for people entering the city, we had a problem.

"Not here," Darius replied. "There are not enough of us to make it worth the trouble, I think."

As the ship dropped anchor, we went below and collected our belongings. In my case, that was a sword wrapped in a length of cloth and a small leather sack with a change of clothing and a few toiletries. It felt odd to wear a dress instead of trousers. I kept tripping over the skirts and hoped we didn't get in a fight before I had a chance to change.

"Here, give it to me," Tijah said as I fumbled one-handed with the hooks on my veil. She stepped back and studied me. "Stop scowling under there, Nazafareen. Try to look meek. Eyes downcast."

I made a rude noise and Tijah laughed. "Just pretend you're wearing a *qarha*. It feels more or less the same. Unless you'd prefer to be arrested at the gates?"

"No, I'm quite happy with the veil," I said, blowing out a hot breath through my mouth. The thin linen flapped up, then settled back down like an albatross coming in to roost.

"Good. You can thank me later." Feet pounded on the deck overhead, accompanied by thumps and shouts as the sails were lowered. "Ready?"

I looked at Myrri, also veiled, who raised an eyebrow. "Ready," I said.

Our ship had once been called the *Amestris*. Two weeks before, she had rescued us from a village on the Midnight Sea and brought us all the way to the Hellespont, where King Alexander's army was camped. As a result, the *Amestris* was a blacklisted ship, so her owner—the smuggler, Kayan Zaaykar —had changed her nameplate to the *Photina*. But her captain was the same man as before, and we bid him a warm farewell as the crew prepared a longboat to carry us to shore.

"Are you sure I shouldn't wait for you?" he asked, rubbing the dark stubble on his jaw.

"When we leave, it will be over land," I replied. "The sea route to Persepolae would take three times as long. And it's not safe. Someone could recognize the ship."

He nodded. It wasn't the first time we'd had this debate. "I'll tell Kayan Zaaykar you landed safely," he said. "Be well."

"And you."

The four of us got into the longboat and sailors lowered it to the water. In a few minutes, they had rowed us to a beach where fishing boats were pulled up. I had hoped never to set foot inside the borders of the empire again, and here I was, heading straight into the dragon's den. I glanced at Darius. His expression gave nothing away, but I knew he felt it too, even more than I did. Dread.

"Which way?" Tijah asked, as the sailors rowed back to the *Photina*.

The veil concealed everything but her brown eyes, which were cool and intelligent. Tijah didn't ruffle easily, nor did her daēva. Once she committed to something, she didn't look back. I wish I had her confidence.

Darius pointed to a fish market at the edge of the harbor.

"We can take a shortcut through there," he said.

The people of Karnopolis were mostly dark of hair and skin, although Darius said the city was a melting pot, drawing merchants and mercenaries and pilgrims from all corners of the empire. The babble of a dozen foreign tongues surrounded us as we pushed our way through the bustling marketplace. Persepolae, the summer capital, was quiet and stately, full of gleaming white marble and strict geometrical designs, but this city hummed with boisterous life. The people were louder, their hand gestures bigger and clothing gaudier. Sleek cats wove between the stalls, hunting for scraps of fish. The tables were shaded by awnings of brightly dyed cloth, forming a maze of light and shadow that echoed with the sounds of full-throated haggling. As we approached the nearest gate into the city, Myrri touched my arm. I felt Darius stiffen.

A body was nailed to the top of the wall with iron spikes, its arms and legs splayed wide. The face had been pecked at by birds and was barely recognizable as human, but the robes were unmistakable. A magus. I had no great love for the priesthood, but judging by the wisps of white hair clinging to his scalp, the poor man had been old enough to be my grand-father. The sight was made even more macabre by the beauty of the massive wooden gate, framed by blue-glazed brick with a mosaic of galloping horses and a border of blue and white flowers.

A few people stared, but most acted as if they didn't even see the corpse, dangling like a broken puppet. From the condition of the parts I could see, I guessed it had been there for at least a week.

"Is that how they punish law-breakers here?" Tijah asked in a low voice. "Gods, I only hope he was dead before they strung him up."

Darius shook his head, troubled. "The satrap of Karnop-olis is not known to be lenient, but I've never seen such a thing before."

"It's a message," I said. "That's the only reason you'd do something like that. To scare people."

We moved away from the crowds to a relatively quiet patch of ground where we could observe the gate. Although the guards seemed mostly lazy and disinterested, I noticed with a sinking heart that not everyone was permitted to pass without question. Every ninth or tenth person was pulled aside as the guards inspected their palms.

"They're checking tattoos," Darius said. He clenched his right hand into a fist. "They must have been warned about us. If they see the triangle..."

He didn't have to finish the thought. The single triangle with a slash through it marked him as daēva. Tijah and I both had two triangles on our palms, one nested inside the other—proof we were human. The tattoos had been inked with the power. Nothing could alter or remove them.

"The magus at Tel Khalujah used to say a messenger could travel the Royal Road from Persepolae to Karnopolis in three days by relay," I said. Our quiet lessons in his study on history and geography seemed like another lifetime to me now, but perhaps they would prove useful after all.

"We have to assume one already has." Darius eyed the four guards, with their spears and wicker shields. "At least they aren't daēvas. Then they wouldn't even need to see my hand to know what I am."

"What next then?" Tijah asked.

"Let's try another gate," he suggested.

We followed the curve of the great wall along the waterfront, but it was the same at the next gate, and the one after that. The guards did not check everyone, but they did seem to be singling out dark-haired young men of a certain age. Young men who looked like Darius.

"This is bad," Tijah said, exchanging a look with Myrri. "Perhaps just the three of us should go through for now. Veiled women won't have a problem." She turned to Darius. "You stay here, and we'll find a way to sneak you in later."

"I don't like that so much," I said. "He's the only one who knows the city. And there's nowhere to hide out here. The *Photina* will be gone by now. Her captain is as wanted as we are, he wouldn't risk staying in port, not even to take on supplies."

"I suppose we could toss the dice," Tijah said dubiously. "We might manage to slip inside."

"I don't like that either," I said, blowing on my veil. I felt sweaty and frustrated. "Darius, what do you say?"

"I have an idea." He smiled, a devilish glint in his eye. "Just wait."

So we stood and watched people and animals and carts go in and out, raising clouds of fine, gritty sand. At least there was no faceless corpse nailed over this particular gate. In the heat, the other one had given off the faintly sweet rot I remembered from Gorgon-e Gaz, turning my stomach to a sour mess.

The sun sat at its peak in the sky when I sensed Darius grow more alert, like a hunting hound scenting a boar.

"Are you going to use the power?" I asked warily. "I hope you remember what happened in Karon Komai. It was as good as lighting a signal fire for the Immortals."

"I remember. And I won't use much. Just a trickle."

I almost objected. If they were close enough, other daēvas could sense the power being used. But I couldn't see any choice. And if we were going to gamble, I'd put my wager on Darius.

A moment later, a cart loaded with huge cedar timbers rolled up the gate. Darius's mind stilled. I knew he had gone to the nexus, the place where he became one with the elements. The cuff warmed against my skin. One of the guards was just raising his hand to wave the cart through when there was a snapping sound and the ropes holding the timbers broke. Yells erupted as ten-foot logs rolled in every direction, smashing into the wheels of other carts and sending the lines of people running for cover. The guards cursed at the driver, who was tearing at his hair and in turn cursing the evil spirits that had brought bad luck and ruin down upon an honest laborer. Two of the guards rushed to the side of a wealthy merchant who was gesticulating in fury at his own ruined cart. The last two looked at each other and shrugged, then began to help the driver retrieve his runaway wares.

"Now," Darius hissed.

Moving fast (but not *too* fast), we joined the handful of people who had been about to pass through the gate before the "accident" occurred. Most had stopped to gawk at the mayhem, and paid us no attention as we slipped into the shadow of the massive wall. Up close, the pitted and weathered mortar looked a thousand years old. Like it had broken the teeth of invaders no one even remembered anymore. Like it had stood there forever and would still be standing when the rest of the world was swallowed up by the desert sands.

As I stepped through the rectangular cut of the gate, I had the sensation of entering the jaws of some great beast and couldn't help but wonder if we would all come out again.

"Let's split up," Darius said the moment we were through. "Follow, but don't let it appear we're all together."

Tijah nodded, and she and Myrri slowed their steps until I could no longer see them. I drew a deep breath, my nose filling with strange perfumes and spices and the dry, dusty odor of sun-baked mud. Mules and oxcarts filled the narrow streets with no regard whatsoever for anyone on foot, or anything coming from the opposite direction. Within a few blocks, I had witnessed two violent arguments over right-of-way, although no one but the combatants paid them any mind. To my relief, the city was crowded enough that four more souls were just a drop in the ocean of humanity. Of course, it also meant finding the Prophet would be like identifying a single grain of sand in the Sayhad desert.

The address we wanted wasn't far from the docks in a seedy area of wine sinks, gambling dens and brothels popular with sailors. I kept my head down and my stump tucked inside my sleeve as we passed a pair of uniformed men with swords and cudgels, City Watch by the looks of them. I no longer wore the scarlet tunic of the Water Dogs, but only two weeks ago I had been a resident of the King's dungeons in Persepolae. And I still wore the pair of gold cuffs marking me as bonded—one linking me to Victor, the other to Darius. Tijah and Myrri wore them too, concealed under long sleeves. A single glimpse of the cuffs by someone who knew what they were and we'd all be in cells.

I held my breath, but the guards strolled by without showing any special interest in us. We could kill them if we had to, but more would come. Too many to fight. For now, we just had to stay out of trouble long enough to find Kayan Zaaykar's contact and pray he didn't turn us in.

The dirty, narrow streets twisted and tangled together like the branches of a thorn bush, and even Darius, who was the best tracker I had ever met, had to stop and ask for directions. Finally, we came to a four-story building that was larger and somewhat grander than its neighbors. A teenaged boy with painted eyes lounged against the wall outside, just under a sign depicting a large—and frankly phallic—shaft piercing a wine cup. His gaze lingered on Darius, then turned to Tijah, Myrri and myself with open curiosity. I guessed not many women turned up on the doorstep of Marduk's Spear, not unless they were hunting wayward husbands.

"We're looking for the owner of this fine establishment," Darius said with a friendly smile.

"Who's asking?" the kid demanded.

"Friends of Kayan Zaaykar," Darius said, dropping his voice.

The boy gave us an unreadable look. He couldn't have been more than fourteen, but his dark, knowing eyes looked closer to forty. "Come inside," he said at last, stepping through the doorway into the cool, dim interior.

Marduk's Spear was nominally a tavern, with tables and couches occupying the ground floor, although the boys serving wine to the sparse morning clientele were all exceptionally pretty. A pear-shaped tanbur sat propped in the corner, its strings silent at this early hour. Arched doors on the far side of the room opened onto a courtyard filled with flowerbeds and more of those strange limbless trees I had seen at the harbor. The boy indicated we should follow and led us into the garden to the shade of a date tree.

It was still early in the day, but the temperature had already grown too warm for my taste. Karnopolis was sticky, damp and vaguely smelly, like the fists of an infant, and I felt a fleeting but sharp longing for the mountains of my childhood. Karnopolis's temperate climate had earned the city its status as the winter capital. The King and his entire court would be here now if not for the barbarian army at his western border—an army I had sworn allegiance to, for whatever that was worth. I somehow doubted I would live long enough for Alexander to collect his due.

"Wait here," the kid said. He darted off, past a few chickens pecking half-heartedly in the dirt and up a flight of stairs, bare feet slapping on the tiles.

"Are you sure this man is a Follower of the Prophet?" Tijah whispered. "He doesn't seem exactly...devout."

"Unless there's another Marduk's Spear, we've come to the right place," Darius said. "Let's just be careful how much we say until we're sure of him." He glanced at me. "I'll take the lead, if you don't mind."

I knew he thought I was a hothead who couldn't hold her tongue, which was true, but I didn't appreciate being reminded of that fact.

"Fine." I wiped a sheen of sweat from my forehead with the sleeve of my turquoise gown. "You do the talking."

A moment later, an enormous man in a leather vest

descended the stairs. His arms looked like they were stuffed with rocks, and he wore a scowl on his scarred face.

"Who's asking for Arshad Nabu-zar-adan?" he growled.

"Kayan Zaaykar sent us," I blurted.

Darius sighed.

"Sorry," I mouthed, clamping my lips shut.

It would have been so much easier if Kayan had just come along, but the smuggler had stayed behind at Alexander's camp. He claimed to be too well known in Karnopolis to risk coming here. But he had insisted the owner of Marduk's Spear was a man we could trust.

"And who's *us?*" the giant demanded.

"Friends," Darius said shortly. "And our message is for your boss, not you."

I wondered how Darius knew the giant was not, in fact, Arshad Nabu-zar-adan, but he was obviously correct in this assumption, because the man crossed his arms—the better to display his bulging biceps—and lowered an impressively ridged brow. It was the sort of head that cracked other heads like eggs. I knew the type.

"Then you're shit out of—"

"It's alright. Bring them to my chambers."

We all looked up at the balcony above. The person attached to the cultured voice had already withdrawn, but it was as if the Holy Father himself had appeared in the clouds, for the giant's demeanor immediately changed to that of a palace courtier.

"Right this way then," he said, baring a handful of teeth in a sweet smile.

CHAPTER THREE

Four leagues due north of the ninety-sixth gate of Karnopolis was a small pond surrounded by trees. No bullfrogs croaked at its reedy edges. No insects skated across its glassy surface. The level of its dark waters never changed, not in the hottest, driest months of summer, nor after the heavy spring rains. It was a lifeless place, because it was not really a pond but a gate, similar to the one leading into the city, except that this gate connected two worlds.

The glen lay deep in the woods, and only a passing fox saw the necromancer named Balthazar ride his horse out of the pond. He emerged perfectly dry and stopped for a moment at the edge, dark hair lifting in the wind. The fox did not like the smell of either the man or his beast. They reeked of unpleasant magic. *Heart thieves*, the fox thought to herself, as she hurried silently back to her pups.

Balthazar took a deep breath, tasting the forest air. Leaving the Dominion always left him with a profound feeling of relief. The shadowlands stole a piece from him, an intangible but important piece, and he was grateful to have it back. It had thudded into him as he crossed the shivery border at the surface of the pond—his magic, what there was of it.

This was the first reason Balthazar was glad to be back in the mundane world. The second was that things moved in the Dominion between the gates, things that hunted his kind, and although Balthazar trafficked in death, he did not relish the thought of his own. He had been lucky this time. None had caught his scent, partly thanks to the talisman of Traveling he carried in his pocket. The journey from Bactria was the longest he had ever spent in the shadowlands, nearly a full day. But it had saved him two weeks of hard riding, and his instincts told him time was running short.

The horse was glad to be out too. It whickered softly, nosing the grass at the edge of the pond. The day was a pleasant one, and the necromancer was in high spirits as he rode out of the woods and found the road to the city. The closer he came to the wall, the thicker the traffic on the road became, but no one gave him a second glance, except to ask for a quick blessing. Balthazar complied with a fatherly smile. He wore the white robes of a magus and knew their nonsense by heart.

Karnopolis had changed little since he was last there, although a full two centuries had passed. It was one of the oldest cities in the known world and exuded the lazy arrogance of a sun-warmed cat. The only major new additions Balthazar could detect were the austere Hall of the Numerators and the much smaller Tomb of the Prophet. Both were near the Temple of the Magi, which was his destination.

Balthazar paused when he reached the enormous marble building and spent a moment looking up at the broad steps and the feckless priests who hurried to and fro. He had decided to come alone for a number of reasons, chiefly because the more of his brethren were in the city, the greater the chance of discovery. They called his kind necromancers because they commanded the Undead, but he disliked the term. Antimagi was a far more accurate title. The powers he served were the exact opposite of the elemental magic of the daēvas and their masters. They took living matter and drained it dry of whatever life force it possessed, swelling the Antimagus with stolen vitality. When Balthazar was chained to his slaves, his strength equaled four men. It was a heady sensation. He could hardly drag his human chattel through the streets of Karnopolis, but he did have the chains and collars in his saddlebag. As he watched the magi scurrying about, Balthazar thought he would not have a great deal of trouble finding new ones, should the need arise.

Queen Neblis had been reluctant to see him go alone, but she had faith in Balthazar's abilities. He had failed her only once, when the daēva called Victor had escaped on the plain, and he felt he had more than made up for it by bringing her the holy fire. Now they needed the Prophet to teach them how to use it.

Balthazar dismounted and led his horse to the stables behind the temple, where he gave a coin to the boy there, tousled his hair, and asked him to take good care of his mount, which was a beautiful black Ferghana. The other horses whinnied uneasily at its presence, but the boy hushed them, grateful for the copper. Balthazar entered the temple through a rear door and went straight to the fire altar. They would give him shelter if he asked for it, and he planned to. It was the ideal place from which to conduct the search. He would be just another magus from the provinces, come to make his annual pilgrimage to the Prophet's Tomb.

It had been a very long time indeed since he had knelt before the brazier. It sat in the center of an otherwise empty room, and the fire within burned eternally, a symbol of the Holy Father and the purification of sin. As Balthazar stared into the flames, listening to the droning prayers of the other magi, he had a sudden, vivid memory of himself as a much younger man. He had worn a short beard then, and the cuff of the warrior magi encircled his left wrist. They had stripped him of it just days before the Druj hordes surrounded the city. He remembered looking out the narrow window of his cell and seeing the endless lines of revenants beyond the wall, their iron swords and fearsome mounts. He remembered the black shadows of the liches, weaving back and forth like snakes, the sound they made. Balthazar had nearly soiled himself watching them.

Now, they obeyed his command.

The magi had called him a heretic and worse for his dabblings. Cast him out. But Neblis had picked him up. And now those magi were all dead, and he was still here.

Balthazar no longer prayed to the Holy Father, but he knew the sign of the flame. Forehead, lips, heart. *Good thoughts, good words, good deeds.* It came as easily to his fingers as if he had just performed it yesterday. He scanned the faces of the other magi at the altar, but recognized none. Back in his day, many of them—all those with the gift, at least—had worn the cuffs. They were at war, and the magi, along with the Immortals, were the first and last lines of defense. But that seemed to have gone out of fashion, or perhaps fewer had the gift. He was glad to see it, because it meant all the magi here would be too young to remember him. The infamous Balthazar. He lowered his head to cover a smile. If anyone knew where the Prophet was, it would be one of these fools.

Balthazar rose and made his way to the guest quarters. The elderly magus there was happy to accommodate a pilgrim from Qaddah. He asked a number of questions, but Balthazar was a fluent liar, and he knew the correct responses. Once he had shaken the man off, he prowled the corridors until he found one of the hidden doors leading down to the tunnels.

He could search them himself, but that would take weeks. A better course would be to at least confirm the Prophet was down there first. In the meantime, he could put the labyrinth to other purposes.

Balthazar looked both ways to ensure he was not observed, then slid the knife hidden in his robes into the crack and worked it open. Dust rained down, a good sign. This part of the tunnels had not been used in a long while. His darkly handsome face cracked into a grin.

That was about to change.

BLOOD OF THE PROPHET

FOURTH ELEMENT BOOK #2

Visionary. Alchemist. Savior. Saint.

The Prophet Zarathustra has been called many things. Now he spends his time drawing pictures of weird-looking goats. That's what happens when you've been stuck in a prison cell for two hundred years. But the man who might be mad, and is definitely supposed to be dead, has suddenly become very valuable again...

It's only been a few weeks since Nazafareen escaped the King's dungeons with her daēva, Darius. She hoped never to set foot in the empire again, but the search for the Prophet has led them to the ancient city of Karnopolis. They have to find him before Alexander of Macydon burns Persepolae, and Darius's mother with it. But they're not the only ones looking.

The necromancer Balthazar has his own plans for the Prophet, and so does the sinister spymaster of the Numerators. As Nazafareen is drawn in to a dangerous game of cat and mouse, her newfound powers take a decidedly dark turn. Only the Prophet understands the secret of her gift, but the price of that knowledge may turn out to be more than Naza-fareen is willing to pay...

ABOUT THE AUTHOR

Kat Ross worked as a journalist at the United Nations for ten years before happily falling back into what she likes best: making stuff up. She's the author of the dystopian thriller Some Fine Day, the Fourth Element Trilogy, the Dominion Mysteries and the new Fourth Talisman series. She loves myths, monsters and doomsday scenarios.

www.katrossbooks.com
kat@katrossbooks.com

ACKNOWLEDGMENTS

To Deirdre, for being my first and last line of defense on typos, grammar and gaping plot holes. And just for...everything.

To Jessica Therrien, for all your invaluable insights and constant encouragement. Your feedback made this book about a hundred times better.

To Holly Kammier, for all your great advice on the publishing process and for inviting me to your wonderful imprint. I'm honored to be part of such a talented group of authors.

To Kat Howard, for asking all the right questions and helping me truly bring these characters to life.

To Damonza, for designing a cover that was everything I hoped for and more.

And most of all, to Nika, for inspiring me to write about fierce girls. You are the original Nazafareen. Thank you for always putting a smile on my face. I definitely see a #1 New York Times bestselling author title in your future.

ALSO BY KAT ROSS

The Fourth Element Trilogy
The Midnight Sea
Blood of the Prophet
Queen of Chaos
The Fourth Element Trilogy Boxed Set

The Fourth Talisman Series
Nocturne
Solis
Monstrum

The Dominion Mysteries
The Daemoniac
The Thirteenth Gate

Some Fine Day

GLOSSARY

Al Miraj. The southernmost satrapy of the empire, it is surrounded by the Sayhad desert. Daēvas are called *djinn* there. Al Mirajis worship their own gods and very few follow the Way of the Flame.

Bactria. The land to the north of the Char Khala range. Once a satrapy of the empire, now the realm of Queen Neblis. It is a wilderness, with all the people who once lived there having fled or been enslaved.

Barbican. The stronghold in the middle of the Great Salt Plain where the daēva cuffs are forged.

Cuffs. Gold bracelets that create a magical bond between a human and a daēva which allows the former to control the daēva's power. In some cases, the wearers will also experience each other's emotions. The cuffs are usually worn for life.

Daēva. Creatures considered *Druj*, or impure, by the magi. Their origins remain a mystery, but they have the ability to work elemental magic. Most daēvas have a particular affinity for earth, air or water and are strongest in one element. However, they cannot work fire, and will die merely from coming into close proximity with an open flame. Daēvas live for thousands of years and heal from wounds that would kill or cripple a human.

Dominion, also called the gloaming, shadowlands or veil. The land of the dead. Can be traversed using a talisman to open gates, but is a dangerous place for the living.

Druj. Literally means *impure souls*. Includes Revenants, wights, liches and other Undead. Daēvas are also considered Druj by the magi.

Elemental magic. The direct manipulation of earth, air or water. Fire is the fourth element, but has unstable properties that cannot be worked by daēvas.

Faravahar. The symbol of the Prophet. Its form is an eagle with outstretched wings.

Gate. A passage into the shadowlands.

Gorgon-e Gaz. The prison on the shore of the Salenian Sea where the oldest daēvas are held. It is also where daēvas are bred. The bloodlines of all daēvas in the empire can be traced back to Gorgon-e Gaz.

Holy Fire. Said to be a gift to the Prophet from the Holy Father. Holy Fire can both forge and break daēva cuffs.

Immortals. The elite division of the King's army. There are always precisely 10,000 Immortals, half of them human and half daēva. They fight in bonded pairs. If an Immortal dies in battle, the cuff is designed to be torn off so the fallen soldier can be bonded by another.

Infirmity. Also called the *Druj Curse*, it is the physical disability caused to daēvas by the bonding process.

Karnopolis. The winter capital of the empire, seat of the magi.

Lich. A thing of shadow whose touch brings death, it can only be unknit using the power.

Macydon. The kingdom across the Middle Sea that invades the empire.

Magi. The priests who follow the Way of the Flame. In the old days, some of them bonded daēvas to help fight the Druj, but this tradition has waned over time.

Necromancers. Also called Antimagi. They are the lieutenants of Queen Neblis. Necromancers draw their power from chains attached to human slaves. When a slave is killed, five Druj Undead are born. Many are former magi drawn to Neblis's power and dark magic.

Numerators. A powerful order in the bureaucracy of the empire, they collect taxes and hunt down illegal daēvas.

Persepolae. The summer capital of the empire.

Purified. The order of magi that guards the holy fire at the Barbican.

Qarha. A protective face scarf worn by Water Dogs.

Revenants. Said to be the corpses of an ancient warrior race come back to life, they stand close to eight feet tall and fight with iron swords. Must be beheaded.

Satrap. A provincial governor of the empire. Satraps are permitted a small number of daēvas to keep the peace.

Tel Khalujah. The satrapy where Nazafareen serves as a Water Dog.

Water Dogs. The force that keeps order in the outlying satrapies and hunts down Undead along the borders. Human Water Dogs wear scarlet tunics, while their daēva bonded wear blue.

Way of the Flame. The official religion of the empire. Preaches *good thoughts, good words and good deeds*. Embodied by the magi, who view the world as locked in an eternal struggle between good and evil. Fire is considered the holiest element, followed by water.

Wight. A Druj Undead with the ability to possess a human body and mimic the host. Must be beheaded.

Zarathustra. Also called the Prophet. The founder of the Way of the Flame and creator of the first daēva cuffs. Considered a saint.

31965904R00195

Printed in Great Britain
by Amazon